Kittens Can Kill

Books by Clea Simon

The Pru Marlowe Pet Noir Mysteries
Dogs Don't Lie
Cats Can't Shoot
Parrots Prove Deadly
Panthers Play for Keeps
Kittens Can Kill

The Theda Krakow Series
Mew Is for Murder
Cattery Row
Cries and Whiskers
Probable Claws

The Dulcie Schwartz Series
Shades of Grey
Grey Matters
Grey Zone
Grey Expectations

Nonfiction
Mad House:
Growing Up in the Shadow of Mentally Ill Siblings
Fatherless Women:
How We Change After We Lose Our Dads
The Feline Mystique:
On the Mysterious Connection Between Women and Cats

Kittens Can Kill

A Pru Marlowe Pet Noir Mystery

Clea Simon

Poisoned Pen Press

Copyright © 2015 by Clea Simon

First Edition 2015

10 9 8 7 6 5 4 3 2 1

Library of Congress Catalog Card Number: 2014951271

ISBN: 9781464203589   Hardcover
      9781464203602   Trade Paperback

Poisoned Pen Press
6962 E. First Ave., Ste. 103
Scottsdale, AZ 85251
www.poisonedpenpress.com
info@poisonedpenpress.com

Printed in the United States of America

For Jon

Acknowledgments

It is part of the misdirection of the mystery writer that we may lead readers to believe we have crafted our work by ourselves. This is not the case. Brett Milano, Jon Garelick, Chris Mesarch, Karen Schlosberg, and Lisa Susser all read earlier versions of this book and gave me great feedback. John McDonough was, as always, generous with his professional savvy, in terms of poisons and police procedure, as was Vicki Constantine Croke, mistress of all things wild. I am forever indebted to Colleen Mohyde of the Doe Coover Agency for her faith in me, and Annette Rogers for her guidance. Moral support and encouragement came from Caroline Leavitt, Sophie Garelick, Lisa Jones, Frank Garelick, and a score of other friends I am probably forgetting to credit. Thanks, purrs, and head-butts to you all.

Chapter One

There's nothing cute about a death scene. Not the shards of the mug that rested in a puddle on the cold tile floor. Not the scent of the tea—acrid and sharp—that now mingled with the mustier odors of a body's last struggle. And certainly not the body itself, sprawled contorted beside the shattered ceramic, one arm reaching out for succor, the other frozen in rigor as it clawed at the argyle wool vest that covered the still chest.

No, there was nothing cute about the tableau that greeted me when I made my way into the kitchen of Mr. David Canaday, Esquire, after twenty minutes of pointless knocking. But the kitten that sat beside the puddle, batting at a metal button that must have popped off the vest in that last desperate effort? That little white puffball, not more than eight weeks old and intent as he could be on his newfound toy as it rolled back and forth? He was adorable. The cutest little bundle a girl could ever swoon for.

He knew it, too. As I stood there, staring, he batted that button toward me. Rolling around on its rounded top, it made its slow circular way toward my feet.

"Play?" The message in those round blue eyes was clear. I was supposed to kick the button back. To get it moving—make it livelier prey than the still man on the floor would ever be again. *"Back to me?"*

The button hit my boot, and the kitten reared up when I stepped back, his front paws reaching up to slap the air.

"No, kitty. I can't." I took another step back the way I had come.

"Play?" And another.

I had no desire to kick the button. What I wanted to do was scoop up this little puffball and run. To remove such an innocent creature from the horror before me. That had been my plan, even before I'd walked into the room. Get the kitten, get out. Get on with my day.

That didn't look like it was going to happen. Not now, and as much as I wanted to snatch the kitten up I restrained myself and, fiddling with my bag, found my phone while I took a third step and a fourth back to the kitchen door. As much as I wanted to grab up the kitten and run for dear life, I knew better than to disturb what just might be a crime scene—or to remove what I assumed to be the only living witness.

Chapter Two

The paramedics arrived first, and for that I was grateful. They had the body on a stretcher by the time the daughter arrived, straps across those jolly blue diamonds and a blanket covering the soiled khakis below. Better still, they were the ones to tell her what that still, pale face should have. What had been patently obvious to me from the moment I'd stepped into the room: Dad was dead. They were taking him to the hospital—that was protocol—but there'd be no sirens wailing because there was no great rush. Lucky for me, she opted to ride along.

I didn't envy the paramedics. The daughter looked like the type who would fight them. Insist on CPR or defibrillation, even as the old man's color faded to a muted version of that vest, the blood slowly settling in his back.

She didn't look much better. Pale as dishwater, with hair to match. That hair, a listless bob, had been dark once, maybe as black as mine, but time had dulled its color and its sheen, much as it had softened what might have once been impressive cheekbones and a jawline that now sloped gently into a chubby neck.

Between that pallor and the way she had carried on, I had thought at first that she was the wife. Then I remembered: the old man was widowed. It was his daughter who had called me, asking for help in settling a new pet with an increasingly shut-in and by all accounts difficult elder.

"It needs everything," she had said when she'd called. "Shots, whatever."

I'd been bothered by that impersonal "it." Sexing a kitten can be difficult, but this smacked of something colder. Still, I'd said I'd call Doc Sharpe, our local vet, to set up a well-kitten visit and silently figured on adding taxi and escort charges. In the meantime, I'd told the daughter that I'd drop by to set things up. As the woman on the phone had gone on, though, I'd begun adding services. Neither she nor her father had expected this kitten. She had errands to run, she'd said, and sounded particularly put out by its sudden, unannounced appearance. It—that impersonal "it" again—had been an unexpected gift, the caller had said. And while that sounded odd, I wasn't going to question it. Not if they were willing to pay.

That gig was shot, I thought as I watched the ambulance from the shelter of an eager rhododendron, blossoms ready to pop. Sure, I could bill for my time. I'd certainly charge for the load of supplies in my car. But I wouldn't count on getting paid, not soon anyway. Spring and my business usually picked up. The tourists started filtering back, and the seasonal condos filled with troubled dogs and angry cats, all confused by the very human idea of relocating for fun. But even though the May days were growing soft, my client base hadn't warmed up yet. I'd been counting on this job for at least a few regular checks.

"Mama? Where did you go?" The soft cry brought me out of my musing. Male, definitely, though still much more a baby than a boy. Spring. I looked through the bush's dark green leaves for a nest. For a den in the dark, damp leaves beneath the trees. *"Where are you?"*

The kitten. Of course. With all the hubbub, the tiny animal must have been spooked. Must have darted for safety and gotten outside. I couldn't recall anyone mentioning the little cat as they strapped the old man to the gurney and bundled his daughter in for the ride.

"Play?"

The kitten was determined, I'd give him that. And he seemed to have gotten over his fright. I looked around. The EMTs had left the door ajar when they first stormed in, and the little fellow probably snuck out. Normally, I'd cheer him on. Self-determination is a virtue that I applaud, but a baby is a baby, after all. And while the east side of Beauville might look nicer than our shabby downtown, part of the appeal was its old-growth woods. I thought of the foxes that would be nesting soon beneath those trees. And the fishers, and a few other predators, all of whom would be looking for a tasty morsel for themselves or their own young. Nature, right? With a sigh that probably revealed more about my human nature than I'd care to admit, I dropped to my knees. Besides, it wasn't like I was doing anyone else any good just then.

"I'm here, little fellow," I called out softly, peering around the shrubbery. "Where are you?"

He didn't answer, not that I really expected him to. I should explain that this is odd for me. I have a sensitivity, you see. Some people might call it a gift. I can pick up what animals are thinking, hear their thoughts like voices in my head. Yes, I know how nutty that sounds. That's why I keep my particular sensitivity to myself, although I have a feeling that others are growing suspicious.

But the thing about picking up animals' voices is that they don't talk like you or I do. They have no need for meaningless conversation, and they certainly don't chatter just to hear themselves speak. And so although I tend to perceive their voices in human terms—that kitten asking for its mother, for example—that's just my weak human brain trying to make sense of what I'm really getting. Which was a young animal coming to terms with its environment. That kitten wanted to play, because playing is its job—how it learns to hunt, to survive. He had appeared to address me because kittens, like all mammals, learn from their mothers, their peers. From the world around them. He wasn't calling to me, specifically. He was reaching out, because he was alone.

Alone. That was part of what I was getting, but there was something else, too—an undercurrent of loneliness and confusion, a jumble of noise and fear and...

"Back to me? Kick it again?"

Boredom? Well, as I've said, play is a young animal's job. And while I didn't necessarily want to play kick the button, I was grateful for the repeated plea. The voice was clearly coming from inside.

I turned back to the silent house. Although I'd walked in with no problem—Beauville still being that kind of place—someone had thought to lock the door. Luckily, the latch was a simple one, and it gave way quickly to the thin blade of the knife I always keep close at hand. This wasn't breaking-and-entering. Not really, I told myself as I closed the door carefully behind me. I'd been hired to take care of a kitten, and that's what I was going to do.

"Kitten? Hello?" As I've said, I wasn't really expecting an answer. What I was doing was announcing my presence, trying to sound as nonthreatening as I could, which for me meant voicing my thought in the form of a question.

"Back to me!" I tried to echo the thought I had picked up. The kitchen remained still and apparently empty. I proceeded through the open archway into what appeared to be a living room. "You there?"

"Play with me!" That insistent voice. *"Why won't he play with me?"*

I didn't have the heart to tell him, but I had to. "He's gone," I said.

"Gone?" The question bounced back, like that button. The small creature was trying to make sense of my response. Of the word. I kicked myself. I wasn't doing the kitten any favors with my euphemism. Animals live or die in the physical world, and despite this one's infant appeal, he probably had a better sense of reality than most of the humans in this town.

"Dead," I said, summoning the memory of the still, cold body.

"Gone?" The damage had been done, and I felt the confusion as the kitten continued to roll that word—that concept—about in his tiny feline brain.

"Catch me!" The button appeared, rolling in a slow semicircle from under a chair. *"Let's play!"*

"Kitten?" I ducked down and leaned beneath the coffee table. There, eyes wide, crouched the little creature. He'd taken refuge from all the commotion. Up close, I could see he was undersized and a little ragged, more ready to pounce than to groom. I reached for him and he reared up, batting at me with cool paw pads. "Okay, little fellow." I scooped him up, and as he nuzzled against my shirt, I felt a wet spot on his back.

"Feels like you've been trying to wash." No wonder his fur looked patchy. "Or did you get splashed?"

〉〉〉

I sniffed the kitten and caught something funky. Tea, I hoped, and not something more gruesome. I didn't think I was imagining a slight mint scent, and any puddles on the floor where the body had fallen had been trampled into dark stains. Mimicking my action, the kitten stretched around to sniff the wet spot, and promptly sneezed.

"Gesundheit, little fellow." He looked up at me, eyes wide, and sneezed again. An adorable little snort, prompted perhaps by that touch of mint. But I've been in this business too long not to think of the other possibilities: feline viral rhinoneumonitis—FVR, better known as feline herpes—for example. Not fatal, but something to manage. At any rate, I held the little creature under the tap for a moment. He was young enough to take my impromptu bath without too much fuss and was purring as I rubbed him down with a dish towel.

"Excuse me." The voice behind me made me twirl around and the kitten jumped to the floor. He landed by a pair of cowboy boots—turquoise blue—attached to jeans that fit like a second skin. On top of these, a woman's face scowled at me, the eyes wide and regal. "But who are you, and what are you doing in my father's house? And what are you doing with my kitten?"

Chapter Three

"Who the hell are you?" I wasn't at my best. I knew it. Dropping by to visit a kitten and finding a dead body will do that to you, and I'd been enjoying my brief respite with the kitten. But even as I grabbed the damp infant once again to my chest, I was beginning to suspect something was wrong.

For one thing, the kitten was squirming. Don't get me wrong. I'm not an animal whisperer. Wild beasts don't go all dreamy in my presence, although I did have a moment with a panther once. I've even got the bite scars—and rabies shots—to prove I'm perfectly capable of provoking animal aggression. But the way I was holding the little cat should have been comforting—body supported, up against my own heart. And the message I was getting wasn't of fear or even a desire get down, but something else again—agitation. Discomfort.

"I'm calling the cops," the newcomer said, still standing in the doorway. And as she pulled her cell from her bag, I suddenly understood.

"You're Judith. In from California." She paused, phone in hand. "Look, the door was open," I said. It had been, originally. "That's how we do it around here. Maybe you don't remember." Her eyes narrowed, and I wondered how long she'd been gone. "Continue calling, by all means." I had more important things to worry about. I had a kitten in distress. "Detective Creighton will vouch for me."

That did it. She hung up and began carefully removing her leather driving gloves, but her dark eyes narrowed as she took me in. "Who *are* you?"

"Pru, Pru Marlowe." The kitten coughed, his body heaving. I knew the drill. I turned him just in time, holding him as he heaved up a bit of liquid and then, with another convulsion that shook his tiny body, what looked like some half-digested kibble. I didn't see anything immediately harmful in the mess, and I made a mental note to check the house plants. Some of them could be dangerous.

That last heave was it, though. Already the fuzzy baby seemed to be better. I put him down as I reached for a sponge to wipe up his vomit. By the time I'd done rinsing the sponge, he was sniffing at the damp spot on the rug and purring. I lifted him up again and absently stroked his velvet-soft head as I turned once more to the woman standing there. "I'm the animal person—the trainer." If it weren't obvious now, there was no hope for it. "Jackie called me."

"Jackie?" I could tell from her tone that this was a quiz.

"Your big sister?" I could pass this one. "She said she needed someone to get a kitten checked out. Get whatever it would need. I picked up a litter box and a scratching post, as well as a bag of kibble."

"*Play.*" The kitten was getting drowsy. I could sense his eyes closing, but still, he looked out at the dark-haired woman before me.

"I could've done that." The peevish tone was fading. More for her sister than for me, I suspected.

I didn't disagree. "She seemed a little anxious." I would give her that. "And she'd called our local veterinary hospital, and the vet there recommended me...." I shrugged, letting her reach her own conclusions. I'm not a behaviorist. I've never finished the training. But Beauville is a small town, and so when somebody needs a pet trained, I usually get the call. I walk dogs, too.

"Huh." Judith pocketed her phone. "What did she say, exactly?"

"That her sister Judith from California had come by with a kitten." I thought back to the call. The woman on the line had sounded significantly older, but there are other things besides time that can age a person. "She said you'd dropped it off—sorry, that's what she said—and 'disappeared.' She sounded like she had her hands full."

She paused and I waited, unsure whether to offer condolences, unwilling to be the one to break the news.

"I didn't 'drop it off.'" Her tone was peevish, her full lips pursed. Judith wasn't angry with me, though. She knew it too, and as she ran her hand through her hair, she shook off the last of her suspicious edge. "I'm sorry. Today's just been…Jackie called me from the hospital. I was on my way there. You said your name was Pru?"

This last was called back over her shoulder. Judith—the glossy sister, as I'd already labeled her—had wandered into a downstairs bathroom and was rummaging through the cabinet, emerging with a couple of aspirin, which she swallowed dry. "My dad's birthday is today—was today." So she knew. It was official. That made my role easier, and I went through the formula then, mouthing sadness and regret while she splashed some water down her throat and on her face.

"I just got in from LA." She looked up at me. "I took the red-eye to be here in time. My luggage is still, well, I don't know. I'm hoping it shows up at some point. The kitten was a present. He's a purebred, some fancy breed. He came with me, carry on, and, so, yeah, I brought him here before I went to track down my bags. I left him with my dad. I thought he could use something in his life that was pretty and gentle and fun."

I bit back my next question: why a kitten? She anticipated it anyway.

"Clearly, living with my sister Jackie, he didn't have much of those in his life." Another sigh. "I didn't expect…"

"I know, I'm sorry." I always tell clients that pets make lousy gifts. If people want animal companions, they should choose for themselves. Now wasn't the occasion to repeat this advice.

She shook her head, stared off into the middle distance. "He's had a bad heart for years. I thought it was under control.

I thought—" She paused to swallow, as tears appeared in her eyes. "I thought Jackie was just worrying. She does that."

"She lives here?" A nod, as she carefully caught a tear on one manicured finger. Maybe the older sister had a reason to sound tired. "Will you be staying here, too?"

"No." She was staring at the kitten now with a look of blank lassitude. I couldn't blame her. "Jackie and I…" She left it at that. "Though I guess I'll have to stick around for a while." She raised her face to mine. The tears were still there, suspended, making her eyes glitter. "I should get over to the hospital. Maybe you could bring in the litter and everything? You know, like you were going to?"

"You don't want to take him?" I had gathered from my brief interaction with Jackie that a pet was the last thing she had wanted before her father had died. I didn't think his loss was going to change that.

Judith looked up at me, her gray eyes sharp.

"I'm sorry," I said again. I wasn't, but it was a convenient formula. "I know you're going to have your hands full, but I need to know what to do with this little guy." The kitten was sound asleep now, soft and quite fluffy, now that I'd dried him with my shirt. It seemed a pity to wake him, so I moved slowly—offering the snoozing bundle to the dark-haired woman.

"No." She backed away. "I'm staying at the Mont." The Mont Chateau, new and very ritzy, presumably did not take pets. Not even pedigreed ones. "You could leave him here, I guess," she said, before I could respond. "Unless you provide boarding?"

I shook my head. "No."

"He'll be fine here, then." She hiked her bag up on her shoulder, signaling that the interview was over. "You can lock up after you get everything set up," she said. "Jackie will know what to do."

"Wait, no." Kitten still pressed against my chest, I reached out to stop her. "You can't just take off."

She turned back toward me, and I shut up. It wasn't the tears, or not only. It was the despair, the awareness of loss that stopped me. Judith Canaday might not be the best sister, but she was a daughter, too.

Chapter Four

Judith took off, and I was stuck standing there, a pint-sized dilemma on my hands.

The younger Canaday sister had said to leave the kitten, but I couldn't see locking him in here, all alone. It wasn't as if I'd be abandoning him—not with food, water, litter, and shelter—but it wouldn't be fair to the little guy to strand him alone just yet. Not a kitten this young. On closer examination, he seemed undersized and a little, well, ratty-looking. His soft fur, downy now that it was drying, made him look rounder than he was. I revised my earlier opinion. He was more like six weeks old. Young to be adopted out. No, leaving him alone wouldn't be fair to him.

Not to mention, to the woman who would come back to find him here. I knew something about death, about hospitals, and I suspected Jackie Canaday wasn't going to be home for a while. When she was, I doubted if she would be in any shape to appreciate—or to care for—a needy infant. A kitten might be cute comfort at some point, but right now? No. I could too clearly recall the day of my mother's death. Grief takes a while to kick in, but exhaustion—that's there from the start. Especially if, as it appeared, Jackie had been her father's caregiver. Her kid sister might not understand, but I did: Jackie was going to be busy with hospital bureaucracy and funeral plans. Going to be busy with the buzz and flutter of her own confused thoughts, while life as she knew it dissolved and rearranged itself around her. The kitten was going to be one more responsibility, a duty she didn't want.

Not that I did, and I found myself stalling as I hauled in the brand-new litter box, the twenty pounds of the fancy no-dust filler, and all the other paraphernalia I'd picked up at the big box store, two towns over. A '74 GTO—two doors, a custom baby-blue—wasn't made for large loads, but it is big by today's standards, which is useful for my job. Sometimes, I think about trading in my car for a truck. It wouldn't use much less gas. Then I think how much of my time I spend on the road, and I know it's never going to happen. Living out here in the boonies, you have to drive. And if you're going to drive, you may as well have some fun.

Four trips later, I'd brought everything in. Still, I didn't want to take off. I told myself I was becoming sentimental—the kind of weakness the rest of the animal kingdom wouldn't tolerate. But it was more than that, and I knew it. Cats vomit for any number of reasons. Sometimes I suspected Wallis—the tabby who shares my house—of bulimia. But kittens are as vulnerable as any baby, and that brief episode—the heave and the shudder—had worried me. No matter how thoroughly this downy kitten seemed to have recovered from his episode, I didn't like leaving him alone.

I also couldn't see hauling him across town to the closest emergency clinic, hanging in the waiting room with every animal that came in. Not yet, anyway. A kitten as young as he was? He'd be exposed to more danger there, not to mention stress and confusion. Instead, I called Doc Sharpe again, getting his voice mail, to see about setting up a proper—private—appointment. Then I took the kitten into the litter box, which I'd installed in the mudroom; these old Victorians were made for real people and real animals, too. Once he'd sniffed that—without sneezing, I was happy to note—I'd opened a can for him, leaving the rest stacked on the counter, right by the bag of kibble. Water, too…check; I'd done it all, even assembled the sisal-draped scratching post.

Wallis would have had a field day with that. A mature tabby with a history I could only guess at, she looks askance at much of what we humans do, particularly at the ways we attempt to restrict the behaviors of the animals around us. If I'd brought something like this post into our house, it would be seen as an invitation to shred—the sofa, the bedspread. Anything, really, except the rope-covered wood.

But Wallis wasn't here, and I needed to do what I could to ease the transition of this small animal into a household that didn't expect and most likely didn't want him. A kitten too young to successfully wash himself. A kitten still calling for its mother. Damn Judith Canaday. Didn't the woman have any sense of what was going on here? Of what her sister was actually dealing with?

The kitten didn't seem to mind. Still sleeping where I'd put him, on an old-fashioned wing chair upholstered in burgundy velvet, he looked as princely as his pedigree. Now, I don't care about papers—as Wallis would remind me, I'm as much a mutt as anything in the shelter. But eyeing the little fellow, the beginnings of the long, silky coat already apparent in the downy fuzz that made him resemble nothing so much as a dandelion gone to seed, I felt relief. Someone—Judith, apparently—had paid for him. That meant he'd be valued by somebody, if not the intended recipient. I don't like how humans think, but I've come to accept it. Besides, it helps with the training.

I took one last glance around. Close to noon, I was already late for my next appointment. I should get going.

I couldn't. Call me crazy. No, never mind, I knew too many people who would be willing to do just that, if they knew the truth. Call me soft and you'd be closer to the reality. I couldn't see abandoning that ball of fluff alone in a house where, unwanted and unexpected, he'd as likely get stepped on as fed.

Scooping up the kitten, I scrawled a note of explanation, complete with my contact info. I didn't need to be accused of stealing a valuable animal. I also didn't want to deal with my own conscience, leaving this little guy here alone. It wasn't his fault that his intended person was dead. At that point, I didn't have any reason to believe the old lawyer had suffered anything but a natural death.

Chapter Five

"Kittens? I don't do kittens."

Wallis is cool in the best of circumstances. When I walked into the kitchen, the still-sleeping ball of fluff clutched against my body, she became icy.

"Wallis, I'm not—" I didn't have a chance to finish. She'd turned her back on me and began to wash. "I'm not asking you to take care of—whatever his name is." It was true. My concern was more basic than that. Wallis does not take kindly to interlopers.

"I'm not going to kill the thing, either," she said, reading my thoughts. *"I'm not a..."* The pause was more for dramatic effect, I suspected, than because she had trouble choosing her words. *"I'm not a human, you know."*

"Thank you." There was no point in apologizing. Wallis knew me well enough to sense my relief, as I told her about the sneezing and then the vomiting. "It might be nothing. Mint might smell like catnip to him, right?"

"Waste if it is," she muttered as she sauntered off. *"Baby that young..."*

Of course. Kittens start off immune to catnip. Some are actively averse to it, which could have explained the reaction. I silently thanked Wallis for the reminder, as I followed her upraised tail into the living room, where I deposited the kitten on my mother's old sofa. I knew from previous experience that it would be pointless to try to isolate the kitten. Wallis could get into every room in the house, and she'd consider any attempt at quarantine a personal affront, and so I did my best to clear my mind of lingering fears and went to catch up on my day.

Wallis might seem cruel, but she had her moments. And I owed her. She'd saved my life, after all, rousing me to drink some water when I'd been felled by a combination of exhaustion and the flu—and, okay, one too many nights of booze and whatever—several years before. I'd passed out, alone by chance, after making it back to our tiny walkup. Could've died, too, not that my date that night would've known or cared, once he'd left me at the curb. That's how I was living then. A big life in the big city.

But I hadn't. I'd heard Wallis—not that I knew who she was—speaking to me. Telling me to drink something. Telling me to move. I had recognized the sense of what she was saying, even if I didn't know where the voice came from. And I'd staggered to the bathroom to put my face under the tap. I'd slept, then, right on the bathroom floor, and after some more water, it had hit me. I wasn't hallucinating. I was hearing my cat.

I'd called an ambulance at that point, scared out of my wits. And once the hospital had pulled me back further, rehydrating me and pumping me full of antibiotics, I'd checked myself into the psych ward. Three days. Observation, they call it, by the end of which I knew I preferred madness. So I signed the forms and blamed the flu. And I came home, to one very angry cat.

That remained a sore point. She hadn't roused me only to have me abandon her. Three days, locked in a city apartment, and she'd been scared, too. These days, I tried to be more sensitive to how my decisions affected her. She, meanwhile, had perfected her aloof attitude, but we relied on each other, still. I knew she cared.

The kitten would be safe with her. I had to believe that. Would I owe her? Sure. But not much more than I already did.

Chapter Six

Not everyone thought as my cat did.

"Kitten? Interesting." With the kitten stashed, for now, I'd gone about my day. But out of sight didn't mean out of mind—as this latest interaction proved. I hadn't realized I'd even been think-ing of the little fellow as Frank looked up at me, the question in his eyes. *"Tasty?"*

"No." I spoke out loud, making my voice as firm as I could. Frank's a ferret, and his query had sounded in my head as his quivering nose sniffed my outstretched hand. I spoke out loud to make a point, however. Mustelids are omnivores and, while I wasn't entirely sure of his intentions—Frank might simply have been asking if I had any spare Cheese Doodles on my person—I didn't like the level of curiosity that was radiating from his shiny button eyes.

"What?" Alfred, Frank's person, sat up with a start. He'd been dozing in his seat when I walked in, his beard cushioning his head as he slumped behind the desk at the town shelter. Alfred is Beauville's animal control officer, but Frank is the brains of the operation.

I'd stopped into the shelter after my afternoon visits—pilling an elderly Siamese and working out an athletic young terrier, whose behavior had improved dramatically once his family paid me to give him the run he craved. Partly, I wanted to see if Albert needed me. I'm not employed by him or by the town. But since Albert himself very rarely does any actual work, he directs a fair amount of assignments my way. The good ol' boy network being what it is, nobody has yet asked why the town is paying a freelancer, like myself, when Albert is getting a salary. Or maybe they do know and don't care. Life is simple here in Beauville.

Partly, I'll confess, I'd come by here to avoid going home. I trusted Wallis with my life. I could certainly trust her with the kitten's. But I knew I'd put her out, dumping that little one into her care. She'd take it out on me, one way or another. What I hadn't counted on was Frank's sharp sense of smell. The masked face looked up at me expectantly, and again, I got an impression of the white kitten I'd left hours ago.

"Not sweet?"

I shook my head. I didn't know exactly what Frank meant, but his persistence unnerved me. Animals don't taste things the way we do. "Sweet," for example, will register to a dog, but not to a cat. Ferrets' taste buds were a mystery to me. Still I didn't like the association of the kitten with anything edible.

"It's nothing." I said, as much to myself as to Alfred, who blinked up at me like a not particularly bright goldfish. "Never mind."

Even as I spoke, I stared at Frank. His moist nose continued to twitch and I could feel his warm breath on my outstretched fingers. But the shiny black eyes that looked up at me read the emotion in mine. I felt the questing of that nose, the curiosity, but also a sense of remove. A recoil, expressed as if he had tasted something bitter. I'd offended the little animal.

"I'm sorry," I addressed them both, as I drew my hand back, and Frank ducked into one of Albert's desk drawers. "I was wondering if you had any more calls?"

Spring is baby season in the animal world. Even up here in New England, the climate grows a little kinder, and food more plentiful. Of course, some of that food is the young of other, smaller animals. I may have insulted Frank by my inference, but it wasn't out of the blue.

Spring is also the time of year that humans notice the other inhabitants of this planet of ours. They hear the raccoons nesting in the attic, the skunks under the porch. They call Albert. And most of the time, he calls me.

I should be grateful. State law allows homeowners to kill so-called problem animals. That is, animals who are simply making the best of a life that now includes us in it. And the folks around Beauville are mostly the kind who will. Fall is the big hunting season around here, but those shotguns are handy year-round—and who's to say whether those particular animals were eating their way into the eaves or simply made good-looking targets on a boring Sunday afternoon?

In an ideal world, of course, we'd all learn to get along. Or quit leaving food out and clean our garbage cans once in a while. Barring that, we can eliminate the animal from the home. It's a tricky business, especially this time of year. You may not care about those helpless babies, but their mother does. You lock her out of the attic where she's nested and she'll move hell or high water to get back to them. If she can't? Well, I'm not sentimental, but that's a bad way to die. Like I've said, nature isn't pretty, but whenever we humans come into contact with it, we make it worse. And spring is when it's at its peak. When I make my money. Which is why I was now staring at Alfred, waiting for my last question to sink in.

"Got a squirrel call you could take care of," he said finally, eyes sliding up to mine. Right. Spring. I'd been out working and shed my denim jacket and the flannel that had covered my T-shirt when I'd left the house that morning. Albert doesn't need the rising of the sap to turn his head. He's pretty basic that way. But the warmer weather does give him more to dream about, at least when I'm around. "I don't know if you want to…"

"Yeah, I'll take it." That got his attention. "What's the address?"

He fumbled with the papers on his desk. He'd expected me to say no. I could tell. Probably only offered it because I caught him staring. I knew I'd do a more humane job than he would, though. Besides, I could use the money.

"Wilkins." He squinted to read his own handwriting. "Laurence Wilkins? Here's the number."

I took the scrap of paper. "Got anything else?"

He started to shake his head, when Frank poked his head out again. I didn't know what powers the ferret had over his human but he was staring at Albert as memory apparently dawned. "Doc Sharpe was looking for you," he said. "Something about a kitten?"

I'd turned my cell off during the run and forgot to turn it back on. I wondered what the vet thought, leaving a message with Albert. But Doc Sharpe was an old Yankee, prone to think everyone was as attentive to detail as he was. I'd give him a heads-up about Albert when I called him back.

"Thanks." I held my hand out to Frank for a farewell sniff.

"Kitten, huh?" His nose quivered over my fingers. *"Remember, Pru, even kittens can kill."*

>>>

I was halfway to my car when I heard my name.

"Pru."

One syllable: that was it. But it was enough. I knew that voice. I turned. The town shelter shares a building with our tiny berg's police department. Sure enough, I had been spotted. Detective Jim Creighton was crossing the lot toward me. Taking his sweet time about it, too.

Tall and lean, Creighton still looked a little like the high school athlete he'd once been. A boy scout, too, I suspected. Not the kind of man I'd have had much to do with during my youth here. Since I returned and he'd become a cop, we'd had some run-ins. I didn't think I'd done anything to get on his bad side, but then again, he picked up more than most would. More than most men, anyway.

"Hey, there," I called back. "You need me for something?" Before I realized what I was doing, I'd run my fingers through my hair.

Creighton had the sense not to comment. He didn't have to. Those baby-blues —almost a perfect match for my GTO— crinkled up in a smile as he crossed the parking lot to meet me.

"I'm on my way over to County," I said by way of explanation. "I've got to talk to Doc Sharpe about a kitten."

He nodded. He'd been at my house this morning when I'd gotten the call. As I've said, we've had some run-ins. "That's what I was trying to reach you about."

I shook my head. "Sorry, I turned my phone off."

"Not a big deal, Pru. But there is a complication."

I waited. Creighton may be my sometime-lover, but he is, as I've said, a cop. He rubbed his face, and I suppressed a smile. He does that when he's tired. He'd been busy the past two weeks, caught up in the loose ends of a drug scam here in town. Between his court appearances and his regular workload—nuisance crimes always pick up again once the weather warms up—we'd not seen each other in a while before last night. Me? I felt refreshed.

"I've been on the phone for the past hour. The Canadays." He didn't have to say any more. When a normal Joe dies, it's sad. You have a funeral. When a big-deal lawyer dies, people start making calls.

"He was an old man. Sick, too, from what his daughter said." I was only repeating what Creighton already knew. "His oldest daughter had moved in with him. She wouldn't have done that if he could have taken care of himself."

"Yeah, well." He rubbed the back of his neck now. I could imagine the feel of his hair back there, cut short but still soft. "The state's calling for an autopsy, and the family is all worked up. But he died alone, so that's the law—no matter what his history."

I didn't argue. I'd been through it. When my mother died, I'd been there, and so the autopsy was optional. I'd been asked, sure, but had said no. What were the doctors going to tell me? That between the cancer and her age, her body had given up the fight? I didn't care which one or another of her organs had called it quits first.

"I've already spoken with the emergency room doctor," Creighton was still talking, "the one in charge of Canaday's care team." I felt myself smiling again, but this time it felt bitter. My mother hadn't had a team. She'd had me.

"Are you trying to tell me that you're going to be working late tonight?" Better to focus on what I had now.

He shook his head. "I wanted to talk to you because I know you're involved, Pru."

I couldn't help it. I caught my breath. He was wrong. This time, he was wrong

"Jim, I don't know—"

"The kitten, Pru. The one the Canaday girl called you about? I won't have the initial report for a few days, and the labs will take even longer. But the initial exam at the ER was pretty clear."

I shook my head, confused.

"David Canaday died of acute myocardial infarction. A heart attack so severe he was probably dead by the time he hit the floor." His voice was matter-of-fact, but I suddenly knew what he was going to say before he said it. "By all accounts, his heart condition was being controlled by medication. He should have been fine. But he wasn't. He's dead. And it may have been because of that kitten."

Chapter Seven

"You can't seriously blame a kitten." Maybe sleep-deprivation was getting to me too. None of this was making sense.

"No." Creighton shook his head, a ghost of a smile on his tired face. "That would be—No." He paused to take a deep breath. "It's more a question of putting together what happened. And once the initial autopsy report is back, the kitten may be needed for testing. Not likely, I know, but the medical examiner is now using the state police labs for toxicology. That means it may take a while; they're thorough. If the family wants something definitive, well, they certainly have the right to push for any number of tests, and the resources, if it comes to that. I don't know how you left it with them, but—"

"I took him." This was my chance to come clean. Not my usual modus operandi, but with Creighton it just made sense. "The kitten, that is."

"*Took* him?" That smile had grown larger. Didn't mean he wasn't waiting for more.

"The other daughter, the one who brought the kitten? She didn't want to deal with an animal right now. I figured nobody would." I quickly ran through what had happened, leaving out the plea I had heard in the little cat's plaintive mew. "I left a note." A thought hit me. "What do you mean, testing?"

Creighton shrugged, and I realized he was staring off at something beyond my shoulder.

"Jim?" I didn't like this.

"Pru." He was stonewalling me. It's a cop thing. But now he was on my territory. I trusted Jim, as much as I was able. But people can take care of themselves. Animals, not so much. Not when humans are involved.

"I'm not letting you do anything to that kitten."

"*I* wouldn't." He started to protest.

"You know what I mean." Curiosity overcame me. "What would you test for anyway?"

He looked as bewildered as I was. "Honestly, Pru? I don't know. Dander, maybe? Maybe just to rule out other allergans? One of the daughters is making noise about it, and she's got the right."

"Jackie, right?" Personally, I'd been relieved when my mother finally died, but when you've been a caregiver for a while, it does tend to define you.

"The youngest." Creighton leaned in as if he was giving me confidential info. Maybe he was.

"Judith?" She hadn't seen her father recently, she'd said. Had just arrived that morning. Maybe she didn't know how he'd declined.

But Creighton was shaking his head. "No, the youngest. Jill. She came in for her father's birthday. Drove down from Vermont and ended up going straight to the hospital. And Pru? She's heard something about what you do. She said she wants to meet you."

Chapter Eight

Great. I watched Creighton walk to his car with his parting words echoing through my head. "Be nice, Pru," he'd said. "She's just lost her dad."

This morning's activities aside, I'm not the most social sort. Albert, the Canadays—that was work. Creighton was pleasure, but I've only recently started letting him stay for coffee. So when I hear that someone wants to meet me—that she'd heard about me—I get worried. Since returning to Beauville, I'd kept more or less on the right side of the law, and I keep my gift to myself. I'd done my time in a locked ward. It had been voluntary—my choice—but it had been enough. Creighton still thought it was cute that I talked to my cat. I didn't want to know what he—or a judge—would think if they knew she talked back.

His unmarked had disappeared around a corner by the time I settled into my own car and turned on my phone. Three messages. Doc Sharpe, at the very least, deserved a call back.

"Pru? Good to hear from you." From anyone else, that would have been sarcastic. Doc Sharpe was a straight shooter, though, if a bit stodgy.

"Sorry to have kept you waiting." He's also the source of most of my referrals. He'd set me up with a guide-dog group that had kept me employed over the winter. I couldn't blame him if the Canaday gig had fallen through. "I went over to see about that kitten—"

"Terrible, terrible." He had obviously heard the news. "But that's why I called you. About the daughter. The youngest one."

"Jill." The one who had been asking around about me.

"Yes, yes, that's her. I have some dealings with her father. Had, I mean, and he sent her to me. She called last week. Knew she was coming in. Didn't know about her father, of course. I mean, that he…."

"I understand, Doc." There was no sense in letting him flounder.

"At any rate, I gave her your number. Least I could do. I meant to tell you the other day, but, well, it's spring."

He meant he was swamped, not that the old dear would ever admit it. Spring meant kitten season. County, the animal hospital where he held sway, had been overwhelmed with unwanted animals since the second week of March.

"Thanks." What else could I say? Maybe she knew about her sister's gift. Maybe she'd chipped in for the little beast. "Was she asking about the kitten? I thought I'd bring him by later. See if you could check him out. He's a cutie, but…" I didn't have to finish. Kitten season was fraught with risks. Unvaccinated, the little creatures were vulnerable to distemper and a dozen other disorders.

"Not today, Pru. I'm…well, we're quite busy." That was an unusual admission for the old Yankee.

"I'm sorry, Doc." I was. I knew I should be helping him out more. "I'll come by later—without the kitten." Something else was tickling at my memory. "Wait, you said you had business with David Canaday?"

"It's nothing. I shouldn't—" I could hear voices in the background. Voices and barking. Someone was calling Doc Sharpe's name. "I'm sorry, Pru. I have to run. Please do give Jill Canaday a call back if she gets in touch. I got the impression that she may have a job in mind."

Good ol' Doc, always looking out for me. I hated to break it to him. "It probably was about the kitten, then."

"No, I don't think so." Doc Sharpe doesn't lose his patience. However, he does get pressed, and he'd come as close to interrupting me as he'd ever done. "Pru, talk to her, please? I think she might be a good contact for you."

A good contact for me? I agreed, since it seemed important to him, and jotted down Jill Canaday's number. I hadn't had to. She had left the next message on my voice mail.

"Pru? Is this *the* Pru Marlowe?" There was a breathless quality to her voice that made me wonder just how young this third sister was. "I'm coming into town to see my dad today, and I'd really love to meet up. I guess my sister called you already, so maybe I'll meet you at the house. If not, would you call me, if you have time?"

I looked at my phone. Eleven a.m. Her father was probably dead already, although she wouldn't have known it yet. I thought about what Creighton had said. It was kinder, probably, not to call. I hit "erase." With that thought in mind, the next message made me feel like a heel.

"Pru, it's Jill again. Jill Canaday." The breathlessness was gone, replaced by a sodden weight that made each word sound like an effort. "I guess you know…well, I know you know. Look, I'd still like to meet up, but maybe…in a few days? Anyway, I'm still planning on being here for the summer, so there's no rush, I guess."

No rush for what? I puzzled that one over as I pulled out of the parking lot and headed home. Animals I understand. People? Most of the time, they didn't make sense to themselves. But that was a question for another time. Right now, I had to talk to a man about a squirrel.

Chapter Nine

Laurence Wilkins didn't answer his phone, which added to the joy of my day. Pest animal removal is never fun, and with my sensitivity the distress is amplified. Imagine evicting a tenant without a good reason. Yes, I know—roof damage. Wiring. But that doesn't matter to the squirrel. Plus, Wilkins was a lawyer, his voice mail had let me know. With the exception of Creighton, I prefer to avoid anybody with a legal background. Lawyers in particular. Talk about vermin, not to mention hard to get rid of.

Still, I wanted to get the job done rather than stressing about it. I'm not the kind to sit waiting at a mouse hole all day. I left a message with the basics—what I could do, how much I'd charge. A girl's got to eat, and I'd be kinder to those squirrels than most. When he texted me back an address on the east side of town, I figured that meant he'd agreed to my terms. If I wasn't worth phone time, that was fine by me.

I didn't know where he was texting from, but nobody answered the door when I rang. At first, I thought he might be with a client. A shingle out by the road announced that the imposing white house at the end of the curving drive also served as his office. But as I waited, eyeing the neoclassical froufrou— the fluted columns that flanked the oversized front door, the ivy swag carved into the molding—I couldn't help but notice why he had called. Over on the side, where a gutter had come loose, the cornice had been chewed through, leaving a gaping hole. Well, I could put a one-way door on that, the kind that lets the animals leave but not come back. After a few days, I'd wire it closed for good.

I rang again and knocked for good measure. Then, since I was here, I started around the side. Yes, there was another hole toward the back, where a modern addition had ruined the big box's symmetry. The office, I bet, seeing the oversize windows with those fancy bottom-to-top shades. Pity he hadn't spent the money on upkeep. I continued my inspection and made some notes. I'd have to come back with a ladder to make sure I hadn't missed anything, but those two holes were a start. I texted a preliminary report to Wilkins and asked for a deposit before I started. From the looks of this place, he could certainly afford me—and he was a lawyer, after all.

> > >

Wallis did not show herself when I got home. I didn't know if that was a message or utterly unrelated, but the way the kitten was sleeping—spread out on my bed—made me suspect the former. Or, possibly, that the young one had run my resident tabby ragged. Wallis didn't like to talk about her age, and I wouldn't dare assume. But she'd been an adult when we began cohabiting, and that had been close to seven years ago now. An afternoon alone with a kitten just might have worn her out.

Rather than seek her out, I settled into the kitchen. I'm not good with paperwork, but I've learned the necessity of sending out bills. Two fingers of bourbon made my monthly invoicing a tad less unpleasant, and the promise of a refill got me to finish as the long spring twilight faded outside. The anesthetic helped, and I poured my second glass with an easy wrist. The paperwork hadn't been that bad, but the numbers would be disheartening if I gave them any thought.

Better to sip the warming liquid and stare at the shadows.

"You know you snore when you drink too much." The gentle pressure against my shin softened the words that sounded inside my head. *"Particularly when you drink too much and don't eat anything."*

I continued to stare and with a bound, she landed on the table in front of me. *"And I'm not old, I'll have you know."*

"I know." I stroked the subtle stripes and she arched her back in pleasure. "Dinner?"

The purr began, low and deep, and I carried my glass over to the counter. I don't cook, not in any real sense. But Creighton had brought over a roast chicken the night before. We'd eaten some of it later, cold, along with the baguette he'd also procured. I'd liked the idea of him bringing me game.

"Does this mean you won't bite my head off?" His tone had been playful, his words accompanied by the offering of a drumstick, torn from the carcass. I'd taken it. I'd worked up an appetite, but I'd only smiled in response. Like I said, I liked the idea of him bringing me offerings. Besides, it wouldn't do for me to let him get too comfortable.

"Sharing the spoils?" I hadn't heard Wallis jump down, but now she brushed against me.

"Shall I warm it up?" I looked down into glowing green eyes and watched as they closed, briefly, in satisfaction. "Okay, then, just a minute."

A turn in the microwave brought out the glorious roasted scent, and my stomach was grumbling by the time I took my own plate over to the table. Wallis, who still preferred hers on the floor, was nearly growling.

"So, dare I ask?" I waited until we'd gone through the remaining breast and thigh. "The kitten?"

"I swear, none of my offspring were that stupid." Wallis had sat back by this point and had begun her post-meal toilette. *"Going on about smelling bad, like he couldn't keep himself clean."*

"He is very young." I pictured the fluffy tyke. He hadn't woken up while we'd been eating. I was so used to Wallis fending for herself that I hadn't left him anything. There was water out, always, but I had left the kitten kibble at the Canadays'. I hadn't even thought to bring him a toy.

"He's already fed." Wallis ran her paw over her whiskers, which already looked spotless to me. Something was going on behind

those smooth stripes, something she wasn't sharing. *"And that button? Talk about child's play."*

I got it then, in full color. Wallis had caught a mouse and eviscerated it, letting the kitten watch. She'd been quick—I sensed impatience rather than mercy—and for that I was grateful. I don't think of myself as sentimental, but compared to my cat, I was an utter softie. At least the kitten had enjoyed the spectacle. Plus, he had gorged on fresher meat than either of us had enjoyed.

"And he learned a thing or two." Another swipe flattened a black-tipped ear. *"By the way, his name is Ernesto."*

She paused. The animals I'd dealt with preferred to name themselves—choosing monikers that reflect their inner selves a lot better than our cutesy handles do. This kitten was so very young, though, I couldn't figure out whether he'd chosen Ernesto or that distant mama had—or if Wallis, in a fit of pique, had dropped that handle on him.

"Ernesto?," I asked.

"Ernesto Vuitton," she said. Another swipe. *"Button. Ha."*

Chapter Ten

When the next day passed without a call back from Wilkins, I had mixed feelings. No, I didn't want to deal with vermin of any kind. But, yes, I could have used the gig. I hadn't heard anything from any of the Canaday girls either, and I was out close to eighty bucks on them. I'd picked up more kitten kibble for the little guy by then. Wallis may have taken the kitten's education in hand, but I wasn't quite ready to trust her to keep him fed. Besides, I'd have to return the kitten eventually, and it would be useful to have some receipts to account for his care.

When the following day passed without a call from either client, I decided to take action. Wilkins I could take or leave, but the kitten was weighing on me. While there hadn't been another incident like the one at the house, I wasn't entirely easy about his health. Granted, I hadn't known Wallis as a kitten, but this little fellow seemed too ditzy to believe. If he wasn't going on about his button, he was calling for his mama. Even the most basic functions—a bath, a drink—brought forth an exclamation of surprise. He was young, I knew that. The world was new to him. But I couldn't rule out brain damage, not after what had seemed like a small seizure. Especially if he was a valuable animal, I didn't want to be responsible for him.

Maybe I was more like Wallis than I'd thought. Neither of us is cut out for parenthood, and I was getting sick of it. Besides, even if I was feeding the little guy, Ernesto—I found it difficult to call such a small animal by such a big name—I wasn't doing him any favors by keeping him here. I needed to return him, or get him placed somewhere while he still had his kittenish good looks. I knew what Judith had said about the kitten's—Ernesto's—papers. I also knew how many pedigree animals—nobody uses "purebred" for a cat—show up in shelters. At best, once Ernesto outgrew his cute stage, I'd be looking for a rescue group, maybe one that specialized in white puffballs with blue eyes.

I tried Jackie first, since she was the person who had hired me, and got her voice mail. I phoned the Mont, after that. They acknowledged having a Judith Canaday registered, but the line to her room went to a recording as well. After leaving my second message, I realized I had another option—a family member who actually wanted to talk to me.

"Jill? This is Pru, Pru Marlowe." I waited to see how she'd respond. Grief is a funny thing, and I was grateful simply to have reached a real person.

"Wow, really?" Not that funny. But before I could respond, the voice on the other end of the line came back. "I'm so glad you called, Pru. I can call you Pru, right? I'd been so looking forward to meeting you and then…"

"I understand, and I'm sorry," I said, as Jill's voice collapsed into a whimper. "I wasn't sure if it was too soon to call."

I waited while she blew her nose. "No, no, I'm glad you did." She sounded better for the brief bout of sobbing. "You're the main reason I wanted to spend the summer here."

"Excuse me?"

"Didn't that nice vet, Dr. Sharpe, tell you?"

"No." This was getting off track. "I thought we should talk about the kitten, the one your sister bought." I didn't want to tell her my concerns over the phone.

"Of course." I heard a voice behind her. One of her sisters' I imagined. "Look, would you come to the house on Friday? We're having people over, after the funeral. We finally got the okay, and—"

"Friday will be fine." I cut her off. I already knew about the autopsy. I didn't need details.

"Maybe after that you could bring the kitten by. I mean, in a day or so." Her comment startled me into silence. "I may as well start right away."

I had no idea what to say to that, but she didn't seem to require an answer. I was left feeling as witless as that kitten.

I have learned to cover my own ass, however, and my next call was to Creighton.

"Hey, Jim. Just a heads-up." He was driving—I could hear the road. That was fine. I planned on keeping it short. "I'm going to bring the Canadays' kitten back after the funeral. Jill, the youngest daughter, just okayed that."

"That's fine, Pru. Turns out we don't need him for any testing."

"No death by kitten?" I was joking. It had been a few days, and I was enjoying my favorite cop's voice.

"Actually, he might have been responsible." That took me aback, but Creighton kept talking. "But I don't think we have reason to hold him for it."

"Excuse me?"

He laughed, and I could almost hear him sorting through his options. "Look, Pru, you know I can't give you details, but I think it's fairly safe to say that the lab won't need the kitten. They've got enough to work with without it."

"So, you do suspect something?"

"Pru..." His voice had the same effect as a growl. Didn't matter. I was already weighing the options. What role would a kitten have in a man's death?

"Was he allergic?" Silence, and I asked the next question out loud. "Why would one of his daughters give him a cat if he was allergic?"

"Look, Pru." Creighton knows me. Knows he has to give me something, sometimes, or I won't shut up. "Nothing is official, not yet. The old guy was on a cabinet full of drugs. Plus, we found an inhaler in his bathroom—the kind that's sold over the counter—and other stuff, too. His oldest is furious with the doctor, of course. Says her father wasn't warned about dangerous interactions." I could hear the wind, some distant jays. Just enough distraction to keep him talking. "Maybe it is his fault." Creighton was musing out loud. "But it seems to me like people need to take responsibility for their own selves. At any rate, the coroner has ordered more tests."

That was possibly the longest he'd ever talked about a case. Then again, it sounded like the death of David Canaday wasn't going to be any of my concern. And Jim Creighton had other thoughts on his mind.

"Speaking of which," he paused, and I was holding my breath. In this mood, who knew what he'd spill? "I don't think I've met this kitten yet," he said finally. "What say I come over tonight and you introduce me to the lethal pet?"

Chapter Eleven

Friday dawned bright and clear. Creighton was singing in the shower as Wallis jumped up on the bed, her ears ever so slightly back.

"Is this going to become a habit now?" She was referring to his staying over. She understood why I wanted him to visit, but half the bed, until recently, had been her territory.

"Don't worry." I kept my own voice soft as I reached to stroke her. Wallis may be able to read my thoughts, but it is easier for me if I conduct our conversation out loud. "You know I can't let him get too close."

"Hmm." That seemed to satisfy her, and she began to knead the thick down comforter. *"And you're getting rid of that infant, too, I trust?"*

I nodded. "I'm sorry. I never meant to dump him on you."

"He's fine. No less intelligent than most males, but the crying has become annoying."

"Crying?" I hadn't heard that last night. Instead, Ernesto had seemed to enjoy Creighton's company.

"Oh, he likes to be played with, all right." She kept kneading. *"He's a weak little thing, awfully dependent on humans."*

"Poor guy." Wallis might be being, well, catty. Creighton and I had been focused on the kitten, after all. But I couldn't discount what she was saying. Ernesto was a pedigreed animal. A show cat. He'd probably been handled since the day of his birth. Fussed over, to make sure he was socialized. Then I'd left him with no company except for Wallis until last night. He had reason to fuss. But …weak? That was worrisome. I thought of the cough. The vomit.

"Not that you're not a great teacher," I added, out loud and hastily, for her benefit—and to cover my own thoughts.

"*I know.*" She had begun to purr as she settled into the down. "*But I think this is something more. Something disturbed him.*"

It wasn't like there weren't other options. Something besides illness. For all that I found Ernesto playing, apparently carefree, he had witnessed a man's death. I doubted that he'd had a chance to bond with old Mr. Canaday, but he might have been held by the man.

I thought of the button the kitten had been batting about when I found him, the pleas for a human playmate to kick it back. Maybe Canaday hadn't been immune to the kitten's charms. Maybe he'd been playing with Ernesto, making the most of an impromptu toy, when he'd started choking. When the pain began to spread. Whether the kitten had been dropped or thrown, or simply witnessed those last agonizing moments, he had seen something confusing. Something potentially terrifying. For a human-oriented animal, that was a lot to deal with.

"And I call myself a behaviorist." I muttered, more to myself than to Wallis, although as I watched, her kneading took on the appearance of a shrug.

"Ah, I see you've got company." Creighton, fresh from the shower, strode into the room. As he toweled off, Wallis eyed him up and down, and I had to resist the temptation to slap her. "How's she getting along with the kitten?"

"Pretty well." I contented myself with putting one hand, rather heavily on her back.

"Think they can get along a little while longer?" He reached to retrieve his shirt, and she nipped at me.

"Probably. Why?" I pulled my hand back, and Wallis and I glared at each other.

"I was wondering if you had plans for the morning." Shirt on, he checked under the bed for the rest of his clothes. "I've got to represent the department, and you've met these people, too."

"Wait." I sat up, pulling the covers up against the early morning chill. "You're asking me on a date—to a funeral?"

His head popped up. "It's not a date, Pru. Don't be silly."

I watched as he retrieved his socks.

"You're going to be meeting one of the daughters after, right?" He sat on the edge of the bed. "And, hey, it wouldn't hurt your standing in the community to show your face. David Canaday was a big deal."

I thought about it while he tied his shoes. He was right about the daughters—at least one of them—and I trusted him about Canaday. But even though Creighton and I had been spending more time together, I still drew the line at being seen in public together. This is a very small town, and I wanted to keep my autonomy for many reasons. He knew some of them and understood—as a cop, he saw our town at its misogynistic, macho worst. My biggest reason—the truth about my sensitivity—would have to remain a secret.

In fact, I could have used some help at this point. But Wallis was simply staring at me, green eyes wide in an expression I couldn't quite read.

"Besides," he added, talking to the mirror, "it would be nice to have you there."

The trump card. Maybe I'm not as tough as I'd like. "Yeah," I heard myself say. "I could meet you there, I guess." As I watched, Wallis slowly blinked in approval. "After I walk Growl— I mean, after I walk Tracy Horlick's bichon."

If he heard me catch myself—I'd almost used the dog's preferred name—he didn't let on. "Great. I appreciate it." He stopped himself in the bedroom door. "Hey, maybe you'll be able to pick up a client while you're there. Just be careful about getting caught up in that family's feuds."

Chapter Twelve

If Growler noticed my clothes, he didn't comment. That didn't stop his person, Tracy Horlick, from raising her eyebrows when she opened the door to me.

"My, what have we here?" Those brows, drawn as an auburn line three shades lighter than her bad dye job, disappeared into her forehead as she took another drag on the ever-present Marlboro and took in my black top and pants.

"Is this a new uniform?" She exhaled, and I stifled a cough. Any response would be seen as encouragement, and I do pride myself on my ability to train even the most recalcitrant beast. After another wave of smoke as she tried again, her smoker's rasp growing louder and more peevish. "Going to rob a grave?"

"Is Bitsy ready for his walk?" I managed a smile. I did enjoy ignoring her. "The weather is so nice this morning."

"Nice day for a funeral." Her eyes squinted, and I began to wonder if some of the smoke was from her brain working. "You're going to the Canaday funeral, aren't you?"

"I am doing some work for the family." I didn't like giving her anything, but I also didn't have all day. "Bitsy?"

"Huh." She turned in. Even from the stoop, I could hear Growler—the dog she called Bitsy—scrabbling at an interior door. "Like oil and water, those girls," she muttered as she shuffled to him. "Wouldn't be surprised if the money just makes that worse."

Money? Hey, the guy was a lawyer. She was trying to get me to respond, I could tell. But none of that money was going to come my way, not unless I kept my reputation. And so as the bichon came racing out to meet me, I ducked down to greet him. "Bitsy! How are you doing?" I rubbed his white curls, and silently apologized for using the name he hated.

"Out," he barked. To anyone else, his curt command would sound like a bichon's sharp yelp. *"What are you waiting for? Let's go!"*

"You're the boss," I replied, standing, having clipped on the little dog's lead.

Tracy Horlick, temporarily mollified, cracked her lipstick into a mean smile. "Don't count on any of the Canaday girls becoming regular clients." She took another drag. "Not like me and Bitsy."

"I should be so lucky." I had kept the smile in place, but I still saw the scowl settling into the old lady's face as she tried to work out whether my words translated into an insult or not.

"What are you playing at, walker lady?" Growler voiced his question as a short yip as he led me to the curb. *"Humans,"* he chuffed, a half-snort bark. *"You'd think you'd have learned to listen by now."*

"I'm sorry, Growler." I was. I'd been selfish, baiting the old lady. "Does she take it out on you?"

He grunted as he watered a tree. *"Huh, Bruce was here. Twice. Lucky devil."* I couldn't tell if I had embarrassed him with my solicitude or he simply had more compelling interests. We walked on. *"Jeff, Douglas…Man, you've got to get over that bitch."* I no longer wondered about Growler's focus on his male colleagues. Given the gender of the woman who controlled so much of his life, I was grateful that he communicated with me at all.

"Get over yourself, girl." I stopped just in time to keep from stepping on the little dog, who was staring up at me. *"You're not the one in charge here. The sooner you realize that, the sooner you might learn something."*

"True enough, Growler." I suppressed a smile. The tiny animal had enough insults to his dignity. "Want to head down to the river?"

His satisfied chuff didn't need a translation, and I let him enjoy the rest of his outing in doggie peace.

Chapter Thirteen

The service was about to start by the time I made it to the church, and a few annoyed eyes turned to me as I creaked open the heavy door. A reasonable crowd, about two-thirds full, spoke either to Canaday's popularity or, more likely, his influence. Canaday had been a big deal, I had gathered. Old lady Horlick's snark about his money had woken some images—things overheard or half-remembered. He'd been a mover and shaker, a town figure. And a hard ass, I now recalled—the kind who was always railing about something. The kind I and my set avoided when we could.

By all accounts, David Canaday was a man my mother would have admired—all law and order, a family that toed the line. For a moment, I had to wonder if there might have been more. My mother had outlived the lawyer's wife, I gathered, and I was gone for a few years. I was pretty sure she was done with men by then, though. Not that other women wouldn't have set their caps for him. A rich lawyer in our town? That would explain the crowd. The church was full of female mourners. With their hard-set faces and short, practical hair, they even reminded me of my mother—the woman she was before I left, at any rate. Then again, looking around, I wondered if their interest had been romantic or even mercenary. Some people believe in a certain order. Not me, but I knew it was true. And maybe there was a reason he had stuck to his daughters for companionship.

Maybe it was those women. Maybe because it was a funeral, but a look around made me think of her. My mom, back in the day.

This hadn't been our church—as much as my family had a house of worship—but she had dragged me to services at the lower-end church across town often enough in her attempt to win me from my father's influence early on. I still remembered the setup and the routine, and that proved useful now. Without much thought, I smiled and bobbed my head as I slipped into a back pew.

As the organ music came to a wheezy end, I spotted Creighton—that short blond crop stood out—and in front of him, the raven black hair of Judith Canaday, a flashy bird among the sparrows. She seemed almost alone in that front pew, but then I saw, off to her left, a dark head dulled with gray. Jackie. It didn't look like the sibs were giving each other any comfort. Trying not to be too obvious, I leaned forward. Jill, the youngest sister, had to be there somewhere, but I'd meet her soon enough. What I wanted to find out was if there were any other family members. Anyone slightly separate from the drama. Someone who lived in town, ideally. I had an outstanding invoice—and a kitten to re-house as soon as I could. A friendly cousin or brother with his own family would save me a lot of bother up front.

That first pew was hard to see, with people shifting on the hard wood, and the rustling of pages around me alerted me to the fact that I'd missed some cue. On either side of me, people were opening black-bound books, and one woman with a face like a battle-ax nodded to the seatback in front of me. I pulled out a prayer book just in time to hear the minister announce a psalm. Switching volumes, I thumbed through to the correct number, all the while feeling my neighbor's eyes on me.

"Do you know who the family is?" I asked. The singing had begun, but as long as my neighbor was paying attention to me, rather than the service, I might as well take advantage of that.

"Shh!" A small, close-faced woman seated in front of me turned with an angry hiss.

"Well, do you?" I was mouthing the words now. Surely the old biddy ahead of me couldn't be bothered by that.

"You are in a church." Staring lady mouthed the words back to me with such care and clarity, I could have read her lips. Since I didn't have to, I only shrugged. She had started it.

"Three girls?" I held up three fingers, and she batted them down. Call me stubborn: that just made me more determined. "Anyone else?" If she wanted me to stop, the fastest way was to answer me. The woman in front of me, the little one, shifted. Around us, the singing had trailed off, and the minister began to talk.

"Bother," said the woman to my left. Or "father," but I couldn't see that as a possibility.

"Father?" I mouthed back. It was worth a shot.

"Partner." Her stage whisper came just as the minister's voice had died away, and this time she was the target of the death glare. I sat back with a nod. This being Beauville, I assumed she meant a business partner, rather than anything more domestic, and that was good news for me. Surely, another lawyer would not be too grief-stricken to take care of the estate's outstanding bills.

"Please rise." We all did, which gave me a better chance to peek through the pews. Yes, up front, a suit sitting near Jackie and Judith. Leaning toward another dark-haired female. Nice suit, from what I could make out. To pass the time, I pegged him for the lawyer. Maybe an old law school buddy of the deceased. The families had vacationed together, and—I was being creative here—the partners covered for each other's affairs. No, I don't have a particularly rosy view of my own species. It's never given me any reason for one.

Mixing and matching the congregation kept me so busy that when the service ended some forty minutes later, I almost missed my cue.

"Peace be with you." The hard little number in front of me was saying to her neighbor. I turned to my source, but the look in her eye stopped me from repeating the same.

"Pru, there you are." Creighton, standing in the aisle, broke into her basilisk stare. "And here I was thinking that you couldn't bring yourself to enter."

"It's garlic that keeps me away. Garlic and silver crosses." I sidled over to him, probably closer than necessary. Churches affect me that way. He stepped back, but he was smiling.

I took that as a green light. "Hey, do you know Canaday's business partner?" I was looking over his shoulder, but the nicely dressed gent had disappeared. "Think you could get me a name?"

"I can do better." He rested one hand ever so lightly on my arm, turning me around and toward the door. "I can introduce you. You were planning on joining me graveside, weren't you?"

›››

We took two cars—Creighton knew better than to protest—and he was waiting for me by the parking area when I pulled in.

"Thought you'd bailed." He leaned in as I walked up.

"I had a call to make," I explained. I'd tried Wilkins again and left another message. "The partner?"

"After," he said, his voice soft. Already a small crowd had gathered by the open grave. A green cloth, looking suspiciously like Astroturf, covered the mound of earth that would soon fill it. But before I could spout off about the hypocrisy of such camouflage, Creighton took my hand. Not out of affection—with a squeeze he directed my attention to the woman sitting in a folding chair by the grave. Jackie Canaday had the worn-down look of a long-term caregiver. Primary mourner, too, I figured from the way everyone seemed to be treating her, greeting her with gentle coos and pats.

Everybody except her middle sister, that is. Judith was standing by Jackie's chair. Up close, the family resemblance was undeniable. Although Jackie no longer had her sister's glossy hair, the two shared a certain bone structure. On Judith, it was striking: sharp cheekbones and a profile that would have looked masculine on a lesser beauty. Jackie's jaw had gone a little slack—I put her close to forty. Closer than I was, at any rate, though the matronly dress didn't help. The puffiness of tears had softened the overall contours, but side-by-side you could see the family resemblance.

You could also see the animosity. Maybe it was the sharpness, the line of pink along those cheekbones, the firm set of the mouth, but Judith looked furious, glaring down at her sister like she was going to attack her. The third Canaday girl, Jill, had to be here somewhere, but I had no idea what she looked like, and she seemed to have no part in the drama being acted out before me.

"Jackie," Another woman—a stranger—bent over the older sister, confirming my suspicion. "I'm so sorry...." Other words followed, muted by distance, moving from Jackie to Judith in dutiful order. I couldn't hear the sisters' responses, but I knew the routine. At least the condolence line was keeping the two women separate. I could almost feel Judith's glare from back here.

"Grateful..." Someone else was talking now. Why the hell did people always use that word? Judith's mood was beginning to make sense to me. Grateful for what? A man came up next. The suit—the one from the church. Jackie took his hand when he offered it and pulled him down closer. Greedy, I thought. Or anxious.

"Is that the partner?" I nudged Creighton and nodded to the couple.

"Uh huh," he murmured back. Behind them, a woman was talking, her voice low and urgent. "Grateful they could even *have* a funeral..." Her voice had risen in excitement, and I turned to look. "From what I heard..." Another voice chimed in.

"Pru." There was a warning note in Creighton's voice.

"Shall we?" The minister's quiet command hushed us all. "If the family would take their places."

"Jill, over here." Another woman—the busybody from the church—gestured toward the chairs.

"Jim?" I was still mulling over that strange comment when the woman from church turned to face us all.

"Please," she said. "We're going to start."

I turned to see whom she had addressed. Another woman was approaching the chairs. As black-haired as Judith, but with the softer face of Jackie, this had to be Jill, the baby of the family.

Seating herself between the two sisters, she pulled Judith into a chair. Only then did she turn toward her older sister to give her a friendly pat. It wasn't appreciated. Even from here, I could see how Judith recoiled. See her glare.

"Our father," the minister began. All three women turned as one, making the family resemblance clear and giving me a chance to think about what could have set the sisters at odds.

I didn't have long to muse. The graveside service was blessedly short. As grateful as I was to be outdoors on a lovely spring day, I was quite happy to join in a general "amen."

Creighton's arm stopped me, though, as I took a step.

"Not yet," he said. Sure enough, I'd forgotten this part.

Two hefty men in dirt-stained work clothes stood back, waiting. I imagined they wanted to get on with it. Have a smoke. Get home. But the minister made one more little speech and then picked a spotless shovel—and things got weird.

Jackie, I could see, had begun to cry at some point during the service. Her head hung down on her chest even as her shoulders bobbed. Jill was fussing over her now. As I watched, she dug a tissue out of her bag and handed it over. With one look at her two siblings, Judith stood, ready to do the honors and, just maybe, show up her big sister one last time.

"Father Paul?" She reached out.

"No!" Jackie stood—flinging off Jill, who sat back with a thud—and strode forward, taking the spade from the surprised minister's hands.

"Jackie." Jill scrambled behind her, reaching for the wooden handle.

"I'm the one who took care of him." Jackie spun around, glared at Judith and then turned to take in Jill, as she brandished the shovel like a weapon. "You didn't know." She spit the words at them, her voice shrill. "You weren't here. Neither of you. But you— Judith—"

"I *what?*" Color had flooded Judith's face, outlining those cheekbones in crimson.

"You know what you did." Jackie's eyes were already puffed, but now they narrowed into slits. Her knuckles, I could see, were turning white as she tightened her grip on the spade. "If it hadn't been for you, bringing that cat…"

"If you had taken better care of him." Judith hissed back, her own hands forming fists at her side. "Made him take his meds. Read the damned labels. If you hadn't left him…"

"I told you." Jackie's voice rising to hysteria. "I had an appointment!"

"Ladies, please." The man in the suit—the partner—stepped in ahead of Jill, who stood frozen at the spot.

Jackie turned toward him, sputtering—"an appointment, and I waited"—but he managed to calm her down. "Yes, you did, Jackie. Nobody's saying you didn't."

It was an odd kind of reassurance, but it seemed to be working. Jackie's mouth closed. I could see her choking back the tears, but she let him take the spade from her.

"Please, ladies." His voice was soothing and calm. "This is a horrible day. For all of us."

Judith glared, but she let it go, and he settled them both back into their seats.

"Thank you—thank you," said the minister, his face glowing with sweat. "I believe we should now proceed directly to the final blessing. Thank you, Mr. Wilkins."

Chapter Fourteen

"Wilkins?" I turned toward Creighton in surprise, my other questions momentarily forgotten. "That's Laurence Wilkins?"

"If you'd *please...!*" Another glare, accompanied by a lipstick scowl. What was it with women and religion? I shook off the memories of my mother and drew my beau aside.

"Jim, why didn't you tell me?" I hissed my question into his ear, as the minister began to drone once more.

"Tell you what?" Creighton drew back and looked at me. "Canaday and Laurence Wilkins had a practice together downtown. Biggest legal firm in town. After your time, I guess."

"He's a client," I explained. "Or, rather, he's supposed to be. I've been trying to reach him for days now."

Creighton shrugged. "I would imagine he's been busy. But, hey, I said I'd introduce you."

With a nod, I followed as he walked into the crowd. Despite the drama—or because of it—the assembly was quiet and attentive, and the minister made the most of it, building to crescendo with his final blessing. A sigh—of relief or disappointment—followed, and people began to mill about. As they did, voices climbed to normal volume again, and I strained for any tidbits. Twice I thought I heard "pending," once "tests," but each time I turned, the speakers dropped their voices. Maybe it wasn't me. With sweeping gestures, the minister tried to move the small crowd back toward the parking area. The two workmen, I could see, were waiting for his cue.

"Laurence Wilkins." Creighton's voice called me back, and I turned as he addressed the silver-haired lawyer. As tall as Creighton, though not as broad in the shoulder, he looked older up close. "I'd like you to meet Pru Marlowe."

"I'm sorry for your loss." I recited the formula as I took his outstretched hand. Large and cool, it closed easily around mine and held it for a moment longer than I would have liked. "And I'm sorry to have bothered you at such a time."

"Marlowe, that's right." He nodded, gray eyes locked on mine. "You've left me several messages."

"I responded to your request." I'm okay with being polite, I don't like being put on the spot. "You called about the squirrels?"

"Yes, of course." Satisfied, he let go of my hand. "I received your estimate and was planning on calling you tomorrow."

"If you like, I can come by tomorrow." I didn't bother to correct him. I provide a service for a fee—not an estimate. "I can put up some one-way gates and in a few days, your problem should be solved."

"Will the work be…" He paused, as if considering his next words. "Disruptive?"

"No more than having animals scurry over your head is." I was getting sick of this guy. Either he wanted my help or he didn't. I made myself think of the money. Swallowed. Tried again. "I'll need to examine the rest of your roof, but as long as I have your permission, I can go ahead. I should be able to put the gates up in an hour or so."

He thought about that. "That might be practicable. I've got clients coming over tomorrow morning."

The shingle. "You work out of your home?"

His nod confirmed it. "I do now. I'm still only semi-retired," Wilkins continued. "Despite anything David could do about it."

As if hearing the implications of his own words, he waved his hands in the air. "No, I don't mean anything by that. It's just that he was ready to let go. To retire—at least from the practice." The lawyer shook his head. "We've been—we were partners forever. My wife and I didn't have kids, and his daughters were like, well…I watched those girls grow up. When he became ill and decided to take things easier—to focus on his charity work—I was in the midst of remodeling. So I just turned it around—made the new wing into a home office. I'd been thinking of it as a satellite, but then we gave up the office downtown, and I now see clients in my home office."

"Well, I'll do my best to stay out of your way." Over his shoulder, I could see the rest of the crowd dispersing. "And if you have any questions, you can call me."

"I will." He was clearly the sort to want the last word. But, no, there was something else. He put a hand out, as if to stop me. "In fact, I wanted to ask you something—"

"Tomorrow." With a smile, I brushed past him. Judith seemed to have disappeared, but Jackie was still receiving condolences. I made my way over.

"Jackie?" She looked up, her face swollen and blotchy, and I caught myself. There was no way I could talk to this woman about a kitten. Not now. "Pru Marlowe," I reminded her. "The animal expert? I just wanted to tell you how sorry I am."

She nodded, but I sensed something beyond a fatigued acknowledgment. Maybe it was the way her mouth tightened up. "If only you'd come sooner," she said, after a pause. The words fell out as if she could not longer restrain them. "If you'd removed that— that animal."

"Now, wait a minute." If I were Wallis, my fur would be rising along my spine. "It's not the kitten's fault."

I felt a hand on my upper arm and shook it off. Creighton should know better by now.

"Pru? Ms. Marlowe?" I turned and instead of my beau, I saw a younger version of the sad, angry woman who was now staring daggers at me. Jill.

"Yes?" I was in no mood for this family.

"I'm so glad you came." Yes, it was the same breathless voice. "Jill Canaday. We spoke on the phone."

I turned back in time to see Jackie storm off. Her coterie—more of those tight-mouthed women—were staring daggers at me. I'd just given them a bit more to gossip about. Not that I could help that. Turning from their basilisk glare, I focused on the woman in front of me.

"Jill, yes, of course." I bit my lip, unsure how to proceed. Behind me, I heard the slow chunk of shovels in the dirt. The gravediggers had begun their work. "About what your sister said." When in doubt, dive in. "You know, it's not the kitten's fault."

"I do." She nodded, and I realized I'd been holding my breath. "I'm sorry you had to hear that. In fact, that's part of what I want to talk to you about."

She tilted her face up to mine, and I was struck again by the family resemblance. Jill's round face might have lacked the fashion model contours of Judith's, her skirt and blouse certainly cost less, but her youth made her pretty. I put her at twenty— twenty-five at the outside—a good ten to fifteen years younger than her oldest sister.

"I'm so glad. I mean, that you'll be taking the kitten." Creighton was behind her and from the look on his face, I knew he was about to butt in. The gravediggers were working in earnest now, their rhythm regular and deep. "Because he needs a home."

"I'm sorry." She had the grace to look distressed, though that could have been the sound of spades. "I'm thinking I shouldn't take the kitten back just yet. Not while my sister is so, well, you know. I didn't mean to lead you on, but I don't really know what I'm going to be doing in the fall. I'd already decided to spend the summer back here. I thought I'd be helping my dad, and now…"

A swallow and a blink pushed back the tears that had suddenly appeared. Chunk. We could all hear it now. Chunk. "But that wasn't all of it. What I meant, was— well…I've heard about you, Pru. I've heard so much about you. I want you to teach me everything you know."

Chapter Fifteen

I had a million better things to be doing than to go back to the dead man's house. Curiosity overruled them all, however. Curiosity and a desire to get to the bottom of this particular puzzle. Creighton looked amused when I told him I was heading over there. Smart enough to suppress his smile, he made some comment about acolytes. He wouldn't say anything more.

"Look," I tried to keep my voice soft. I'd taken his hand by then. Usually the combination does the trick. "I just want to know what's going on, okay? The Canaday who hired me is not going to take her dad's kitten. I don't think she's going to want to pay me, either. And the sister who bought the animal can't take him. She's staying in a fancy hotel for the duration." I paused, waiting. I got nothing. "So this third daughter is it. Only, I don't know what's up with her."

"Watch out, Pru." A dimple twitched in his cheek. "These Canaday girls—they're a whole new breed of animal."

"I'll watch it," I snarled. I hadn't wanted to be roped into this whole funeral shindig in the first place. I liked even less thinking that I was going to be even further ensnared.

By the time I got to the house, it was already full. Casseroles and platters of cold cuts covered the dinner table, and I saw one of Creighton's deputies loading cheese on an overfilled sandwich.

"Ms. Marlowe." Wilkins turned to acknowledge me. He'd been talking to Judith, who turned and blinked at me as if we'd never met.

"Pru Marlowe," I extended my hand to her. "I'm the one who took your kitten in."

"That's right." She looked me up and down before turning back to the lawyer. "Maybe she can talk some sense into Jackie."

"Excuse me?" I don't like being talked about as if I weren't there. In that way, I'm like Growler.

"Sorry." She smiled, full wattage, and I remembered—she'd been living in LA. "It's just ...my sister has gone a little over the edge. She's so into being the mother hen that she doesn't know what to do with herself."

A look around revealed what Judith was talking about. Even now I could see her older sister putting together plates of food, wrapping up sandwiches in plastic like she was about to launch a campaign.

"Was she always like that?" As I watched, Wilkins made his way over to help her or to calm her down.

"Well, since this latest development," Judith answered, her voice cool. "You heard about the autopsy?"

I nodded. "I gather there are some loose ends?"

"Aren't there always?" Judith shrugged. It had the effect of sending a ripple through her coal-black hair. "Jackie just can't deal. Ever since Mother died, she's been high-strung, but I've never seen her like this. I used to feel bad for her, but you know, she could have left."

I kept my voice cool. "Like you did?"

One eyebrow arched. "I have a right to a life. For what I wanted to do, I couldn't wait."

I nodded. "And how's that working out for you?"

"Fine, thank you." She turned, meeting me stare for stare. "I remember when you left town, too."

Point. I smiled, the closest I would come to a submissive gesture. Judith Canaday would be a formidable opponent if I were ever in a competition. As it was, I noticed the few men in the room hovering. Maybe it was just as well Creighton had not tagged along. I looked back over at Jackie. She was fussing in the kitchen, rooting around in a cabinet. Wilkins had his hands full, balancing a plate of cookies and a cup and saucer, his temper starting to fray.

"Jackie!" I heard him bark. "It doesn't matter. Go sit down."

I couldn't have said it better myself. She shot him a pained look but obeyed, drifting off to the living room.

"You think you'll stay?" I turned back to the woman before me. She had caught me watching the lawyer and smiled now, a slow smile.

"Why should I?" Judith's voice was low. "What's left for me here?"

A home, I could have said. A sister who would probably welcome you. A father whose overriding presence had been abruptly removed. Any of those would have been true. None of which I wanted to say. Instead, I found myself at a loss for words.

Luckily, I didn't need them. Before I could form a more polite answer, a sudden rise in volume from the other room caught my attention. Panic sounds the same in most species.

"What's wrong?" A woman's voice spiked. "What is it?"

"Nothing, nothing." Wilkins, his voice deep and reassuring. "She just needs some air."

The crowd parted as the lawyer came through, one arm around the youngest Canaday girl.

"Poor thing." I heard another woman say. "She loved her father."

"We all did." I turned to see Jackie, returned from the living room, her voice strained. "We all loved our father. We all lost him!"

"Of course, dear." One of the matrons stepped in, as much to smooth ruffled feathers, I thought, as to offer real comfort. Any talk about the autopsy was over, at least until the social equilibrium was restored. Everyone was fussing about Jackie now—the town's notables focused on her, and on the little sister who had left the house on the lawyer's arm.

But there were three Canaday girls, and I turned to look for the other daughter. The one who had not seemed so upset. She had stepped back, I saw then—away from the hubbub by the food, from the drama surrounding her sisters. Judith was watching the room, I could see that. What she hadn't realized was that

I had turned to watch her. And what I saw was chilling. For once, for maybe the first time in a long time, the woman before me wasn't the focus of anyone's attention. And in the calm privacy away from the spotlight, she had dropped the cool mask. Her striking features showed the grim set of rage.

Chapter Sixteen

"You should have seen your face." Later, back at my place, Creighton was having a good laugh at my expense. "I can't believe that little chit of a girl managed to shake you up like that."

"You don't—" I stopped myself. He was talking about Jill, not Judith. I was still mulling over what I'd seen—that sudden transformation. So instead I told him about Jackie, flailing, her outsized grief grabbing all the attention in the room. And only then about Jill's strange request. With his cop instincts, Jim had homed in on the one Canaday girl who had really gotten to me.

"You don't know how presumptuous Jill was being. I studied for years to get where I am, Jim," I barked out now.

"Well, you didn't have to poison her." Creighton was joking. He knew—he had his sources—about Jill getting sick at the gathering.

"Jim." I wasn't even going to respond to that. Besides, if he knew she had gotten ill, he also would have heard that she'd recovered. "I wasn't the caterer. But, wait…" I turned to look at my beau. "Why are you talking poison?"

The autopsy. "Jim, was Canaday poisoned?"

"Pru, you know I can't talk about this." He put his hand on my mouth before I could speak. "But just to shut you up, darling, I will tell you that there's nothing to say."

"The medical examiner is doing more tests." The hum of gossip at the funeral. The talk of delays.

His raised eyebrows were the only confirmation I would get.

"You really are becoming a gossip," he said out loud. "Seriously, Pru, maybe you should take this girl up on her offer."

He knew that the sofa we were now sitting on, as well as the house where I had retreated after the debacle at the funeral, was mine only because of my mother. Just as he knew that the labors that had taken up the rest of my day were more on the level of petsitter than animal professional.

"You know, it wouldn't kill you to open up a little." The bourbon had loosened his tongue.

"Are you sure you're talking about that girl, Jim?" I wasn't just deflecting his attention. This was an ongoing struggle between the two of us.

"She wants to learn from you. She admires you." He took a sip. "She seems nice."

"Maybe you're jealous of her interest in me." I was teasing, sure, but not entirely. I'd rather pawn my hunky beau off on a new girl than risk him knowing the truth about me. I liked having some company. I don't like being locked up. "Maybe you want her for yourself."

"I know what I want." He put the glass down, and then he showed me.

>>>

I slipped out of bed before he woke the next morning, anxious to avoid any further questions. This close to the solstice, the sun was up as early as I was, sneaking through the shades with a soft light that almost had me reconsidering my harsh stance. Wallis was waiting in the kitchen as I came through, and she tilted her head as I reached for my jacket.

"Gotta get going." I kept my voice soft.

"Don't you want to know what's up with Ernesto?" Without any apparent effort, she leaped to the windowsill and waited while I opened the window. The air that came in was cool, but as she flexed her whiskers, I caught the rush of new life it carried.

"If you can give me a quick rundown." Creighton had a cop's senses. He'd be up soon, despite the bourbon and my best efforts to lay him out.

"I *don't have to.*" She flicked her tail. *"He will."*

"Ernesto?" I looked around. Sure enough, the kitten had entered the kitchen and now stood looking up at me, imploring. With a sigh of resignation, I bent to pick him up, but rather than allowing himself to be cuddled, he strained toward Wallis. I put him in the windowsill and marveled at how he mimicked her pose. The scrawny kitten was learning balance, if not poise.

"He fell." He was staring out the window, his mouth slightly open as he took in the scents. *"Fighting it. Grabbing at it."*

I drew back. Was this little creature reliving the death scene? Had he been traumatized? I knew animals didn't view death the same way humans did. They were much more prosaic about mortality. As carnivores, they are part of this bloody cycle in a more immediate, visceral way than we humans are. But had the kitten bonded with the dying man? Had he been scarred by his fall?

I got an image of hands grasping and then that button, rolling around on the floor. *"Yes! The button."* And I got it. Ernesto wasn't reliving anything. He was watching the world outside.

This was his frame of reference. Not that prey animals were toys, but that play was serious work for him. Every time he had jumped on that rolling button, he had been exercising his instinct to pounce, to hunt.

He was learning to be a cat.

Chapter Seventeen

Albert didn't like lending me his truck. The Beauville animal control officer—think "dogcatcher"—particularly didn't like that I wouldn't give him the keys to my GTO in exchange, which meant he was stranded in the office until my return. But not only was I doing him a favor by taking the Wilkins case off his hands, I was protecting his pride. Albert was afraid of heights, I'd discovered, the first time a homeowner had asked him to go up a ladder. I'd covered for him then and not let on to the boys at Happy's, our local watering hole. That gave me leverage now, when I needed something besides my old muscle car to do my—or, really, his—job. His ladder had been in the back of the shelter since that first unsteady climb, and that saved me a trip, too.

"Be back by lunch, Pru." He surrendered the keys finally. "Okay?"

"I'll do my best." With a quick wink at Frank, who had popped out of his person's vest, I took off. Back to Laurence Wilkins' place.

Quarter past ten, and the day was gearing up to be a warm one. In a month, I'd work up a sweat hoisting a ladder. The same breeze that had flooded my kitchen had hung around, though, and I welcomed the sun on my back as I settled Albert's cheap aluminum deal against the side of Wilkins' house. Careful as I could be, I couldn't help crushing the first leaves of his foundation planting. It was a pity. That greenery would soften the boxy look of the new addition, if it survived. But I had a job to do. Already, I could hear the chirps and squeaks of life inside the roof. Happy sounds. Homey. Shaking them off, I went back to the truck for the wire contraptions.

"Ms. Marlowe." The lawyer had come out to his front stoop. "You're prompt."

"Who's there?" A sharp bark, inquisitive rather than alarmed. *"Who?"*

"Going to get these up and be out of your hair." I showed him the little wire boxes. Although they look like traps, they allow animals to get out, I explained. But once out, they can't re-enter. "I'd give them forty-eight hours," I said. "If you hear anything after that, give me another call."

"Who?" Someone was getting impatient. *"Is it her? Her? Her?"*

"You have a dog?" The bark was audible, after all.

"What? Oh, yes." He turned back toward his house. "A Shetland shepherd. Biscuit. She was my wife's."

"I'm sorry." He'd mentioned her. I tried to remember what else he'd said.

"Thank you." He looked down at the stoop, embarrassed, I thought, by his emotion. "That was close to ten years ago, and she'd been ill for some time."

I nodded. Some people think of grief as a weakness, as if time and anticipation make it less. Another bark rang out. Someone was still feeling the pain. Someone was also, I could hear, bored and sick of being cooped up. "You know, I also walk dogs."

"Good to know." But he was looking toward the road. Silly me, I had thought he was checking up on me. That he'd want an explanation of what I was doing. He was simply taking the air.

Or waiting for someone, I realized as I went back to work. One day after his partner's funeral. Well, life goes on.

Chapter Eighteen

I was up on the ladder when the first car appeared. A late model sedan, big, dark, and formal looking. An older woman, perhaps, looking to revise a will. Another lawyer, seeking to finalize some corporate paperwork. Whoever it was would be a break from the chirps and squeaks around me. My hammering might not be understood—not exactly—but my presence, so close to a nest, was. I was a danger, a threat, though not quite as deadly as those squirrels feared. Well, they should be grateful, I told myself as I turned to watch the big car. Life was hard all over.

The sedan had been idling at the curb, but now it parked and the driver stepped out—Judith, in the dark suit she'd worn to the funeral. She stood, leaning against the hood of her car and stared into space. She must be early for an appointment, I realized. And that meant I could grab a few minutes of her time.

"Hey," I called, or tried to. In lieu of a third hand, I held my nails in my mouth and only managed a grunt. Judith looked around—but not up. Instead, I heard a rustle on the window. Old man Wilkins, only a few feet beneath me, was peering through the blinds. I couldn't tell if he had heard my smothered greeting or he was checking to see if Judith had arrived, but I wouldn't risk disturbing a paying customer. Instead, I took the nail from my mouth and used it as I'd intended. Two more, I'd have the one-way door in place.

Three minutes later, the first opening was wired shut. And Judith was still outside, leaning against the sedan's hood. I watched her with interest. As I'd learned yesterday, the dark-haired beauty was very conscious of being looked at—and very different in her unguarded moments.

Not that there was much to see. Despite her dramatic coloring, she looked pale and drained today. Her body language radiated fatigue and something else. Determination? Yes, that was it. I could almost feel her gritting her teeth. She had just buried her father, so perhaps there was a reasonable explanation for the tiredness that dragged down her wide, elegant mouth. The set of those lips? Well, she was at the lawyer's, her father's former partner. This couldn't be a pleasant duty, though it was apparently a visit she had to make. As to whether she felt responsible for his death, and whether that added to the weight of this particular visit, I couldn't tell. Not by looking.

I turned back toward the house so I could grab both sides of the ladder and took a step down. As much as I could get from watching her, I had responsibilities too—and they included two more holes to patch. Another step. Albert's ladder was in about as good shape as I could expect, and I lowered my weight carefully, half expecting each rung to give way beneath my feet.

The sound of the engine made me pause. I turned my head half expecting to see Judith driving away, and was a little surprised to see another car pulling up instead. An older model—smaller—with the dents and dust that indicated an owned car, as opposed to some airport rental. Jackie, wearing another shapeless dress, but looking to my first glance a little less tired than she had been. Of course. The oldest daughter had been worn down by the constant care of the invalid father. As terrible as grief might be, at least she was no longer also weighed down by that particular responsibility. The middle girl had arrived fresh and rested, to be met by tragedy.

Remembering the scene at the grave site—and Judith's cold anger when her sister had had her meltdown—I waited. I needed these women on my good side—at least one of them—and I know enough not to get between two animals fighting. But whatever had sparked between them yesterday had died down.

Judith had clearly been waiting for her older sister and walked over to greet her. They didn't hug. Maybe they weren't a hugging family. They did talk, heads down for about a minute. I was too far away to hear what was said, but some kind of truce seemed to have been made. Even though she had been here first, Judith hung back as Jackie began walking up the path to Wilkins' front door. From my perch behind an eave, I saw her step onto the granite stoop. Judith followed a few steps behind.

I carried the ladder over to the new extension. I'd missed my chance to confront either sister without it being obvious that I'd been watching them. I might as well do my work. But before I could start on the second gate, the sound of another car stopped me. Beauville is a quiet town, and here on the moneyed side, traffic is as rare as street people. Still, I was kicking myself as I saw a little Mini Cooper pull up, bright red and as perky as a robin. Of course: Jill. Whatever was going on with the lawyer, all three daughters were involved.

"Jill!" Jackie called out and turned back down the path to face her.

Judith hung back, greeting her baby sister with a snarl. "You're late."

"I know." The younger daughter alone was casually attired, wearing jeans and a pullover that may have fit our town's dress code but made her look out of place among her sisters. "I got lost. I'm sorry."

"It's okay." Her oldest sister reached out an arm, as if to draw Jill in. "I'm glad you're here." Jackie had dropped her voice, but near as she was to the house, I heard her. I also heard a snort— Judith, who rolled her eyes in case anyone had missed the point.

"What?" Jackie turned on her, the truce forgotten. "She lost her way, Judith. That's not a crime. She hasn't been back for a while."

"Little Miss Perfect lost her way, all right." The venom in Judith's voice surprised me. "And you know this because you're the good girl. The one who stayed."

" I stayed here because *someone* had to." Jackie fired back. "You weren't going to take care of him. Not you, no—"

"You love it." Judith was practically hissing. "You define yourself by it. Jackie, the good daughter. Jackie, the caretaker. Jackie, the *responsible* one. Who wasn't home the one day our father could have used some help!"

"Someone had to shop. Had to cook for him. And if *you* hadn't brought over that— that *cat...*"

"She's here! She's here!" The sheltie's high-pitched bark added to the cacophony.

If I could have climbed higher onto the roof, I would have. Although I was partly behind the eave, if any of them looked up, they'd see my ladder—and, soon after, me. As much as I enjoy a good drama, I had not asked to see two sisters flaying each other, and I certainly didn't need to be labeled a busybody.

"Judith! Jackie!" Jill's voice broke through, loud and clear. "Stop it, please!" For a moment, I was afraid she'd seen me. I expected her next words to refer to the woman on the ladder, with a caution about airing dirty laundry in public. "This is hard enough," she said instead. "Please, shall we?"

A door must have opened, because suddenly the sisters had a canine escort. The sheltie, her gray muzzle showing her age, did her best to scamper up to the trio.

"She here? She here? Greetings!" Now that she was out, the sheltie's communication was silent, the only outward sign was in the enthusiastic, if slightly stiff, wag of that flaglike tail.

"Hey, girl." Jill bent to pet the eager arrow head, so like a collie's. From the way the sheltie strained upward, I got the sense that such affectionate gestures weren't a frequent occurrence in the Wilkins house, at least not since Mrs. Wilkins had died. But, wait, the gray muzzle wasn't directed toward Jill.

"Who's there?" One sharp bark. The sheltie might be old, but she had a good nose.

"I'm a friend." I concentrated on reaching the little dog. *"A friend."*

I flattened myself against the wall and waited. Judith and Jackie must have gone ahead, and I heard Jill hurry to catch up, the dog following close behind with a soft chuff. *"We'll see."*

The silence that followed lasted for a few seconds, then the birds started up again. The sisters had gone inside.

I wasn't crazy about the idea of hanging out any longer, but I wanted to get the job done. I don't think I've ever been more careful about moving a ladder than I was this day. Hell, I would have carried it around the long way, rather than be spotted by the feuding family, only a quick reconnaissance trip had reassured me that the shades in Wilkins' home office were drawn three-quarters of the way up.

Still, I was quiet as could be as I leaned my ladder up against the new construction. The spring earth was soft and moist, the plantings here a little farther along, and the base of my ladder dug in soundlessly, releasing the scent of leaf mold and new life as I secured it. The sun was warm on my back as I climbed up to the second squirrel hole. A pity, really. Spring days like this one were all too rare. I could have enjoyed a little manual labor today, if my mind hadn't been preoccupied with keeping unnaturally quiet.

"Mine! Mine!" Spring is nesting season for most creatures, and off in the woods, a crow was defending his territory.

"Here! Here! Here!" A thrush called out. Not, I realized, responding to the crow but to a more dangerous threat. *"Here! Here!"* Yes, she was trying to draw off a predator. Offering herself up rather than let some beast—was it a blue jay? A hawk? —get at the fledglings I could just envision at the edge of her panicked cry.

"The entire estate." I nearly dropped my hammer at the sound of the voice, so near by. "In excess of two million," the voice continued. I looked down. Yes, the shades were drawn nearly to their apex, but on top the windows had been lowered, to let in that soft May air.

I went back to my business, holding the squirrel gate up against the soffit as I fitted a nail up to the bracket. Animals take care of their young, lawyers as well as birds. The daughters had come together for the reading of their father's will, perhaps the last duty of Canaday's former partner.

"Feed me, feed me." Ah, the thrush had returned home. Her fledglings had no idea of what she had risked. Only that they were hungry. My heart went out to the mother bird who, even now, was refocusing on her young ones' insatiable appetite. *"Feed me!"*

I'd finished the gate and now held up a piece of wire netting to bolt alongside. Squirrels don't dissuade easily, but this was thick enough so that even a nesting mama would have trouble gnawing through it. Four quick taps, and it was up. Leaning over, I looked at the other side. I didn't know who had the nerve to shortchange a lawyer, but somebody did. From the ground, this addition looked solid. Out of sync, maybe, with the precise balance of the original architecture, but nice enough. Those big windows would look out over the back lawn, if Wilkins ever lowered those shades.

Up here, though, I could see a different side of the story. The squirrels had chosen this space for a reason. This had been a big job. Expensive, no doubt. But the money hadn't been well spent. Shoddy workmanship had left a gap between the gutter and the roof, allowing rain and ice melt to soften the wood framing. If this weren't relatively new, it would have already rotted through. As it was, it was easy for some determined rodent to gnaw an opening. I held the second piece of netting in place and debated the larger question. Should I tell Wilkins? I'd be doing him a service, alerting him of upcoming maintenance issues. Then again, I might be drawing down his wrath —and legal expertise—on someone I knew. Much of Beauville's original population still cobbled together jobs, changing from season to season with demand. Maybe what I was seeing was careless. Maybe it was the result of one job too many. An out-of-work teacher trying his hand as a carpenter. A contractor cramming in too many gigs during the good weather. I thought of that frenzied thrush. *"Feed me! Feed me! Feed me!"*

Life was hard all over.

"What?" One word, so loud I almost fell off my ladder. "Are you kidding me?"

Jackie, I thought. She had an edge to her voice that her sisters lacked.

"Please, Jackie, sit down." I was right. Wilkins sounded like he was doing his best to calm her.

"Judith." Jackie ignored him, using what I recognized as a command tone. "Look at me. Did you know anything about this?" I couldn't help myself. I leaned toward the window.

"Wait, you automatically think that I…?" Judith, her temper rising.

"Please, Judith. Jackie." The voice was soft, the tone placating. Jill the peacemaker, trying to quiet her sisters.

"Your father's wishes were clear." Wilkins again. I leaned further. Too much, almost, and had to catch myself on that loose gutter. "…finish her education." I missed something—and the lawyer had lowered his voice further. Well, he had known I was up here from the start. "You have the house," I heard him say. "He made a point to leave you the house."

"I don't care about the house." Jackie also didn't care who heard her. "You know that— I— We were all his daughters and I— I'm the one who…"

"Jackie." Judith cut in, her voice growing sharp. "Please."

"You weren't here." Jackie, her voice growing more shrill by the second. "You never visited. You got away. You ran—"

"Jackie, please." Wilkins again, trying to be reasonable. "I know how strongly you felt about your father. But I always tell clients, money does not equal love."

Even I winced at that, and the three women in the room below all burst out in aggrieved protest. Wilkins must have realized his misstep, because he kept talking, his deep, low voice bulldozing over the higher-pitched complaints.

From my perch, I pictured him looking through papers as he lumbered on about probate and "eventual disbursements." A charity that could be written off. Judith, it seemed, would be getting an annuity. "He remembered each of you," he said. "And as soon as the medical examiner signs the death certificate, we can begin the process."

Another outburst followed. Still, he kept on talking, seemingly intent on wearing them down.

"I'm sure there's nothing amiss," he was saying. "Nothing the three of you, his heirs, need concern yourself about."

I'd stopped listening around then. I had enough to get the picture. The estate would be held up until the medical examiner signed off. David Canaday had left most of his money to his youngest. And Jackie, at least, was pissed.

As quickly and as quietly as I could, I finished tacking up that last piece of mesh. All I wanted to do was to get away. No way was I going to tackle Wilkins today; his limited people skills had already been stretched to the limit. But before I could make good my escape, the front door opened. I leaned into the roof, hoping to make myself less visible, and watched the scene before me.

Judith was the first out, her arm around Jill, who appeared to be crying. Maybe the meeting had reawakened her grief. More likely, I thought, her oldest sister had scored a few hits. As I watched, Judith bent over her kid sister, offering her comfort or pledging support, while she walked her to the little sportster. As she walked to her own car, I could see the toll the meeting had taken. Judith looked tired, possibly ill.

Jackie, meanwhile, was lingering by the house. Hoping for a last word, I thought. A chance to change what she'd heard. At one point, I thought she was going to ring the bell again, but she didn't.

"She's gone." I'd almost forgotten the aging sheltie. She'd walked out with the sisters, I realized, and now whimpered softly, her black leather nose sniffing at the open air. *"She's left me."* With a low whine, she turned and head back into the house.

"Mine!" That crow again, in the woods.

Chapter Nineteen

Maybe I should have let her be. Maybe she shouldn't have dumped a kitten on me. I'd already left several messages for Judith Canaday, so once I was done with my afternoon rounds I figured I'd try again. As I suspected, she'd retreated to her fancy hotel. She hadn't had the sense to refuse all calls.

"Judith? Pru Marlowe here." I made a quick decision. I didn't know what was going on with that family, but I wasn't supposed to know anything. Besides, no good would come of putting her on the defensive. And I like having a little more knowledge about a situation than anyone expects. "I'm calling about the kitten?"

A sigh. In anyone else, it might have been grief. In this case, I bet she simply didn't want to bother.

"Jackie doesn't want it, right?" At least she remembered how we'd left things. Which, of course, was my cue to fill her in.

"I wasn't sure where everyone stood." I wound up my summary. That was true on more levels than just the one where a cat was concerned. But there was that, too. "I didn't feel right leaving the kitten alone with everything going on," I went on. "Besides, I was going to have him checked out by a vet. Or did you have that done already?"

"What?" She had barely been listening. "No. It's a kitten."

Sometimes I don't know why I bother. Cats need vaccinations, same as children, and that bout of sickness—almost a seizure—had been preying on me. Distemper usually moves fast—in days, if not hours, it can kill. But there were always outliers. Individualized manifestations. Secondary infections. Not that the woman on the phone had a clue.

"Judith." I fought the urge to bark at her. I've trained parakeets that were smarter. "When you purchased the kitten, did you get papers?"

"Of course." She was offended. I could hear it.

"Did these include certificates of vaccination?" I was hoping so. After all, kittens can get shots as early as eight weeks, and I was hoping this little fellow was right about that age.

"I'm not sure. I didn't check."

I bit my lip. Some airlines insist on seeing vet certificates before they allow an animal onto a plane. Then again, Judith had the kind of assurance that would probably make mincemeat of most airline staff.

"Look, you're staying at the Mont, right?" I took her silence as assent. "I can be over there in fifteen minutes. Twenty at the most. I'll go through the papers."

"This isn't the best day." I could hear the edge creeping into her voice.

"I won't take long." Still in training mode, I ignored her implication. "See you soon."

Dealing with one of David Canaday's daughters was not how I wanted to finish my afternoon. But waiting on her pleasure would be worse, and so I hit the highway with a roar. Two hundred horses don't mean anything, not if it's powering a lunk of steel. But I had one of the first of the remodeled GTOs, the ones that carved off some of that dead weight. I could feel the 350 cubic inches singing as I shifted. I was almost sorry when the Mont came into view as I took that last turn, right where the hills start, in record time.

The Mont Chateau. Judith had done well by herself. While her sisters were living in their father's old house, Judith was luxuriating like a tourist. Built to resemble some kind of French country house, the Mont didn't look that out of place in our green hills. The combination of stone and half-timbers sort of fit the background, but not the Belleville budget. Even in high season, we were more motel than Mont, and as I took the curving drive up to its entrance, I found myself wondering about Judith's lifestyle. About her expenses and her expectations.

The valet was trotting toward me before I'd stopped, but I waved him off. Sure, he was bored. This place couldn't be half-full. No way was he driving my car. I parked at the side of the traffic circle in front of the entrance and pocketed my keys. One look at my face and he backed off, nodding. He didn't know me. He didn't have to.

"Judith Canaday?" The woman at the front desk looked just as bored. She knew to hide it, though, with a smile that gauged my chances of being able to afford a room there perfectly.

"I'll ring Ms. Canaday." She had already turned away, her hand on the receiver.

"No need." I'd seen the room number—502—and headed toward the elevator.

"Miss!" Her voice, shrill and a little peeved, followed me. Not even the lobby fountain, replete with cherubs, could drown it out. Never mind. I kept walking. If she called security, I'd find out soon enough.

"Pru." Judith met me at the door, alerted from the lobby no doubt. "I'm afraid we may have a problem."

"Oh?" I followed her in to a room that looked like any hotel room anywhere. Any hotel room that had a glass-walled bathroom and a floor-to-ceiling window, that is. "What's that?"

"The papers." She picked up a jacket from the back of a chair. I'd already sat on the lipstick-colored loveseat. "I seem to have misplaced them."

"Misplaced." She was busy hanging the jacket. It seemed to need a lot of attention. So I decided to backtrack a bit. "Judith, would you tell me why you gave your father a kitten?"

"Why?" She was brushing invisible lint off the jacket's lapel. "It seemed like a nice thing. You know, what do you give the man who has everything?"

"Your father had everything?" I couldn't help it—my eyes darted from the glass brick to the bathrobe laid out on the bed.

She looked at me suddenly, her gray eyes sharp, and then turned away. "He was comfortable. And very self-sufficient."

I nodded. That, at least, jibed with what I'd heard. "When was the last time you'd seen him?"

She shook her head and reached for another item that apparently needed brushing. "I don't know. A year ago? Maybe more?"

"And you decided to visit now?" I wondered what the thread count was on those sheets.

"It was his birthday." A shrug, that hair glistening blue-black. "A big one. Jackie was planning a party."

"Somehow, I can't see one of Jackie's parties being high on your to-do list." Maybe it was my tone. She turned for real then, and it looked like the air went out of her.

"No," she agreed, sinking into the chair. "I'd heard that he wasn't doing well. That maybe it was time..." She looked toward the window. I didn't think she was seeing the view over the valley.

"Time?" I waited. If she'd hoped to ingratiate herself, she'd put it off too long. I wondered how big that annuity was—and how much she might need it.

"Time to make peace," she said at last. "I left home rather impetuously. It was— we didn't leave things on good terms." She licked away the last of her lipstick. "He didn't approve of California. Of my acting."

"You're an actress." That was something to keep in mind.

"I've had some commercial work." An edge, a little defensive. At least that was what she wanted me to hear.

"That's a hard life." I didn't add anything about her age. She was closing in on thirty, maybe more. Close to my age, and in a very different profession. As an actress, her time to make it had come and gone.

"I get by." That aristocratic chin had come up. She was defiant, I'd give her that. "I have friends." Another shrug. "Had friends."

That confirmed it. "But you needed money." Another quick look, sharp and hard, before those thick lashes fluttered to soften it. "You wanted to make sure you were in your father's will."

"I wanted to visit my father." She enunciated every word carefully.

"Whom your older sister had moved in with." I could have laughed. This was an old story. Usually it doesn't end in death. "Your kid sister was the baby, still in school."

She shot me a look. I waited. "Jill was smart. Smarter than me," Judith admitted. It seemed to cost her. "I can't blame her for that."

"But you had a role too," I said. "You could be the prodigal daughter, coming home to be celebrated."

"If that's how you see us." Her voice was suddenly weary. "You didn't know my father. He wasn't the sort to celebrate."

"Oh?"

"It wasn't just that he was strict." Her mouth was set in a tight line. Without the lipstick it had begun to look hard. "He was …unforgiving. You either toed the line or…"

"And you were out?" I didn't want to give her anything. Not after what I'd heard. But I understood. She hadn't come home in time. I had.

She sniffed suddenly and reached for a tissue. "Sorry."

"Not a problem," I found myself sympathizing. "He might have forgiven you, you know."

"Not with Jackie around." She shook off the suggestion. Tried to shake off the tears. "She wasn't going to let that happen. Maybe that's why she…" She left her sentence unfinished, but her glance said it all.

"Do you think your sister did something?" I chose my words with care. I was remembering that day—when David Canaday had died. Judith had shown up and almost immediately ducked into the bathroom. Had she found more than aspirin? Had she known something else would be there? "Are you saying she had something to do with his death?"

"I'm not saying anything." Her voice had taken on a singsong quality. "After all, I wasn't around."

"I haven't heard that there was any evidence," I paused. That was a cop word. At the funeral, Judith had talked about her father's "meds." About reading "the damned labels." "That there was any sign of anything other than natural causes?" I was pushing. "Your father did have a bad heart, right?"

Another shrug. How strange, I thought, that before the reading of the will, Judith had laughed off the idea that there was anything amiss. Dismissed it as part of Jackie's neuroses. What was it old Horlick had said? Money really did change everything. Money—along with the continued interest of the medical examiner.

"You know, Jackie was saying the same thing about you. That you brought him a kitten to provoke an allergic reaction." I was playing with fire, and the spark in her eyes confirmed it. I expected her to lash out. To reveal something about her sister—or her own dark motives.

Instead, I got tears.

"How dare she?" Face in her hands, Judith collapsed on the bed. "When she— when she knows!" She was sobbing now. "She must know. Jill must have told her."

I waited. "Judith? What's going on? Knows what? What would Jill have said?" I was beginning to have my suspicions. This hotel, her look. Her so-called profession—and Jill's aspirations. "It's the kitten, isn't it? He's not a pedigreed animal at all, is he?"

She shook her head. That glossy hair covered her face, but it couldn't block the sound as she gasped. "I—it was silly."

"Judith?" I almost reached out for her. She almost had me.

"Stupid." She sat up and swiped at her face. Stood and walked to the window. "Not silly, stupid. I thought things would be different. The way they were before Jill grew up."

I held my breath. Judith's sorrow had turned cold so fast, it had sucked all the oxygen out of the room.

"I gather it was Jill, not Jackie?" I kept my voice as gentle as I could. "Jill who was your father's favorite?"

"Our father? Ha!" Judith barked at the silent hillside. A minute passed, maybe more, before she turned toward me, a sad smile playing on those wide lips.

"He used to call me his kitten."

Chapter Twenty

It didn't mean anything, I thought, as I drove away with my mind more on the woman I had just left than on the road. Part of that was because I had left Judith without any resolution—and without any plans for the kitten.

"I can't have him here." She'd remained adamant, even as I'd pushed the point. "Those are Frette linens," she'd said, as if I'd care. She must have seen something in my face. "Isn't there a shelter in town?"

"I'm not—" I caught myself. A woman who valued sheets over a life wasn't going to understand. "I'll figure something out."

Even before I left, I'd begun running through the options. The shelter was not one. Cute as he was, Ernesto would be just one more kitten among dozens of others—and even if he were adopted, it would mean a lost opportunity, and possibly euthanasia, for another.

As I thought this through, I could hear the opposing argument in my head, sounded in the voice of my tough-minded tabby. Young animals die. That's how nature works, and why adult cats keep producing litter after litter. Didn't matter. Wallis might not care—might tell me she didn't, anyway—but I did. No, this family had brought this kitten into my life. Somehow, I'd make them find a home for hm.

The question was how? None of the sisters seemed like a good bet, especially not the way they were fighting now. I couldn't see the little puffball becoming a pawn in their battles. I had tried Judith then. "Maybe you could take him back with you?"

She gestured to the clothes she had just hung. "I don't know when I'm going back, exactly." She'd regained her poise. "I do have other business in town."

I wondered what that business could be. She'd referred to friends, and I didn't see her as any more sentimental than my cat. If she were looking up people from her past, I would put money on it that these were business contacts rather than old high school buddies. And while that might have nothing to do with me—or with Ernesto—I was realizing how much of an impact money was having on us both. The lack of it, specifically. What I didn't know was how to find out more. Or if Judith Canaday was simply waiting around until the full autopsy report came back.

"Does this have to do with your father's estate?" Nothing ventured, nothing gained.

"My father's affairs are none of your business." She pulled another blouse out of the closet. "And, really, Ms. Marlowe, now that you've gotten my dirty little secret out of me, I think you should leave."

"Some secret," I muttered as she turned from me. I didn't know if she meant that the kitten was a rescue—or that she had cherished her father's pet name for her. She'd clearly been the pretty one among the Canaday girls. Still was, if you counted all the props.

That was it. Her clothes. Hadn't she said she'd barely had time to drop the kitten off?

"I see your luggage arrived after all." I stood, but made no movement toward the door.

"Yes, the airline found it and had it delivered." She turned on the full wattage of her smile. "And there I was, running around for no reason. Now, if you'll excuse me?"

I'm not usually at a loss for words, but right then I was out of questions. I'd let her walk me to the door as a strategic retreat. I needed some answers, but I might have to get them elsewhere. After all, I had more sympathy for Ernesto the kitten than for this self-assured beauty. And the visit hadn't been completely pointless. Judith Canaday had revealed herself to be a liar. And while she might still turn heads, I had the feeling she was very aware of the clock—and of how quickly overripe fruit can go bad.

As much as anyone, she should have had some feeling for a discarded pet. One that all too soon would no longer be considered cute.

Chapter Twenty-one

"So what kind of business could Judith Canaday have back here in Beauville?" I hadn't found a satisfactory answer by that evening, so I tried bouncing it off my bedmate.

"Why do you care?" Creighton leaned back against the headboard, sheet pulled up to his waist. "She's no threat to you. I can't see that one working with animals," he added, to make sure I got the point.

"That's for sure." I agreed, accepting the implied compliment. I was feeling good. Curious, sure, but he didn't have to know why. Except that he was waiting, his blue eyes cool. "The sisters are fighting over the estate." I threw him a tidbit. "It's getting nasty."

"And you know this how?" He was giving me the cop look now, face as impassive as those blue eyes.

"You could say a little bird told me." I paused to see how Creighton would respond to that. "Why?"

"Interesting you should say that, Pru." His voice was as cool as his body was hot, but I didn't like the way he was looking at me. "Interesting phrase. Especially seeing as how you're working for the family."

"But I'm not." I reached for the beers we'd left half-finished, handing him one. I needed to distract him. "At least, nobody's paid me yet. Or even paid me back."

"I'm sure they'll each have enough to cover your costs." Placing his bottle on the nightstand, he slipped out of bed and reached for his pants. "No matter what you think you know."

"Anything you want to share?" I wasn't going to beg him to stay. That's never been my way. Didn't mean I wasn't the slightest bit put off by his getting dressed. "I was working on Laurence Wilkins' house and I overheard some squabbling, okay? He's got a squirrel problem."

My beau paused, and I had the uncanny feeling he was waiting for more.

"What?" I clasped my hands behind my head. "You were the one telling me about the tests going to the state lab, about the medical examiner asking for more tests."

"I shouldn't have said anything." He shook his head as he buttoned his shirt.

"It was bothering you." I took a swig and waited, but his lips remained set in a straight line as he pulled on a shoe. "At least you didn't find out that he was intentionally poisoned."

Shoe untied, he looked up, too fast for it to be a coincidence.

"What? He was?" Any chance of appearing uninterested went out the window, but I was too curious not to follow up. "I thought you said he had a bad heart. That he was on medication and that something…"

He smiled then, a thin smile. "Is this you trying to talk me out of going back to work?"

That was new information. "Jim, you serious?" It wasn't late. We hadn't even eaten the pizza he'd brought over.

He stood, tucking in his shirt. "Sorry, Pru. I stopped by because I said I would and then…" He looked around the shambles we'd made of the bedroom. "But I've got a ridiculous amount of paperwork."

"That autopsy report." I leaned forward, wrapping my arms around my knees and gave him my best come-hither look. "If you've got it in the car, you could bring it in here, you know. I'll heat up the pizza while you read it over. I won't bother you while you're working."

He laughed out loud. "Pru, you always put me in a good mood. Even when you don't mean to." And with that, he was gone.

"*You expected something different?*" Wallis met me by the bathroom door, as I emerged from the shower. Like all cats, she is fascinated by our bathroom habits, even as she distrusts large quantities of water. "*You're the expert on training.*"

"Point taken, Wallis." I toweled off and found my own clothes as my tabby watched. "So, where's Ernesto?"

"*I was waiting for you to notice.*" Wallis sat up, wrapping her black-tipped tail around her forepaws. "*You haven't asked about him all day.*"

"I've been busy, Wallis." I pulled on my jeans. "Busy at least partly on his behalf. In case you haven't noticed."

"*Just thought you might be interested in what he has to say.*" Always nonchalant, she began to wash her face.

"What is it?" She kept washing, one black paw sliding over her ear. "You do that when you're trying to hide something."

"*I do this to stay beautiful, without getting into...*" Another swipe, bending her black-tipped ear forward. "*Water.*" The word dripped with disdain, and the taste of fur.

"Wallis?" Creighton's desertion hadn't left me in the best mood, even if—as Wallis was so quick to remind me—I had set the standard for our minimal relationship.

"*Ask him yourself.*" With a shrug, Wallis turned and, tail high, walked off.

It took me a good half-hour to find the kitten. My old house is full of nooks and closets, and after my romp and the rest of the beer, my strange sensitivity wasn't working at its best. Sure, I could hear where Ernesto was, more or less. But hearing a tiny voice call out "*mouse hole!*" and following that voice to a fold in the living room rug is a different matter. As to whether we did have rodents in the living room, well, that I chose not to explore. Wallis and I might not have an exact division of labor, though each of us considered ourselves the more put-upon in the household. Rodents in the furnishings, however? That was clearly my tabby roommate's area of expertise.

"Keeping ourselves busy, are we?" I was down on the floor when I found the kitten. As his overheard exclamation implied, he was half in what to him constituted a "mouse hole," a rucked-up fold of the carpet. "Are we having fun?"

The round kitten butt wiggled as Ernesto attempted to turn around in the hole. I was tempted to extract the little creature, but life with Walllis has taught me that felines value their dignity, even small ones.

"*I am on duty.*" The tiny cat finally managed to back out and blinked up at me. "*Looking for mice!*"

As if aware, suddenly, of how he must look, he lifted one paw in a perfect copy of Wallis' grooming motion. Only the kitten lacked the mature tabby's poise, and ended up falling over onto the floor.

"*Meant to do that!*" He struggled back to his feet.

"Of course you did." Behind me, I could sense the slightest ladylike snort. "Wallis?"

"*Tell her, kid.*" Wallis wasn't joking now. "*Tell her what you told me.*"

I looked from the kitten to my tabby. She was focused on the kitten, but he seemed oblivious.

"*Mouse!*"

"What is it, Ernesto?" I made a point of using the small cat's name. In my experience, most animals respond well when we respect their selfhood. Not that I thought the little fellow would have anything to tell me. Then again, I didn't want to see Wallis discipline the poor thing. And before my tabby could pick up on that thought, I asked again. "What do you want to tell me?"

"*Playtime.*" Those round eyes looked up at me. "*He played with me.*"

"That's nice." Unlike Wallis, I couldn't get mad at a face like that.

"*Back and forth.*" He tilted his head and blinked. "*And then he was gone.*"

"He is gone." I paused, sorry I had ever used the euphemism. "I'm sorry."

"*Never you mind that.*" Wallis reared back, as if to cuff the kitten. "*You go on.*"

"*I told her.*" Ernesto drew back. "*Playtime.*"

"Come on, Wallis." I reached for the kitten. "Cut the kid some slack."

"*Fine.*" Wallis turned and stalked off, leaving me with a sulking kitten, no wiser than I'd been before.

Chapter Twenty-two

The phone woke me, but I ignored it. Sure, I may work out of my house. That doesn't mean I ignore business hours—or my own rules. People who call before nine can leave a message. I am not an animal trainer for nothing. Besides, between Wallis' sulking and Ernesto's newfound curiosity—what Wallis would term neediness—I hadn't slept well.

"Pru?" I waited until the coffee was brewing before I hit playback. "This is Jackie Canaday." The slight edge of hysteria was familiar, as was the voice. "I'm calling about the kitten. Please call me back as soon as possible."

I stopped and turned. This was great news. It was also, I could see, still a quarter to nine.

"Mama?" Tiny claws, like needles, grabbed at my ankles. That did it. I made the call.

"Jackie." If she was comfortable using my first name, I'd use hers. Another rule of training: start off with the power dynamic you want. It's a lot easier than trying to change it later. "Pru Marlowe here. You called about the kitten?"

As I talked, I looked down at the fuzzy baby. He was still holding onto my leg, his blue eyes fixed on mine. He couldn't know who I was talking to on the phone, could he?

"Yes, thank you." I did some quick calculations. If I left now, I could bring the kitten over to her before walking Growler. "I'm sorry to have been remiss."

"Not at all." The kitten's fur was downy, and without thinking I held him against my cheek. "You've had other concerns, and it's been no trouble having him here."

"He's at your house?" Her voice tightened.

A little purr, barely audible. *"Mama!"*

"Yes." It's hard to get stressed while holding a kitten. Besides, I'd left a note explaining that I'd taken the kitten for the time being.

"Mama!" He rubbed against the phone, and for a second I considered putting him on.

"Why?" I'm not that kind of a person. I was, however, beginning to feel the slightest bit of anticipatory regret.

"Well, I thought you'd be taking him to that animal hospital."

I winced at my own forgetfulness. Of course, the well-kitten visit. "County," I clarified. "Yes, Doc Sharpe—the vet there—had to delay our appointment, but I can easily run the little guy over there before I bring him to his new home."

"Oh, that won't be necessary." The little nose, damp and cool, against my cheek.

"You have your own vet?" Maybe I'd find a reason to visit this little tyke. Training, maybe. Or to clip those pin-like claws.

"No, I'm afraid I'm not being clear." Something was bothering this woman. Even with a kitten pressed close to my face, I could hear it, in her voice ratcheting higher. "You see, I don't want you to bring that animal here. I want you to bring it to the vet. And I want him to put that animal to sleep."

Chapter Twenty-three

My surprise did us all a disservice. At least, I figured it was my startled reaction that caused Ernesto to lash out, scratching my cheek and eyelid. But it wasn't the shock—it stung rather than really hurt—that made me curse out loud, scaring the poor kitten and putting the woman on the other end of the line on the defensive.

"Well, I never!" I hadn't known people still talked like that.

"I'm sorry, Jackie." I had lowered the frightened feline to the floor, and now focused on trying to save his life. "I was—a cat scratched me as I was talking to you." It wouldn't help the kitten to name him as my assailant, but sometimes the handiest excuse is the truth.

"That's what I mean." She kept on talking. "They're vicious animals, and this one—this one killed my father."

"Jackie…." I didn't know where to begin. "Look, if you don't want the kitten, I can understand it. I can help find a new home for him. You don't even have to see him again."

"I've never seen him—seen it." That edge of hysteria again. High-pitched, like a mosquito in the room. "That's not the point."

"It's exactly the point." I couldn't let her continue. "I understand. You're upset. But no vet is going to euthanize a healthy animal simply because—"

"Aren't unwanted kittens killed every day?" She interrupted me. "And if I bring this one in and talk about what trouble it's been?"

"What trouble?" The scratches were forgotten, even as I wiped my cheek. "I'm sure if you met him. If you held him. He's a kitten—"

"He's my *property*." She barked, her words clipped tight. "I am inheriting my father's house and all property within. And that kitten was a gift to my father." She paused, and I scrambled for an appropriate response. "If you won't do as I ask, then you have to return it, and I will take care of it. Any other action is theft, plain and simple."

She hung up then, which was a good thing. Nobody would be served by me tearing her a new one. My coffee had finished brewing, and I poured it into a travel mug as I looked around for my feline housemates. That poor kitten had disappeared. Just as well, I realized. I couldn't tell what Ernesto could pick up from me, and it would do him no good to share the thoughts that were whirling around my head.

I was surprised to see Wallis as I stormed toward the door.

"What?" I didn't need to be polite. She would know from my thoughts what had just happened.

"So much for 'Mama.'" She flicked her tail. *"I tried to warn that kitten."*

"She's mourning her own parent." I didn't know why I was defending Jackie. Maybe because I'd spent time with her sister the day before.

"Exactly." Wallis would be more sympathetic to Judith, I realized. The middle sister was the one with the feline self-possession, not to mention the good looks.

She looked up at me. *"Well, aren't you, too?"* Her voice sounded in my head.

"Wallis, please." My tabby's ability to read my thoughts made conversation confusing. "And for the record, yes, I do find Judith a little easier to understand than Jackie. That doesn't mean I like her."

"Maybe you're not the only one."

"Excuse me?" Wallis gave me the look she usually reserved for the kitten. "I'm sorry, Wallis, I'm not getting what you're implying."

"Pru, please." Wallis' eyes closed, her ears rotating slightly. I could feel her straining. She was searching for a way to explain. *"Can't you see beyond the obvious?"*

"What?" I was getting angry now. More at my own stupidity than at my cat. "Jackie wants to get rid of the kitten. Doesn't want it around her house." That was it: *her* house. "Is this about the inheritance? That she's getting the house? She can do with it what she wants?"

Another slow blink. From a cat that signaled approval. It also drew my attention to her eyes. Clear and cool and green, they were beautiful and alluring.

"This is about Judith, isn't it?" I was thinking aloud, but I could hear Wallis start to purr. "This is Jackie getting back at her sister for being beautiful. For being their father's 'favorite.'"

Another slow blink, the eyes closing.

"But Judith wasn't the favorite, not at the end." I assumed Wallis could read my memories. Still, it helped to say things out loud. "Jill was. And Jill is the one who started the investigation into their father's death."

Sisters. As the pieces fell into place, I thanked whatever gods there were once again for being an only child.

"Jackie can't lash out at Jill, so she's striking out at Judith. Is she going to keep trying to prove that Judith's gift caused their father's death? Or did Judith find something in the medicine cabinet—something that should not have been there? Does Jackie have something to hide?"

But Wallis was asleep.

Chapter Twenty-four

Some people say you shouldn't drive with your emotions. Me, I'm not one of them. As far as I'm concerned, the car is the apex of human achievement. Driving is my best outlet—as well as my one financial indulgence. Not that I'm stupid, far from it. Anger just makes me cooler. Hones the edges, so to speak. And with my particular set of high-test wheels, I need to be razor-sharp. Especially when I'm driving fast, which I was.

Driving and thinking, I'll admit, with the one helping the other. Maybe it's something to do with blood flow—the oxygen from the rapid shift and the growl of the engine. But as I made my way into town, I had an idea. Something that just might work.

The exchange with Wallis had suggested it—my reaction to the tabby's implacable stare as much as anything. Jackie Canaday was in mourning, the first sharp stages of grief. But there was something else going on with her, too. I'd picked it up from the start. A strange hysteria that hinted at more than sadness.

Jackie felt guilty about something. And she wanted to pin that guilt elsewhere. On the kitten, if she could. On one of her sisters, if not. Now that was not my responsibility. Hell, if Jackie had hastened her father's death, it wasn't my problem. I could even understand the temptation in retrospect. What I couldn't stomach was her callous attitude toward the kitten. It didn't seem likely that anyone would euthanize a healthy animal But if she surrendered it now—during kitten season—and if the tyke had another seizure…No, Ernesto was the one innocent in this whole story. The Canaday sisters could turn on each other, for all I cared. I wasn't going to let that poor kitten be their fall guy.

I slowed as I drew near my destination, more to think, than to admire the scenery. Beauville is beautiful this time of year. The trees are more or less leafed; the new foliage throwing a lacework of shadow across the road. Under the trees, I knew, those same shadows hid death. Spring was more than kitten season, and baby animals everywhere were the most vulnerable. My connection with one such creature shouldn't have meant a lot. It was more that I felt responsible—that my species was responsible—that got me. Wallis would say I was a hypocrite. At least, she'd imply as much with the angle of her tail or a turn or her ears. I couldn't argue. I knew we were a mean and silly species. And maybe that could be something I could use.

Jackie said that she had inherited her father's house, and that fit with what I'd overheard. But I assumed that the title—like the rest of the estate—would depend on the resolution of a death certificate. Plus, if she and Judith were contesting the will, then the delay might be even longer. Legally, the kitten might still be in limbo. It was a small edge, but I'd take it. Sometimes, I thought as I pulled up at the rundown white ranch, our human prissiness could be an advantage.

Sometimes, I realized with a growing sense of glee, our nastiness could be, too.

> > >

"Mrs. Horlick." I was almost crowing as I bounded up her cracked concrete walk. "So good to see you."

If I'd startled the old bag, she didn't show it. Sure, she blinked as I greeted her, but that could have been from the smoke. As usual, a Marlboro hung precariously between her lips as she stood in her doorway.

"You're bright-eyed this morning." She flicked the ash into the shrubbery and waited for an explanation.

"Got a new client." My grin was real. I was enjoying this. "A lawyer."

Her eyes narrowed, and this time I didn't think it was because of the smoke. "A lawyer?"

"Laurence Wilkins." I was hoping that she wouldn't question my newfound openness. "He's got a squirrel problem."

"He's got more than a squirrel problem." She took a drag. I waited.

"Really?" It seemed I needed to prime the pump. Back behind her, I heard a clipped bark. Growler had heard me arrive and was anxious for his walk. I needed to hurry her along. "Problems with a client?"

"Aren't you the curious one?" Another flick into the bushes. "I'm going to get my dog."

"You should know better, walker lady." Growler had accepted my apology before the end of the block. Gruffness aside, he knew me as an ally. *"That one...huh!"*

He squatted to illustrate his point, and I struggled to explain.

"I'm looking for gossip," I said, unsure how the word would translate. "I need to know the dirt."

The shaggy white head tilted up at me, and I realized I felt ashamed.

"I'm trying to find out how bad a fight is." I pictured the sisters and the house. My best chance with the kitten might be a prolonged dispute about the will. Wilkins didn't know what I'd overheard, so I couldn't ask him directly. "It's to help somebody."

It was a sad excuse.

"That one doesn't help anyone." He turned and trotted on. I followed. *"You should know that, walker lady."*

He walked on. Sniffed a sapling whose new leaves were still small and perfect, watered it, and looked back at me. *"And you think you're the one holding the leash."*

Growler was right, up to a point. As much as I might buck at authority, I needed clients like Tracy Horlick to pay my bills. And to try to outplay her at her own game was risky.

I was considering my other options even before we finished our walk. Tracy Horlick greeted us at the door with a smile that made my skin crawl, which confirmed Growler's warning.

"I was wondering where you were." She'd applied more lipstick in the interim, and it cracked as she bared her teeth.

"I gave Growler an extra long walk today." The smile I gave back was just as real. "The weather's so fine."

Her eyebrows went up at that. "Don't think I don't know what you're up to."

I shook my head, confused. She couldn't know that I'd taken the bichon down to the river as a peace offering. He'd even let me brush him quickly before we'd turned onto his block.

"There's a new girl in town. Doing what you do." Tracy took a long drag and waited for her words to sink in. "From what I hear, she's going to need the work, too."

"Excuse me?" I had other things to do. Places to be.

"Jill Canaday." Another drag, an excuse to examine me between those half-closed lids. "She's not going to get anything by the time this is over. Not with what she's been up to, so she's gunning for what you've got."

Chapter Twenty-five

Growler barked— *"No!"*—just as Tracy Horlick's snark hit home. Thanks to him, I didn't bark back.

"Really?" I'd responded, managing to be a little little less brusque in my response.

The old lady had just grinned, if the stretching of her mouth could be called that. And I left, feeling like a fool.

What to believe, what not? That was the problem with using Tracy Horlick for information. Had I been played by the youngest Canaday girl? As I'd bent to unhook Growler's leash from his collar, I'd taken a moment to collect myself—and to give the fluffy white dog an ear scratch of thanks. He'd tried to warn me. I prided myself on denying his person the pleasure of my shock, though from her evil leer, I must have shown something before I turned away.

Tracy Horlick had given me something, though. That comment about Jill needing the work? That fit with what I'd suspected. The older sisters were contesting the will. I wasn't surprised. Whether they would have a case, I didn't know.

I had planned to follow up with Laurence Wilkins. The one-way squirrel doors should be enough to solve his problem, but lawyers are trickier than squirrels, and I wanted this client to feel like he'd gotten his money's worth. What I didn't know yet was how to ask about these feuding sisters. After all, I wasn't supposed to have heard anything and my little-bird excuse wouldn't fly with a lawyer. That didn't mean I wasn't going to try.

Jackie's call had reminded me that I had other duties. As worried as I'd been, I had neglected to follow up on Ernesto's care. On the spur of the moment, I turned and headed toward County General. If nothing else, the drive would give me a chance to strategize my approach to Wilkins.

Maybe I could pose it as a question of custody, I realized, as I pulled into the animal hospital's lot. I doubted the deceased had had a chance to include his new kitten in his will, if he would have even bothered. But maybe there was precedent—something I could use to keep the kitten out of Jackie's hands, anyway.

That was a problem I'd tackle later, though. Right now, I had a very particular errand in mind.

Spring hits us hard out here in the Berkshires. After months of cold and mud, suddenly the natural world wakes, shaking off its winter stupor and embracing life. And creating it: spring is known as kitten season in the shelter world because of the sudden influx of baby animals. And so stepping into County, which also serves as our local shelter, meant facing a cacophony of crying babies, both animal and human. Adoptions and surrenders were in full swing by now, and that was hard on everyone. Sure, Junior has found the right puppy. And even though Doc Sharpe runs a tight ship—no animal would leave its mother too early—that doesn't mean the puppy isn't scared and confused as it is separated from its mother and placed in a carrier box for the first time. Same thing for Molly the moggy. It's not her fault that nobody noticed she wasn't a kitten anymore—and that they ignored Doc Sharpe's advice to keep her indoors. Now she's been scooped up from that nice bed she made in the laundry room, she and her kittens, and is wondering why they're all stuck in a metal cage instead.

For most people, it's noisy. As I walked through the crowded waiting room, it was maddening—the cries of confusion, of anguish, of joy. I tried to focus on the latter: the reunions, the dawning realization that the hard times in the wild were over. I've been learning to tune out the voices, to get some control over this strange sensitivity. Wallis says it's a skill her kind master as kittens, learning selective deafness. Still, it was hard for me, and I must have been standing in front of the reception desk looking blank for several moments before a popping sound broke through.

"Earth to Pru." Pammy was chewing gum. She was also twirling one strand of her dyed blonde hair. It was an impressive feat of coordination for her, and to impress me further, she blew a bubble. When it popped, she pushed the gum back into her mouth with a lacquered finger, tilted her head up toward mine, and asked again. "Can I help you?"

"I'm here to see Doc." I resisted the temptation to answer honestly: *No, but maybe you can help yourself.* "Would you buzz me in?"

A raised eyebrow showed she was considering turning down my request, but laziness got the better of her. Rather than query her boss, she hit a button.

"Thanks." I called as I walked by her, another bubble on the way.

The working part of the hospital wasn't quiet, far from it. But it was better—the whines and whimpers toned down to a manageable roar, one I was able, with a little concentration, to put out of my mind.

I found the white-haired vet seated at the desk in his office. A tiny room, overrun with books, it served as a consulting room for the people who determined their animals' lives. Doc Sharpe looked up when I entered, knocking on the opened door to announce my presence. He had a book open before him—an old-fashioned ledger that seemed to contain more red ink than black—and he pushed his glasses up a potato of a nose and nodded toward the one guest chair. I removed the pile of folders from it and sat.

"How may I help you, Pru?" Unfailingly polite, he managed a smile, but I hesitated. The old vet looked tired.

"I think maybe I should be helping you more, Doc." I looked around. A tray of vials had been laid out, probably by Pammy. FVRCP the labels read. Feline distemper. Good. I had a specific favor in mind, but it couldn't hurt to start by offering one of my own. "At least with the animals, if not with all this paperwork."

He managed a smile that looked more like a grimace. "If it were only the animals, I could keep up."

I nodded. The old Yankee and I were alike in that way. Work was our tonic. "Is it billing?"

"Not exactly." He rubbed his eyes, dislodging those glasses. "More our funding. Things may be looking up, however."

"Oh?" This was great news. County General, as its name implied, was largely supported by public funds. Those covered the basics, barely. Any extras—and that meant my work as a freelance behaviorist—came from the Friends of County, a non-profit whose books grew and sank depending on the weather, the stock market, and the popularity of other causes as the hip charity of the moment. "Did we get a new Friend?"

He shook his head. "Lost one—what does my granddaughter call them? A frenemy? David Canaday. In fact, well, his demise might prove timely." He looked up at me, blinking. "He'd been a supporter, but he'd always insisted on looking over our shoulders. Looking over every expense. He called me, you know, the morning he died. I was…well, to be honest, I was avoiding calling him back. I thought…I didn't know what to think."

"It was probably about the kitten." I kept my voice soft. No wonder the old vet felt so guilty. "That's all, Doc. I'm sure. The little fellow was a gift to Canaday from one of his daughters."

"Maybe you're right. I hope so." A slight smile played at the edge of Doc's mouth. "It's funny," he said. " I never had any reason to believe that the man was fond of animals." He looked back down at the ledger, at all that red. "He certainly was not fond of animal-related charities."

"Well, the kitten may have killed him. At least, one of his daughters thinks so." I gave Doc the outlines of the story—allergy, bad heart—end of story. He had the grace to look shocked.

"That's terrible. His poor daughters."

I nodded. This was playing the way I wanted. "His oldest wants the kitten killed."

"Well, I can understand the sentiment." A frown creased his round face.

"Doc, there's no reason to take it out on a kitten!" I had looked to the vet to be on my side.

"No, no, I agree." He raised a hand, as if to block my objections from proceeding further. "And I'm not saying it should be done. Simply, I understand the emotion. Something you, Pru, might want to work on."

"Doc, you work with a lot of the same animals I do," I countered. This wasn't what I had come here for. "If seeing how we treat them doesn't turn you off the human race…"

"I understand what you are saying. Honestly, I do." He cleared his throat, usually a sign that he was about to say something that made him uncomfortable. "But, Pru, at times I have come to wonder if, well, you have either made a conscious choice to consign yourself to the outskirts of society or, if perhaps, you might benefit from some kind of assistance with, well, socialization."

That shut me up. I knew Doc Sharpe worried about my ability to support myself. I didn't realize he worried about my emotional health as well.

"I do fine socially, Doc." I wasn't about to spell out my relationship with Creighton.

"I don't mean to pry." That hand again. Poor Doc. He's got a Yankee's reticence for talking about personal matters. To go this far meant he really must be worried, and so I bit my tongue. "This matter did predispose me to pursue a proposal, however."

"Yes?" Tongue biting only goes so far.

"She should be here by now." He looked past me to the open door.

"Wait." I twisted around. I'd been ambushed.

"Hi, Ms Marlowe—I mean Pru." Jill Canaday was standing in the doorway, looking pretty and fresh in pink scrubs.

"You look nice." From my mouth, it wasn't a compliment. Doc Sharpe probably got that. I heard a small choking sound behind me. Jill Canaday simply blushed, the pink in her cheeks bringing to mind her older sister's more dramatic coloring.

"Thank you," she said. "If I had known you were coming in today, I would—"

"What?" I had been startled. I hate being startled. "Avoided me until you'd stolen all my clients?"

"Pru, please." Doc Sharpe hates conflict. "She's not—"

"I'm not getting paid." Jill broke in. "I'm here as a volunteer. Honestly, Pru. I was only going to say that I would have arranged to meet you here. I just want to learn. "

I eyed her. Cute as a kitten, this one, but kittens could kill. I wanted no part in training her—or in letting her learn anything about me.

"Ahem." Doc Sharpe can make even clearing his throat sound reticent. "Pru, if I may, this is the—ah—kind of situation we've discussed."

"You've talked about, you mean." I was beginning to feel cornered. Those distressed barks and whimpers were leaking through. I could feel beads of sweat on my brow, down my back.

"Pru, are you feeling ill?" Doc Sharpe stepped toward me.

"I'm fine." Now it was my turn to bark. "But I don't like to be—"

I stopped myself. What was I going to say? Ambushed? To Doc Sharpe—to any outside observer—I was the one with the power here. Jill the acolyte, looking for guidance. No, I had enough problems without getting a reputation for misogyny. Any more of one, that is. Besides, I needed something from this family.

"Surprised." I finished my sentence with a smile to match the one on her pink face. "I'm so sorry, Jill. I've just had a lot on my mind."

"No problem." She certainly bounced back. "But since you're here, maybe we can talk sooner. I was just about to clean the cages in the cat room. Want to come with me?"

I paused. Okay, I got it. She was doing the kind of volunteer work I really didn't want to do. Unless this was all an act to lull me into accepting her. Doc Sharpe was looking at me. Waiting.

"Sure," I kept the smile in place. "I'll be with you in a minute."

I watched her go before turning to the old vet. Maybe I could turn this to my advantage. "Doc?"

I waited for him to apologize. Waited for his usual reticence to play out with a downcast gaze and an open, if vague, offer. I'd worked with Doc Sharpe for some years now. Long enough to think I knew him.

"Yes?" When he looked at me, gray eyes light and clear behind those glasses, I was a bit taken aback. He didn't think he'd wronged me, I realized. He thought he'd done me a solid.

"About the kitten..." I hesitated. I'd been going to ask if he could sneak the little fellow in. Give him his shots and maybe make up a story about quarantine. Just until I had things figured out. "You know, the one I got from the Canaday family?"

He reached up to rub his eyes again. Took his glasses off to do so. Allergies, I thought. As well as fatigue and money woes.

"Pru." He shook his head, his fingers still pressing into his eyelids. "You aren't helping yourself, you know." His voice was sad as he reached behind him for a tissue. Dabbed at those reddened eyes. "Give the kitten back to Jackie Canaday, Pru. You've got to start making people your priority."

When I stood, it wasn't anger. It was more a straight animal instinct—the desire to flee from a place that felt confining. Dangerous. But as I did, I saw that tray. Those vials. I pocketed two of them, as well as a hypo. And with a few mumbled words, I took off.

Chapter Twenty-six

I couldn't run. No matter how much I might want to, I knew better than to act suspicious. Couldn't take my booty and scamper. If I were lucky, the vials wouldn't be missed. I had no idea how many kittens came through here, but I knew there were a lot. Just as I knew for sure that Pammy wasn't always careful or neat. If there were a discrepancy in the numbers, she'd take the heat—for carelessness or loss. Was I endangering some other animal? I thought of what Doc had said, about the hospital's money woes, and I put them from my head. I was doing what I could for the one animal in my care. Doc Sharpe would understand. I'd make him—if I were caught.

As I closed the door behind me, I had managed to mutter something about Jill. And so now, to make that part of my story true, I went to find her, walking down the long hall to the animal rooms, all too aware of the glass vials bouncing in my pocket.

I found the youngest Canaday in the first cat room, cleaning cages. To do her justice, Jill didn't ask me to help. Instead, she went about her work with the minimum of cooing or complaining while I leaned back and watched. She'd removed the cage's occupants—in this case, a new mother and three nursing kittens—to a travel case as she emptied their temporary home of soiled newsprint and food. The kittens were oblivious; they didn't care as long as mom was nearby. The mother, however, was a bit anxious. Change was scary, especially now that she had little ones to care for. Where was her safe closet nest? Her person, the little girl who always brought treats?

I couldn't tell her. Didn't want to tell her that her kittens would probably be taken as soon as she had weaned them. And that her chances, if her family wouldn't take her back, weren't the best. Instead, I did my best to tune out the feline queries and contemplated how I could use this time—since I probably couldn't bill for it.

Jill was the first to break the silence.

"I really do admire you, you know," she said, as she wiped down the tray. "I've been hearing about your work with animals for ages."

"From Doc Sharpe?" A twinge of guilt, easily dismissed.

"No," she shook her head. "From my father."

That made me stand up straight. "I didn't think he was much of an animal-lover." I was downplaying even Doc Sharpe's restrained comment. Then again, I was fishing.

"No," she shook her head as she reached for the paper towels. "That's not true. He just believed that things should be done a certain way. That's what makes it weird that Judith would…" She broke off. The kitten, I knew. I figured Jill was either too young to know about her sister's pet name or Judith had invented that story for reasons of her own.

"I gather that Judith and your father had a falling out?" She'd raised the topic. That made it fair game.

"Yeah, before she left." She wiped down the tray and turned away, looking around her as if for a misplaced sibling.

More likely, she wanted the bottle of disinfectant. I reached for it and paused. The way Judith had put it, her wanting to leave had been the problem—not the solution. As I handed Jill the spray bottle, I asked, my tone as even as I could make it. "Do you remember what they fought about?"

A shrug as she spritzed the empty cage. "I was so young then, I don't really know." She paused and looked back at me. "She'd been taking courses at Berkshire Community for a couple of years by then, off and on, but I don't think she was ever really the college type. So when her job ended and she and Dad started fighting, I guess it made sense for her to leave."

She handed me back the bottle and started refilling the cage with clean bedding.

"I get it. I mean, I didn't visit as often as I should have. Maybe once every few months. He talked about you, though—my dad did. I guess he kept seeing your name in reports. And when I was home, I heard him on the phone arguing with Dr. Sharpe about you."

The expense. Of course.

"And that made you want to seek me out?" Something wasn't scanning here.

Another shrug. "My father could be difficult. But I—I could usually see beyond that." See how to manipulate him, I translated. "He listened to what Doc Sharpe said, you know. He wasn't a bad man."

No, not if you were the one getting all his money. I waited. It's a cop trick. Facing silence, most people rush to fill in the blank. Jill was better than most, I'd give her that. She finished up the cat room and I followed her to the small mammal cages before she started talking again.

"So, you're wondering what I'm trying for," she said, looking at me with a hopeful smile.

"Not really." That was true.

"I want to work with animals." She opened a cage that housed a family of gerbils. They seemed pretty calm as she reached in for their food dish, as calm as gerbils can be, anyway. "Like you do."

"There are a lot of good animal behavior programs." I waited, letting in more from the gerbils. No, they weren't overly concerned. Then again, gerbils aren't the best judges of character. "You're up in Vermont? I can give you some recommendations."

"No." She shook her head as she replaced the dish. "I mean, I am taking some classes. I'm thinking of veterinary school. But I want to do what *you* do. You make their lives better."

I looked at her. She appeared serious, which only made me more uncomfortable. "Well, if you want to help, you can try working on your sister."

"What?" She shook her head, uncomprehending. "You mean Judith?"

"Jackie. She wants to have the kitten put down."

"What? Why?" Her surprise seemed real. Then again, I doubted the sisters talked much.

"She seems to blame the kitten." I watched her, waiting for a reaction.

Jill shook her head in disbelief. "That's crazy. You won't let her, right? The kitten—where is it? Is it safe?"

"He's safe." If her sister hadn't shared the kitten's location, I wasn't about to. "For now. But if you want to help an animal, I would suggest starting at home."

She nodded. "I will. Jackie's not herself. She's been going on about that day, about visiting with our lawyer, Mr. Wilkins." I *bet*, I said to myself. But Jill didn't miss a beat. "After—when all this stuff with my father is straightened out, will you think about taking me on?"

"I'll think about it," I said. For sure, I would. Talking about Ernesto had made me antsy to get home to him. I fingered the vials in my pocket—and thought about the woman who had brought the kitten into my life. "Hey, what did Judith do here, anyway?" I asked. "Before she took off for LA?"

"Didn't you know?" The round face that looked up at me was all innocence, eyes as wide as Ernesto's. "She took care of Mrs. Wilkins in those last few months. Everyone thought she was going to become a nurse."

Chapter Twenty-seven

I left County with one answer but a lot more questions. Some of those I floated, asking in an offhand way as I drifted toward the door. Most of them were pointless. Jill didn't remember Wilkins' wife, Melissa, well. Didn't recall anything more than a pale woman on a daybed and didn't think her sister did much more than sit with the ailing woman, since Judith had been just a few years out of high school at the time. But what she had told me did leave me with a little more understanding for Judith. I'd been a caregiver, too. I wouldn't volunteer to do it again either.

It also made me wonder about their father. After all, from what Jill said, her middle sister had been quite conscientious. Surely, she was allowed to make some choices for herself, after her one charge had died? Unless, of course, he thought her early choice was the one she should stick with. Maybe he had some inkling of his own future incapacity then. Maybe his kitten was supposed to become a house cat.

I was thinking about Jill and her sisters as I drove. I'd originally meant to go back over to Laurence Wilkins' house. Check on those squirrel gates, and see if I could connect with the man himself. Now I had an additional reason to want to talk to him. I wanted to ask about Judith and about his wife. In particular, I wanted to know what had happened after his wife died.

First, I had to make use of those vials. The day was fine, and I'd have plenty of time to check in on the lawyer later.

"I'm home," I called, as I came through the front door.

"*Clearly.*" The word was accompanied by a small thud, as Wallis jumped off the windowsill to greet me. "*You've been…*" She sniffed the air around my legs, "*social.*"

"It was work, Wallis." I reached to stroke her, my hand releasing a flurry of fur that drifted in the breeze. "And you're shedding."

"*No manners.*" She sat and twisted herself, as if to lick the exact spot where I had pet her. "*No manners at all. Just like a kitten.*"

"Speaking of," I looked around, ignoring her rebuff. "Where's Ernesto?"

"*He's…*" The taste of fur so strong, I reached up to my own lips. "*Somewhere.*"

"Wallis?" This was what I'd feared. She was losing interest. Then again, I'd never had any desire to parent a child either.

"*Please.*" Even her voice sounded fuzzy. "*He's old enough to know what he's doing.*"

I wasn't sure about that, but I tried to keep my thoughts to myself as I went in search of the kitten.

"*Play?*" He found me first, barreling out from behind the sofa to tackle my foot. I lifted him to my lap as I sat, even as he sighed, his sides heaving with disappointment. "*Button?*"

"Sorry, kiddo." With my left hand, I stroked his back. With my right, I slipped the vial and hypo from my pocket. But if I was hoping to inject the kitten without his noticing, I hadn't counted on a young cat's curiosity.

"*Toy?*" One small paw came up to bat the vial.

"Not quite." Releasing him, I opened the vial and filled the needle. In my last practicum, I had gotten this move down. "Medicine."

He looked up and then started, as the needle made contact with his flesh. "*Oh!*"

"Sorry, kiddo." I smoothed his fur, hoping to distract the little fellow from the spot where I had punctured his hide. Treats would have been better, but I hadn't thought that far ahead. I couldn't think of how to explain what I'd just done. I could at least have provided the feline equivalent of a lollipop. "There, all done."

"*Sick?*" Those blue eyes looked up at me. I blinked back. This little fellow got more from me than I had thought.

"Not now, Ernesto." Even as I said it, I realized I was prevaricated. Getting the vaccine was certainly better than getting the disease. That didn't mean it was entirely safe. "Now you're going to be fine." I really hoped I wasn't lying.

Chapter Twenty-eight

In an ideal world, I'd have stayed with Ernesto all day, watching to see if he had a reaction. In an ideal world, my bills would pay themselves, too. And so after making myself a turkey sandwich—and making sure that both resident felines had their share, minus the bread and mayo—I turned my thoughts toward business.

"Watch him?" Wallis was still lapping at the thigh meat I had left for her, but a single flick of her tail acknowledged my silent plea, and I set out again.

With my windows open to the spring afternoon, I let my thoughts fly as I drove. Left to their own devices, they hovered around the Canaday girls. What can I say? My mind is more crow than swallow. I am drawn to carrion.

It wasn't only the backbiting and jealousy that drew me. It was curiosity. As an only child, I'd fantasized about having a sister. Someone to keep me company when our parents fought. Someone who could explain why my father was never home, and my mother was always angry. Of course, in time, I figured out the answers to that last bit by myself. By the time I took off, I was grateful to have so few ties to cut.

In her way, I figured, Judith was the most like me. She had fled from the traditional daughter role. Taken off and started some kind of life for herself out on the West Coast. It didn't seem to be working out as she'd planned, otherwise, she wouldn't have come back hoping to win her father over, I suspected. She certainly wouldn't have lied about the kitten's origins. That didn't mean it hadn't been the right move for her. I didn't know the age difference between Judith and Jackie, but Judith looked at least a decade younger than her sister. That could have been because she'd had her taste of caregiving and decided to take care of herself. Whatever she gave up when she ran off, she certainly seemed better off.

Then again, I could see Jackie's side, too. I'd come back to Beauville for my own reasons. I had needed to get out of the city, away from a life that had driven me too hard and too close to the edge. It was an accident of timing that my mother was in her final decline when I returned, though caring for her did make a good cover for what was really a full-on retreat. Still, I had done what I could, taking on responsibility for the old house and my not-so-old but more decrepit parent.

Of course, I hadn't been alone. My mother had had the sense to set up hospice care for herself while she could, and much of what I did was follow the instructions of the professionals who came by with increasing regularity. In fact, much of what I had to do—set up a hospital bed, do the laundry, do more laundry, sit and wait—was precisely what I needed, not that I'd known it at the time. My brain was soothed by the simplicity of the routine. Life pared down to its basics. But emotionally? It was exhausting. My mother was strong. She was a fighter. That only made it worse to watch her lose her abilities, day by day, knowing full well how the battle would end.

From what I gathered, I didn't think Jackie had ever gotten away. I doubted she had felt like she had much of a choice but to care for her father as he stumbled and declined. Yes, I could see what she'd gone through, too.

Not that her suffering gave her license to kill a kitten.

Unless she didn't mean it. As I drove, this option began to seem more viable. There was an edge of hysteria to Jackie. She seemed to be wound so tight, her voice a little too strained and loud for the circumstance. So maybe the kitten thing was simply part of that. She was angry. She had lashed out. I should have seen her for what she was—a sad and aging woman who had given up much of her life and now felt she'd been cheated. It was a reaction, nothing more. After all, who would really want to hurt a tyke like Ernesto? Unless the kitten was a stand-in for her sister. Jill might be too young to remember their father's pet name. But Jackie? I bet she remembered everything.

Which left Jill. Whatever Judith had once been to their dear departed dad, by the end, her younger sister was clearly the loved one. The baby. From what I'd gathered, she'd not escaped, she'd been launched. Sent on her way with her father's blessing only to return every few months, at least according to what she'd told me. And yet, she was the one who wanted to go into animal care—the field her father had been so critical or, rather, suspicious about. No, I told myself as I pulled up to Laurence Wilkins' house, I didn't understand sisters.

I did know squirrels, however. Squirrels and, I liked to think, dogs. I listened for the dog Wilkins called Biscuit as I walked up to the house. That poor sheltie wasn't happy, and if I could, I'd help her out. Shelties, like so many breeds we've made pets of, are work dogs. Shepherds. From the little I'd seen and, more importantly, heard, the old gal was bored. Granted, at her age, she might have other issues. We don't often hear of dementia in animals, but it happens. But the way she was still harping on her lost mistress spoke as much of her lack of present-day occupation as of grief. The lawyer's wife had been dead—what?—ten years? If this dog had been mourning her mistress all that time, it also said something about Laurence Wilkins' insensitivity, as much as about the little sheltie's loyalty.

She still made a good watch dog, though. No person answered the door, when I rang. But one bark—alert and inquisitive—responded. Wilkins was out. His dog—his wife's dog—was not.

"Biscuit?" I asked the air.

"Who?" The bark was short and sharp. A warning, as much as a question. Age hadn't muted the faithful dog's hearing.

"I'm a friend." It's hard to communicate an abstract concept. *"A friend of your person."*

"*Who?*" The same bark, the same question. Maybe the old girl really did have some dementia.

"*Biscuit*—" I caught myself. One of the first things I'd learned, once this sensitivity had manifested itself, was that animals have their own names, their own ways of referring to themselves. The dog Tracy Horlick knew as Bitsy, for example, was really Growler. "*Who are you?*"

Silence, though I got the sense of a low whine, heavy with longing. "*Sheila,*" the answer came back finally. "*She called me Sheila.*"

"*Pleased to meet you, Sheila,*" I responded. The formalities are different for animals, but with her inside the house and me out, she couldn't exactly sniff me.

"*Are you a friend?*" The thought was accompanied by a sweet taste—malt, maybe, mixed with peanut butter—a favorite of dogs.

"*Next time,*" I promised myself as much as her. "*Next time, I'll take you out, too.*"

〉〉〉

As I pulled the tarp off of Albert's ladder, I wondered what the sheltie had made of the squirrels. She'd have been aware of them—and they of her, for sure. Maybe the rodents had picked up on the little dog's advanced age. Or maybe they'd simply taken the risk. Had Sheila been frustrated by their continued presence, their incursion into a house she must consider her own? If so, would she consider me an ally—or a competitor?

Not the latter, I hoped, as a third possibility flashed through my mind. Maybe the sheltie had made peace with the invaders. Could a canine find common ground with a creature her person considered a pest? It was possible, I thought. Loyalty—and gratitude—could be funny things.

I dismissed this train of thought as I positioned the ladder. And once I had climbed up to the roof, I couldn't help but pride myself on a job well done. As far as I could tell, nothing was stirring under the eaves. The wire mesh had been chewed, and when I touched it, I received a flood of memories. *Nest, babies.*

Safe at home. I jerked back as if burned. Yes, some squirrel had nested here. Raised her babies. But that story was over now. Those reflective thoughts merely memories. It was late May, and the spring had been a warm one. Those babies might still be spending time with their mother, but they were adults for all intents and purposes. And they were out of the good lawyer's roof. My work was done. I'd send an invoice to Wilkins. Maybe offer to do another inspection in the fall. I had to come back with Albert's truck for the ladder, anyway.

"Nest, babies! Nest!" It wasn't only the squirrels who had family issues to deal with. I started down the ladder with the late afternoon bird chatter ringing in my ears. Spring. It's a noisy mess, and I looked forward to the day when I could truly block it all out.

"Mine!" A discordant caw broke into the chatter, rough and loud. That crow again. The one I had heard out here last time. Amid all the anxious peeping, his voice was singular and clear. *"Mine!"*

The sounds hit me so hard, I had to close my eyes. Dizzy, I put my hand out, touched the warm slate. *Nest. Babies…* No, I couldn't go there. I had a job to do, and I had done it. More mercifully than many others would have. I had to work on stopping this. On not hearing every voice. I descended the ladder and folded it once again. My job here was done.

Chapter Twenty-nine

I tried to put those voices out of my mind as I made my way home. The spring weather was mild. I had more important things to worry about. My own nest to protect, so to speak. What did Jill really want, for starters? That was what I needed to figure out. On the surface, she was the solution to my problems. Want to learn how to work with animals? Here, take your father's kitten. Two birds with one stone.

Until the situation with her sisters settled down, though, I didn't feel comfortable entrusting Ernesto to her. Wallis may scoff at my atrophied instincts, but something was hinky with that family, and Jill was a part of it. Even if Jackie had called me in a fit of grief-induced pique, giving the kitten to her youngest sister wasn't likely to improve that particular relationship—or get my bill paid. Of the three, Judith probably had the best claim on the little cat. I didn't see her changing her tune anytime soon, though. And considering what had happened to the last creature in her care, well, maybe that was just as well.

Speaking of instincts, Wallis was waiting when I got home.

"How is he?" I hadn't realized till the words were out of my mouth that I'd been worried. "Is Ernesto okay?"

"Relax." She stretched on the word, extending one hind leg in a perfect balletic line. *"He's fine."*

"No reaction to the vaccine?" I wasn't sure how much Wallis had picked up.

"I didn't say…" another stretch, *"…that."*

"Wallis." I caught my breath. Cats cannot be hurried. "Where is he?" If he were having a reaction, I promised myself, I would rush him back to County General. I would confess to Doc Sharpe. I would…

"It's not his body." Wallis cut into my thoughts, her tone acid. *"It's his mind. What did you tell him, anyway?"*

"I didn't." I paused. What had I been thinking when I'd injected the fluffy little creature? Had I given him a preview of distemper—or of County? "Why?"

"He's been going on about his mama again. And that damned button. Oh, and he has a new word: medicine." She used the word gingerly, and I wondered how she understood it. *"Oh, I understand enough, Pru. I know that you dosed him with something. And Ernesto knows it too."*

This was the problem with this so-called gift. Well, one of several. When it worked, great. I'd been able to help some animals—some people, too—by serving as an interpreter between the species. These days, though, it felt more like a burden than any kind of blessing. Either I heard what I didn't want to hear—what I didn't *need* to hear, I reminded myself—in order to do my job. Or what I could get wasn't useful. If anything, it created more tension. Someone else would probably fawn all over that cute kitten. Me? I wanted to shake him. Or at least demand that he speak more sensibly.

I was becoming my mother.

I was also like her, I realized, in that I was waiting on a man. Creighton was becoming a habit. Not a bad one, but not good either. We were getting closer, and I knew what was coming next. Already, he'd started—pushing me to open up, as if that were possible for someone like me.

It wasn't just my natural reticence. I know I'm more like Wallis than she would ever admit. But more than my privacy, my sense of personal space was at stake. Even if I wanted to—and, yeah, I got the temptation—it wasn't like I could tell Creighton what was going on. Sure, he'd shut me out from what he knew about the Canaday investigation. Kept me from info that could have made my life—and Ernesto's—easier. But he could—and did—claim work. Privilege. Privacy. Even as I pushed, I had to respect that.

I didn't have a similar excuse. Yet there was no reasonable way to share what I was dealing with. That my one benefactor was pushing me to take on a protégé of my own, an impossibility that could threaten my freedom. That my cat was giving me grief for not understanding a kitten's problems. That my nerves were frayed and battered by the constant assault of all those voices. No, for all our growing intimacy, there was too much that I had to keep from him. It was a lousy deal and getting harder. It made me want to drink.

With a sudden surge of energy, I reached for my jacket and my car keys. Doc was right about one thing. I'd been too much of a hermit. Winter can do that to you, as can having a semi-regular bedmate. Spring was here, though, and I didn't like to rely too much on any one man. Besides, I needed information about the Canadays. About lawyer Wilkins, too, if I could get it. I was headed for Happy's.

Chapter Thirty

Happy's is as close as I come to a family institution. Back in the day, my father used to hang out here, drinking away whatever money he'd managed to earn. Not that I crossed paths with him. When he was around, I was too young for our town's one dive bar. Too much my mother's daughter, wondering and wishing why Daddy didn't come home for dinner. Why Mommy had to work so hard.

By the time I gave up wondering—gave up trying to make things right with Mom, too—my dad had moved on. Supposedly with another woman, one of many who was more tolerant of his drinking. In reality, he was driftwood, chasing a dream in a bottle. When he died, it didn't make much difference to us. My mother got some money since neither of them had bothered with a divorce. But he'd been gone so long by then, the mourning was itself a memory.

Still, Happy's had some resonance for me. Virtually windowless—the small slit in the front nearly obscured by that neon beer sign—it was a claustrophobic time capsule. The Berkshires the way they used to be, before the yuppies and their money. Happy, the original owner, was an old-style barkeep. He'd be behind the thick oak bar himself most nights, pulling drafts for working folks, pouring out shots without comment. I didn't know if he ever smiled—the name was typical of the dark barroom humor. What I did know was that he was gone by the time I came back to town. The new barkeep could have been his brother, though I never bothered to ask. A face lined like an old hound's, mouth aged from keeping mum. When I took a stool at the bar, he poured me a shot of bourbon without my having to ask. It had been a while, but at Happy's—at all the real bars I'd ever frequented—they remember.

"Pru." I turned. This early, the bar was nearly empty. I hadn't seen Mack come up. Then again, the back booths are dark for a reason.

"Mack." I raised my glass, then turned away. Life hadn't been easy for my onetime beau, and I didn't like to see him this way, strung out and grubby.

"Want to join us?" His voice still had that lilt in it. That bit of a tease. I wasn't interested, but I turned to be polite. Sure enough, there were two others in one of the four booths that lined the wall. Men I knew from around. Nobody I wanted to know better.

"Thanks, no." I faced the bar. Happy—or whatever his name was—kept busy, wiping down the glasses. That was okay. I didn't need his help.

"Suit yourself." Mack slid onto the stool beside mine and nodded toward Happy. The barkeep remained stone-faced until I nodded, too. Mack and I went way back. I could stand him a drink.

"Thanks," Mack said, his voice low. He closed his eyes while he drank, like he'd needed it. "You look good," he said, finally. "How you been?"

"Good." It wasn't like I could confide in Mack, but he was easier to lie to than Creighton. "Work's good."

He nodded, like he knew. "I hear you've been getting jobs over on the east side."

"Albert tell you that?" Albert was a regular at Happy's, kind of a mascot. He'd probably spun giving me the Wilkins job, making himself the boss and me the worker bee.

Mack smiled, the old, slow smile. Only now the creases in his face emphasized how thin he was, how worn. "I still have my connections, Pru. In case you ever need to draw on them."

He was still confident, I'd give him that. Plus, he had given me an idea. "Yeah, maybe." I looked over at Happy again. I wasn't flush, but I could pay for information. He brought the bottle over and filled both our glasses. "You have any dealings with the Canadays?"

Mack perked up at that, or maybe it was the drink. "Old man Canaday? Yeah, he wasn't one of the Happy's gang, but I knew him, if we're talking about the same guy."

"Lawyer? East side?" I paused. He probably knew. "Recently deceased?"

Mack nodded. "Yeah. Guy I know did some time with someone. " I waited, but he'd stopped. "Long story. At any rate, he was out of my price bracket, even on those rare occasions when I did get caught."

He was flirting again, his voice lifting. I put it down to the drink, more than my interest, but that didn't mean I couldn't use it. "What about his daughters?"

The smile became wider now. "Why Pru, I didn't know you swung that way. Though maybe it explains some things…" He leaned in, the invitation implicit.

"Are the Canaday girls gay?" This was interesting. I didn't know if it meant anything, though.

"The oldest? Who knows." He leaned back on the bar. "She's the kind who's happy with any attention. Something wrong with that one. The second girl? She was a looker. Kind of reminded me of you." A sidelong look, one I'd have fallen for a year or two before. "There was another, too."

"Jill." I filled in the blank. Mack was quiet. Remembering, I thought, or maybe just lost in a bourbon daze. "Jackie was the oldest, then Judith." I said to prime the pump.

"Judith, yeah." He nodded. "She used to come in here every now and then. It was slumming for her, though. Not like you." He turned, and for a moment, I felt it. Those eyes. Even now, threadbare, he still had it. Then he smiled again, wider than before, and I saw the space where a tooth had gone missing. Saw the wear and tear. "Then you left, too." The smile faded into the melancholy of the serious drinker. My window of opportunity was beginning to shut.

"What else can you tell me about them—the girls or the father?" I nodded to the bartender, but also held up my hand. I wanted Mack to know I'd see him right, but not just yet.

"The father was a hard ass, like I said. Real strict, real law and order." A snort—half laugh, half belch—as he heard his own words. "I mean, more than some lawyers around here."

Happy came closer. I put my hand over my own tumbler. It was still half-full, and I wasn't going to need any more. "And the girls?"

"The girls were, well, what would you expect?" He pushed his glass toward Happy, unaware of how hungry he looked. "Judith, yeah, she was the one. Put that much pressure on a girl, and she's going to bust out."

"I gather her father wasn't pleased when she went to L.A." I wasn't sure what I was looking for. Something that would explain these women.

Mack nodded. "There was some kind of a blow up, I know that. Funny thing was, I'd thought she'd straightened out. She stopped hanging out here, anyway."

"She have something else going on?" I asked. He shrugged, and I motioned for Happy. I was losing Mack, and I needed more. "You think she could have hurt anybody?"

I was thinking of Laurence Wilkins' wife. Wondering why she'd left.

Mack's answer surprised me. "I wouldn't have been surprised if she'd taken a shot at her dad," he said, his words beginning to soften and slur. "Turned them against each other, their dad did. Sisters are supposed to be close. That's what I'd always heard. Those girls looked out for each other, at least at first, when their mom died. By the time Judith left, they were on each other like wildcats. Man, women can be vicious."

"Thanks, Happy." I turned away as the bartender poured, unwilling to see the naked thirst on my ex's face. I'd never loved Mack. Never trusted him, entirely. But we'd been running partners as much as lovers, off and on for quite a few years. If he said that Judith was capable of killing her father, I had to take that seriously. As for the sisters turning on each other? That I'd already witnessed.

Life in a small town wasn't for everyone. Men like Canaday and Wilkins can master it. Others, like Mack, get crushed beneath its wheels. Seeing him this way made me all too aware of what I might have become, except for a few small twists of fate. Spending time with him made me long for Creighton, for his straight-ahead nature, for his solid charm and lack of decrepitude.

All the reasons why I couldn't have any kind of a future with him, not and be honest about who I am. I stared into my glass, knowing that I wouldn't see anything at the bottom. And when Happy came back one more time, I let him fill me up.

Chapter Thirty-one

I woke with a start, my heart pounding. Alone, I was glad to see, and as I licked my dry lips I remembered why. My feral ex had shown more enthusiasm for the bottle than for turning my self-pity to his advantage. Well, my mother always said I should be grateful for small blessings, though I doubted this was what she meant.

I clambered out of bed, desperate for some water, and tried to reconstruct the night. Mack kept drinking, I knew that, and while I had enough sense not to match him, I'd clearly gone too far. I'd pushed him on the Canadays, I recalled. Not that it had gotten me much more: the sisters had fought. Jackie had been the dutiful one. The one who stayed. Mack had hinted at something more—called her a dark horse, in fact. When I'd pursued, though, he'd backed off, leaving me to wonder if he had just been talking to hear himself speak. To keep the bourbon coming.

Judith was more interesting to him. She was the wild one, the one who had gotten away. But even Mack had sounded puzzled by her defection. Said she'd seemed to settle down before she left. Before the big blowout with her dad. He didn't know anything about her working for Wilkins, though. Certainly nothing about Wilkins' wife. And I didn't want to share my suspicions with the bar.

That left Jill, the baby. By the end, she had been her father's favorite, not that he'd been easy on any of the girls. Beyond that, she was a blank. That could have meant anything. She didn't drink, or didn't drink at Happy's. Didn't party with Mack or any of his friends. In a way, those two were synonymous. All Mack had really cared about was the bottle. Even I, his former flame, seemed most compelling when I signaled for one more round.

Mack had always lived on the edge—mixing handyman work with the kind of shady deals that come through a small town. He'd gone too far in recent years, at one point turning up as a suspect in a drug-smuggling ring. But he'd kept his easy charm throughout, leaving me to hope that he'd surface, maybe on the arm of a wealthy widow, somewhere down the line. I couldn't see it now, not with that damaged smile. His sunken cheeks, the hollow look in his eyes, seemed to foretell what waited for me if I couldn't find a way to make peace with this world. That, I thought, taking another long drink of water, must have been what woke me. That, and my painfully dry mouth.

Thirst sated, I returned to bed, pausing only to remove the few clothes I had fallen asleep in. My wallet was still in my jeans, I was glad to note. Not that I expected there to be any money left.

"I've got to stop living like this." I spoke to the ceiling.

"*You've got to stop drinking,*" a voice responded.

"Wallis." It wasn't a question. "At least I no longer think I'm going mad."

A small snort, as the tabby landed on the bed. "*That's why you're sleeping so soundly?*"

She was pissed, I could tell. When I toss and turn, she can't spend the night on the bed.

"I'm sorry, Wallis." I could close my eyes now without the room spinning. "I was just thinking about Mack."

"*Mack, huh.*" She was kneading the comforter now, so I didn't bother apologizing again. "*It's not me you want to make peace with.*"

"What?" When you're trying to get back to sleep, a voice in your head can be most annoying.

"*You're going to keep having nightmares.*" More kneading, until she plopped over on her side. "*Not that a furry-tailed rat would bother my conscience at all.*"

"You don't have a—" I sat up, suddenly awake. It wasn't Mack. It wasn't even my own overconsumption that had caused me to toss and turn until I woke up, pre-dawn, with a dry mouth and a throbbing head. "The squirrels."

Wallis turned slowly, an appraising look in her cool, green eyes. *"Like you care."*

"I don't, but…" The protests. The voices I'd worked so hard to suppress. Either my inebriation had lowered my defenses or, more likely, my increasing alcohol intake had been insufficient to block out what I had heard—but not wanted to take in—earlier at Laurence Wilkins. That squirrel? The one who had made a nest inside his roof? She wasn't simply complaining about having to move. And I wasn't simply ousting a female and her adult offspring. I'd been wrong. Whether because of the long, cold winter or some other variable that I hadn't taken into account, I'd been wrong in my flip decision. Since when do animals consult calendars? Since when do I expect them to obey our rules? No, the cries of distress I had tried so hard to block weren't as simple—or as minor—as I had believed. They were the sounds of a mother, crying for her young. For her infant, trapped to starve and die alone, by the one human in town who ought to have known better.

Chapter Thirty-two

I made myself wait. I couldn't be scaling people's houses in the pre-dawn dark, not unless I wanted to get shot. That meant—I checked the clock—one hour, maybe two, and to pass the time I stared in the darkness, waiting for the cracks in the ceiling to appear. Fighting the urge to close my eyes. Sleep wasn't an option, though my alcohol-soaked brain needed the time to recover. I wouldn't let myself, even as Wallis curled up for a late-night snooze. Now that I'd let myself hear the desperate cry, I could barely stay in my skin. I lay there, staring at the ceiling. Had my mother felt such pain at losing me? I doubted it. Then again, she knew I could take care of myself. I had left home of my own volition. Left her, too.

It was too late to make any kind of amends in my own family. Maybe not too late for the squirrel. Despite a stirring that let me know Wallis' thoughts on my belated sympathy, I had to try. I had to…

My eyes snapped open. The room was bright. I'd slept—actually overslept—fatigue and booze overcoming guilt. Pulling on last night's jeans, I tore outside. Growler—and Tracy Horlick—would have to wait. I was heading toward the road.

Where I stopped. An unmarked car, Creighton's, blocked my driveway.

I got out. Jim Creighton was in the driver's seat, head back, mouth open. When I rapped my knuckles on the window, he blinked awake and started his car to roll the window open.

"Good morning." He may have spent the night in his car, but he looked in better shape than I felt.

"Jim, what the…" I drew back, suddenly aware of my breath. "Look, I have places to be."

"Did you say you were making coffee?" He smiled as he sat up. "Why thank you, I'd love to."

"Jim." He didn't wait for me to answer. Closing the window, he once again turned the key, leaving his car, parked in front of my driveway. I stepped back as he opened the door, but I wasn't about to give in. "Jim, what are you doing?"

"Coffee, Pru?" He made a show of pocketing his keys, and then turned toward the house. "Or do you really want to risk your license with a sobriety test right now?"

I thought I was fine. I felt fine. I couldn't risk it. And so I returned to my car to fetch my own keys before leading Creighton back up the drive.

"This isn't funny, Jim." I wasn't fighting him. Didn't mean I had to like it. "An animal's life may depend on me."

"And what about your life?" He leaned back on the kitchen table as I heated the water, not even starting when I slammed two mugs down with unnecessary energy. "What about the lives of everyone else on the road?"

"I know how to drive, Jim. Better than most of the tools out there." I had to stop talking. Counting scoops seemed particularly difficult this morning. "Eight."

"That was ten, but I don't mind." His voice was even and low. "I like my coffee strong. What I don't like…" He'd come up behind me. I waited for him to pull me close, to feel his breath in my hair. He stopped before he reached me. "Is you, driving drunk, careening home at all hours of the night."

"You're watching me?" I spun around, spitting my words. "Keeping tabs on me? What, do you think you own me now?"

He didn't back away, I'll give him that. He did, however, look sad, as he slowly shook his head. "No, Pru. I don't own you. That doesn't mean I don't care about you. And I do worry about you sometimes."

I stared, waiting.

"I saw your car behind Happy's." He exhaled in what might have almost been a laugh. "What a name. I can't believe that place is still around. Anyway, I thought about going in to look for you, but I didn't, okay? I did some errands, got some dinner, and when I saw your car was still there, I started to worry."

"No, I know." He raised his hand to stop me before I could start in on that one. "I know you can take care of yourself. Even the men who want you are a little afraid of you."

I raised one eyebrow, but my straight-living beau wasn't flirting now. "But I've seen you drink, Pru. I think you've been drinking more. You're your own worst enemy. That's what worries me. And so, yeah, when I saw your car was still there, I waited. Didn't mean to stay as long as I did, but I did. And when you came stumbling out, sometime after two, I meant to stop you, to give you a ride home. Hell, maybe even see if you wanted some company. But you were too fast for me. You peeled out before I could get into gear."

He stopped and stared at me. I heard what he was saying. He'd let an intoxicated driver go.

"You could have pulled me over." It was a simple statement of fact.

He seemed to accept that. "Maybe I should have. I thought about it. I also thought that if you saw my lights, you might just hit the gas."

I nodded. He was right.

"I didn't want to spook you. I also thought, just maybe, I could talk some sense into you. Not when you got home. Man, I'm impressed that you managed to unlock your own front door. But this morning. Only I'd kind of hoped you'd be sober by the time you found me out there."

"I am sober, Jim." I reached for the carafe and carefully filled the two mugs, making sure my hand didn't shake. "Now I am, anyway."

"Good." He pulled out one of the chairs for me and took the one facing. "So, Pru, you mind telling me what the hell is going on?"

Chapter Thirty-three

I'd have loved to, I really would. Sitting and sharing an early morning coffee with Creighton was as close as I was likely to get to another human. But what was I going to say? That I needed to push him away before he found out that I could hear animals? That I *thought* I could hear animals, anyway? Jim Creighton was a cop through and through, a Boy Scout at heart. No way was he going to accept that my sensitivity was anything other than a major malfunction. Even if he cared for me—and I was willing to believe he did—it wasn't in his nature to accept the truth. We were doomed either way, and this way I could at least enjoy his company a while longer. And my freedom. No, I'd been hospitalized once before. I wasn't going back.

What I ended up telling him was a version of the truth. That I'd had a disturbing visit with two of the Canadays and had needed to blow off steam. And that I'd woken in a panic, realizing that in my distracted state I had miscalculated. I had done the unthinkable. Walled up a squirrel's nest while ignoring the signs of nursing babies inside. If he'd pressed, I would have come up with some gibberish to account for my certainty: say that I had heard them squealing, or that nursing mothers made some kind of special cry. He didn't, and as I went on he actually seemed touched by my distress.

"Why don't I give you a ride over there?" He reached across the table to put his hand on top of mine.

"Thanks, but really, you don't have to." I took his hand. If he sensed the sadness in me, he could attribute it to the squirrel. Or, hell, to the drinking. "I'll take some aspirin for the headache, but I'm fine now. Really." I hefted my mug. "See? Steady as a rock. Ready to climb ladders."

More than forty minutes had passed since I'd first banged on his car window. I did feel better now, the caffeine and the extra time working their magic. Creighton still looked uncertain, and I did my best to meet his gaze.

"I'm sober, Jim," I said again.

"I believe you," he said, finally. "I just wish…" He withdrew his hand to rub his face, and I saw what the night had cost him.

"It's not you, Jim." I reached out, took that hand between my own. "Some things are just not meant to be."

"You talk as if you believed in a higher power." The half-smile again, mirthless and grim. "And here I am, thinking that we're adults and we have choices." He stood up before I could respond, pushing the chair back with a rough scrape. "Look, thanks for the coffee, Pru. And thanks for not killing yourself last night. Or anybody else."

"Creighton, I—"

"Go save a squirrel, Pru." He was halfway to the door. "Who am I to say what your priorities should be?"

"*Territorial.*" Wallis' voice, sounding in my ear, made me jump. The tabby herself came up beside me and jumped to the windowsill. "*I once knew a tom like that.*"

"He's not being territorial, or not entirely." We watched as the tired man stalked back down the driveway to his car. "He cares. He was worried about me."

"*Really now.*" Her tail lashed back and forth. The early morning air full of life. "*Hasn't he heard that the female is the deadliest of the species?*"

Chapter Thirty-four

I wasn't sure if Wallis was simply showing off, but Creighton had a point. Alone in my car, I could admit that. My hands were steadier, my mind more clear than an hour before, and I felt grateful for the enforced respite that made me confident on the road—on the ladder, too, I realized, as I shimmied up as fast as any squirrel. I'd even formulated an excuse, should the lawyer stick his head out and see me. Next day follow-up, I was prepared to say. All part of the service package.

My plan was to remove the one-way gate, replace it with a loose piece of mesh. That would look good, in case Wilkins bothered to check. It wouldn't stop a determined mother, however. As I worked with the claw end of my hammer, rocking out the nails I'd placed so carefully only a day before, I could hear voices in the lawyer's office. Or not voices—the tinny sound of a speaker phone, the caller growing more agitated as the call went on.

"Hang on." Laurence Wilkins voice broke in, his voice loud and live. "I've already told everyone. Everyone knows."

I got the second nail out as the caller kept talking, the voice too low for me to make out the words.

"Jackie, please. You don't know what you're asking." That caught my ear, and I paused. But when the caller—Jackie Canaday?—kept on at the same volume, I went back to the task at hand.

"No, I can't. Until it's official, we can't do anything." Wilkins again. I had the wire door off, and positioned the new mesh in its place. "I know what you're saying, but my hands are tied."

Women. These sisters, at any rate. Jackie was worse than any magpie I'd ever heard, and Canaday was saying just the wrong thing to calm her. She must have called about the will. With a quick tap I tacked one corner of the mesh to the soffit. And then I stopped.

I'd let myself be distracted. My lawyer and his feuding clients were diverting, but they weren't why I was here. What I needed to do was tune them out and focus on the squirrels I had come to rescue. That was what had woken me in a panic last night. That might even have explained some of my despair the night before.

I'm a realist, no matter what Wallis might think. I knew that there was a chance—a good chance—that whatever baby had been separated from its mother had died overnight. I had no idea how old the infant was, though the image I had gotten was of a nursling, still blind and helpless. I also knew that wasn't a tragedy. There's a reason rodents reproduce so prolifically: Even in the kindest of worlds, fewer than half of that female's offspring would live to their own sexual maturity. No, what I was doing was for my own peace of mind. Trapped between my own species' selfish nonchalance and my secret sensitivity, I needed to tread a fine line. If the baby hadn't survived, so be it. I simply didn't want to be in the middle. I had to try to undo what I had done.

With that thought in mind, I braced myself, holding onto the edge of the gutter, I focused all my thoughts on hearing something—*anything*—from inside that hole.

And got nothing.

I shook my head, hoping to clear the last of the hangover from my brain. Closed my eyes, and leaned forward. Waiting to hear an echo, or the tiniest peep.

"Baby?" I startled, and had to grab the gutter to keep myself from falling backward. *"My baby?"* The cry, barely an audible sound, wasn't coming from the hole in the rotted wood. What I was hearing was the mother in a tree somewhere behind me. It was a seeking cry, the sound of a parent desperate to find a lost child.

Clearly, I was in the way. I pulled the mesh out, glad that I had only started to tack it in place. Mesh in hand, I started down the ladder. Maybe that infant was still alive— probably not, but if I was going to have any peace, I needed to let that mother squirrel have something like closure. I had to let her return, to see what my ill-considered actions had done.

"But what if I could have done something?" The speaker phone again, but the content stopped me in my tracks. Had my two worlds overlapped?

"Jackie, please." Wilkins again, and I realized I'd been holding my breath. Of course the people inside the office were not talking about my sins.

"My baby!" I was hit with the loss, the confusion. The despair. *"Where are you?"*

I had to think. Rather, to stop myself from thinking. Hearing animals as I do, it's too easy to anthropomorphize, to attribute human emotions where they don't exist. I wasn't hearing despair, not the way I would feel it. Not even as my poor mother, tough as she was, must have. Animals don't believe in fate like we do. They don't strain to see beyond the horizon. What I was getting was the instinctive panic of a mother who has lost her young. Within a certain window, an infant that has gone astray may be redeemed, and a mother, at least if she's a mammal, is programmed to find her child, rather than let all that gestation go to waste. What I was hearing—feeling, rather, as a high keen inside my head—was nature's way of telling me that this window was still open. Might still be open, I corrected myself. If the mother and her infant could be reunited.

I looked up at the opening. *"Baby!"*

I looked at the neat work I had done the day before, the heavy wire mesh covering the soft wood. From the open window, voices reached me.

"Breaking a will is a difficult matter, and I cannot in good conscience advise you to pursue this."

Lawyer speak. Wilkins. My client.

"Baby!"

I climbed back up, pulling my hammer from my belt. Using the claw, I started ripping out the nails. When the mesh was free, I let it fall and cocked my head, listening for a whimper. For the sound of life. Instead, I heard the lawyer. "This is your sister you're talking about."

Forget my client. My obligations concerned a lot more than money. I continued to work. The soffit, the gutter, a bit of the clapboard. The wood was rotten and came off easily, as that squirrel had known. I didn't care. Wilkins was going to have to replace this anyway. I was doing him a favor.

The morning had grown warm, and I was sweating by the time I stopped, having made a hole big enough for me to stick my head into.

"Hello?" I did just that, speaking softly into the dark, damp space. "Anyone there?"

I didn't know if a squirrel could read my mind like Wallis could. I didn't know if I would simply scare a truly wild animal. I wanted a response, any response. Just to hear if there was any reason to continue.

"What the hell are you doing?" It wasn't the response I expected, and I bumped my head pulling it out. Down below me, Laurence Wilkins was leaning out of his office window, a mix of anger and disbelief on his face. He was looking up at me, but he quickly followed my gaze down, to see the shreds of his new addition lying on the ground. "What the…?"

I couldn't blame him. Listening to Jackie rant would try anyone's patience. That didn't mean I didn't have to come up with an excuse, and the one I had prepared seemed insufficient to explain the damage.

"I should have alerted you." I was stalling. I even cleared my throat. "I realized I needed to get complete access to the area under your roof, in order to assess the state of the infestation." It was as many big words as I could throw together. "Better to be safe than sorry," I threw in.

His eyes narrowed, and I waited for the angry dismissal to come. If I were lucky, he would stop short of suing. But just as I was gathering my breath for another try, he ducked back into his office, slamming the window shut behind him.

I took a deep breath and looked around. The mother squirrel, the one who had been crying, had taken off. The slam, if not the shouting, had driven her away. I looked at the hole, taking in the quiet, the immensity of that quiet, and what it meant. And then I retrieved the wire mesh, torn and bent as it was, and nailed it back over the hole, using the one-way gate to help plug the opening. Knowing full well that nothing was going to come out from under that roof alive, no matter how long I waited.

Chapter Thirty-five

"Late night?" Tracy Horlick asked like the question was rhetorical, but I chose to ignore her insinuating tone.

"Animal emergency," I said, with as little emotion as possible. "Sorry."

Between oversleeping and going to Wilkins' house, I'd rung the old lady's doorbell about an hour after my usual time. Anyone else might have already taken their dog for a walk, but when I'd checked my messages, I hadn't seen one from Tracy Horlick. I figured that she preferred to pay me—and to see what she could squeeze out of me.

"That's a new term." Arms crossed over her faded housedress, the old lady eyed me. Clearly, I was going to have to do better if I expected to free Growler from her clutches.

"Would you rather we skipped today?" I was in no mood to play.

"I could get the Canaday girl, you know." Her eyes narrowed, waiting for a response. "At least, if she doesn't go to jail."

"Where do you get your information?" At this point, I was honestly curious. I knew Tracy Horlick had several sources of gossip. I suspected she picked some up with her unfiltered Marlboros as well as from the hair salon where she got her dated 'do lacquered every week.

"You're not the only one with bad habits." She smiled and drew a battered pack of cigarettes out of a pocket. Shaking one out, she stuck it between her lips and still managed to mutter, "that's how."

"You should quit, you know." I'd lost all patience. "It's bad for Growl—Bitsy, and he doesn't have a choice."

"Huh." She turned and retreated to get the dog she called hers. "I'll look into that."

"*You never learn.*" Growler and I were halfway around the block before the little white dog would even address me. "*Maybe if you listened…*"

"I'm sorry, Growler. Truly I am." Despite the harsh terms of his captivity the bichon was well trained. Between his person's insensitivity and my tardiness, that meant the poor dog was near to bursting by the time I got him outdoors. "But old smoke-teeth wasn't the reason I was late today."

I wanted to tell him about the squirrel, though I didn't know how he'd react. Wallis would have snorted in the feline equivalent of a laugh if she'd heard how badly I wanted to save a mere rodent. Jill Canaday, though, she might have understood.

Then again, she might have found reason to blame me. Reason to poach my clients. Maybe, I thought, these were all the same struggle. We do what we need to in order to survive. A safe place to live. A livelihood.

There was something off with the Canadays, though. Something the delayed death certificate didn't quite explain. The medical examiner's office was backed up. Everyone knew that. It didn't mean anything. Unless, of course, someone knew that it did—and was desperate to divert suspicion. Jackie had been the first to make accusations, crazy as they were, and it seemed like she was still at it, trying to enlist the lawyer to her side. There was an edge to her I couldn't figure. Nerves and something more—could it be guilt? Nerve was what Judith had in spades, though it hadn't helped her bluff her way back into her father's good graces before he died. And there was something about the way she had left town. Something Jill had been willing to hint at, maybe for reasons of her own?

Not that any of them had a case. It was all backbiting and gossip. Besides, they weren't my concern. That mother squirrel—thoughts of her were preying on me.

"If you'd only pay attention." Growler was grumbling, a low growl starting in his chest.

"You're right," I admitted. "This whole thing started because I didn't let myself hear what that mother squirrel was telling me. It's all my fault."

"Deaf as a white cat," Growler was going on. *"And just as dumb."*

〉〉〉

My phone was buzzing as I got back to my car.

"Oh, hi, Pru." Jill Canaday, sounding all girlish and eager. "Are we still on for today?"

"Are we—" I caught myself. I had said I'd meet with her today. Running into her at County only set the groundwork. "Sure."

"I can come to you." Her eagerness made me think of a puppy. If only I hadn't met her sisters, I might have bought into it.

"Look," I needed to make myself clear. "I don't know exactly what you're expecting from me. There isn't much I can teach you that you can't get from a reputable animal behavior program and working with me won't count as a practicum for any degree program. I'm not qualified." That was all true, as far as it went. Whatever special skills I did have, I neither could share nor would want to.

"Oh, I've taken a bunch of pre-vet courses." She jumped right in. "But that's all theory and memorization, at least at this point. I want to spend time with you. See if I can handle the work and, well, if I have a gift for it. Like you do."

I felt my own low growl starting, and was grateful for the electronic distance of the phone. "A gift?" I had to find out what she knew.

"I can pay you." She misunderstood me. At least, I thought she did. "For your time, that is. If I can shadow you, spend some time with you. The career counselor at school recommended I do that before I commit to a degree program. And you're, like, the best at what you do. Dr. Sharpe was going on about how good you are with all different kinds of animals."

"What I do isn't very exciting." I was wavering, the mention of money, more than the blatant flattery getting to me. Not that I dislike a compliment, and name-dropping Doc Sharpe did serve to remind me of his preferences in the matter. All in all, I felt myself being manipulated into assenting. Jill Canaday was either very lucky or very skilled. "And some of my clients might prefer their privacy."

"I understand." Smart, I was thinking. She knew she'd won, and she was giving me my own small victory. "You just tell me when to get lost."

I thought I had already tried that, and held my tongue. Then it hit me. If she came to my house, I'd get to see her interact with the kitten. You can tell a lot about people by the way they treat animals in their care. Besides, I wanted Wallis' take. I might be, as Growler pointed out, clueless and deaf as a white cat. Wallis was a tabby, though, and she had earned those stripes.

>>>

When I pulled up, I saw her, leaning against the sporty little Mini.

"Cute car." Not my type, but it was.

"Thanks." She stood at my approach, fumbling, one hand behind her back. "It was a gift. You know, for driving back and forth."

I nodded. Her father really had been indulgent. Then I saw what she was hiding—a lit cigarette.

"You can't do that." I tried to keep my glee from my voice. Here was my answer. "You can't work around animals and smoke."

"Oh, I don't," she said. "Not anymore."

I stared at her cupped hand, unconvinced.

"It's an e-cig." She held it out to me, and I took it. Long and slender, with a glowing tip, it resembled one of those fancy European brands that used to be targeted at pretentious college students. I sniffed it. Sure enough, the "smoke" was steam.

"This works for you?" I handed it back.

She nodded and pocketed the device. "I hardly ever use it anymore." An awkward shrug. "I guess I'm a little nervous."

"Well, you don't have to be." My words, if not my tone, were welcoming—as welcoming as I could manage, anyway. For a moment, I'd thought I'd seen an out. Now I was back to square one, with an acolyte I didn't want. Or necessarily trust.

"Well, come on in." I led the way to my door.

"So how many animals do you live with?" I'd automatically headed toward the kitchen and now found myself making coffee. My mother would have been proud.

"One." At least she hadn't asked if I had any pets. "Wallis. She's a tabby."

As if on cue, Wallis entered. *"A female."* She brushed up against Jill's legs. *"How interesting."*

"How pretty she is." Jill bent to stroke Wallis' back. "May I pick her up?"

"Ask her yourself." I tried to catch my cat's eyes, but she was too busy nuzzling up to the visitor. "She seems quite interested in you," I noted.

"She's a love bug." Jill cradled her hand around Wallis' soft body and lifted her in her arms. "She's purring."

"Putty in my hands." I couldn't help a chuckle. Jill thought it was for her.

"Is she not usually this friendly?"

"She's a very discerning animal." There, nobody could take offense at that. Besides, it was true. Unlike me, Wallis was quite happy to use her looks and her affections to get what she wanted. Two could play at that game. "And you know how to read her."

Jill tried to hide her smile in Wallis' fur, but I saw it. So did Wallis, I thought, as she twisted in Jill's grip. "Oh, she wants to get down."

"Rule one," I said as Jill released the tabby to jump to the floor. "Animals tell us what they want, if we let them."

"Well, that was pretty basic." Jill accepted a mug, and we both followed Wallis over to the table. "What I want to know is how you establish a connection with an animal. From what Dr. Sharpe has been telling me, you're really a genius at it."

"So you've been spending a lot of time at County." I worked to keep my voice as soft as Wallis' fur. "Thinking of picking up where your father left off?"

"Oh, no." She answered easily, as if her father hadn't been the scourge of the veterinary hospital. "I'm not a watchdog type. Dr. Sharpe knows that."

"Mmm." I tried to sound noncommittal. If Doc Sharpe was hoping to get some of the Canaday fortune, I wouldn't sabotage him. "Well, it never hurts to be observant. Animals tell us what we need to know. Look at Wallis, for example." My tabby was sitting, ears perked up, tail coiled loosely around her front feet. "What do you see?"

"Besides a very pretty girl?" The flattery card seemed to come naturally to her. "I see that she's alert—those ears of hers—but that she's not scared or anxious. Is that what you mean?"

I nodded. "Now, what would you expect if she was frightened?"

Ten minutes later, we'd run through the basics of feline displays. Wallis had settled into her sleeping sphinx pose, but I was having trouble hiding my own frustration. Short of putting my ears back and hissing, I wasn't sure how to get rid of this girl. Nor was I sure how to ask her what I wanted to know.

"So, you drove down from—where do you go? UVM?" She nodded. We'd finished our coffee. Might as well cut to the chase. "You're going back to finish?"

"In the fall. I think." That was an open answer, and I waited. "There's so much to clear up with my father's estate…"

I was supposed to express empathy at this point. But I had my own agenda. "I am sorry, Jill. Can't your sisters take care of things?" I paused to see if she'd pick up on my cue. She didn't. "Your older sister was living with your father, wasn't she?"

A slow, sad nod. "Yeah, I think maybe it was too much for her."

"Your father had resources. She could have hired assistance."

"You clearly didn't know my dad." Jill was almost laughing. "No, he had definite expectations for his daughters."

"And yours was to go to college?" Another nod. "And Judith?"

"She was always the rebel, from day one."

"Always?" I thought about Judith's story. About being her father's favorite. It was possible Jill was too young to remember those days. Anything was possible.

"Yeah," said Jill. "It's funny, isn't it? They usually say it's the baby of the family who escapes. But Judith and my dad were always locking horns."

"So you must have been surprised when she came back for a visit." I waited to see if she'd bring up the kitten. "Especially with a gift like that."

"Yeah, she couldn't have known about the latest complications." She saw my look. "He was on ACE inhibitors. For his heart?" I nodded, not knowing where this was leading. "Some people develop a cough from those, and Dad did. Sometimes it can develop into adult asthma."

"So maybe Jackie wasn't that far off base." I was trying out the idea.

Jill looked at me, waiting.

"That the kitten might have been intended to—ah—hurt your father?" I'm cool, but even I didn't want to spell it out any clearer. A feline as an allergy trigger. An intentional asthma attack.

Jill shook it off. "He was more of a danger to himself. He had an inhaler, NSAIDs, a whole bunch of other things in his house that he shouldn't have had."

I must have looked surprised, because she kept on talking. "Pre-vet's pretty much the same as pre-med," she explained. "But all those drugs? It just doesn't seem like my father."

"He was a sick man," I said. "Maybe he wasn't thinking clearly."

"No, but Jackie was there." Her soft mouth set hard. "She should have been."

Maybe, the thought struck me, she had. Jill was certainly pointing me in that direction, with her hints and her face clenched in anger. But I couldn't ignore the obvious—Jackie wasn't the only one who knew about the old man's medications apparently.

"I can see you going to vet school," I said. I was trying to make it sound like a compliment. "You do have a way with animals. Wilkins' sheltie really liked you."

"Oh, poor Biscuit." Her face softened at the thought of the little dog, as I had hoped it would. "He doesn't pay enough attention to her, so I try to, whenever I can."

I smiled to cover my own thoughts. For someone who was only in town every few months, Jill Canaday had built up quite a relationship with the dog she called Biscuit.

Chapter Thirty-six

I couldn't totally discount what Jill was implying. David Canaday was, by all accounts, headstrong. Not the kind of man to listen to his daughter. And Jackie herself had brought up the possibility of a drug interaction—had blamed the doctors, Creighton had told me, for not informing the family.

Still, it wouldn't be a bad strategy—an accidental interaction that you could then pin on someone else. It was probably a safer bet than introducing an animal into a home and hoping for an allergic reaction. Especially if you already had some medical knowledge, and lived only a few hours away by car.

"So, what's up with the kitten?"

Jill's voice broke into my thoughts. I'd missed something. I looked down at Wallis, but she was deep in a dream.

"I have him isolated and would like to continue observing him." I did my best to cover. Wallis would fill me in later. "He's been agitated and he was vomiting."

She nodded. "Maybe I should take him with me today then. I could bring him into County. Maybe Dr. Sharpe would let me assist with his checkup."

"Well, why don't we wait until things settle down a bit." I wasn't about to confess to the purloined vaccine. Not to this girl. Not now.

"At the very least, let me pay you back for what you spent on the kitten."

That I wasn't averse to. I dug out the receipt. Forty-seven dollars, not including my services. Well, it was better than nothing. She dug out three twenties.

"Do you have change?"

I opened my wallet to find a scrap of paper, an old business card—and no cash. Damn, I'd forgotten Happy's. How many rounds had I bought? Had Mack—? No, it didn't make any sense to even wonder. If he was that low—and I wouldn't be surprised—then I couldn't really begrudge him the forty-odd bucks I'd had the other day.

"Sorry." Now it was my turn to feel stupid. "Look, you can get me next time."

"No, really." She pressed the bill into my hand. "Let me pay you while I can."

"You're expecting your situation to change?" That surprised me.

A grim smile. "You don't know my sisters, do you?"

Chapter Thirty-seven

With one last longing look at Wallis, Jill took off, leaving me with more questions—and sixty bucks in cash. I wondered how many rounds I'd bought last night. Or for how many people.

That scrap of paper—it was cardboard, really, a square with a phone number scrawled on one side. I recalled one of Mack's friends, a beefy guy, handing it to me. I'd been talking to him about something—someone—when he had to get going. I was about to toss it when I saw the other side—Randy's, it said in block print, Smokes and Novelties. I didn't know if Jill's vapor device counted as the latter, but I couldn't ignore the coincidence. Besides, I vaguely recalled the big guy saying something about Jackie—or, no, Judith. Maybe it was both.

I called the number. "Randy's Smoke Shop, hang on."

I hung up. I knew the shop. It sat on the same strip as Happy's and was probably the same vintage. In my day, it had been a head shop, selling rolling papers and bongs. I'd bet it now had cigars and high-end humidors, trying to lure the tourists. But the lug I had spoken to was old school, however he made his money. And if he'd given me his number last night, he might be able to share a little more today.

The late afternoon sun gave everything a golden glow as I drove back into town. Not even spring could brighten up Randy's Smoke Shop, though. Separated from the rest of the small development by one empty storefront and another whose streaked window displayed dust-covered plumbing supplies, Randy's represented old Beauville as much as Happy's did. My past, what I had tried to run from. Maybe it wasn't a coincidence that Jill had a habit she was trying to kick. She was a part of this town, as much as Tracy Horlick. Or…

In a flash of memory, I remembered just how the bell over the door would jingle. I'd first come here as a child. Taken here by my dad to buy loosies—single cigarettes—during one of those times my mother had cut him off. I'd been fascinated by the store then. Its rich, spicy smell, the pipes and cigar boxes. Randy's didn't have a wooden Indian. Beauville didn't have the money for that kind of thing back then. But it was the place for serious smokers, with its jars of loose leaf and other paraphernalia that, by my teen years, would be replaced by bongs and black-light posters. In those days, it had been a man's shop, no question. Probably still was, I thought as I sat in my car, looking through the window.

Well, that could be an advantage. After all, someone in there had approached me last night just down the street at Happy's. I got out of my car and glanced at the window. Whether by accident or by design, it was blocked—vintage posters and some that looked newer, advertising candy flavors in day-glo colors. Hand-written brags about lottery winners already fading, and a notice about a boat for sale that told those interested to ask for Randy, who I gathered was still the proprietor.

That bell, a tiny jingle, brought me back. It also brought out the counter help—a big guy, more fat than muscle, with salt-and-pepper bangs that fell over his face in a style that suggested minimal maintenance. I remembered those bangs from last night. I had pushed those bangs back, I recalled, wincing at the memory.

"Are you Randy?"

As his smile dawned, I realized my mistake. He saw it, too. "Sorry, old joke," he said, holding out his hand. "Randy Jr.—the only Randy now. How can I help you?"

"I'm Pru." We shook. "From Happy's?"

"Yeah, I remember." He nodded, then tossed back those bangs. That gesture. He'd been talking about Judith—or was it Jackie? I used to be able to hold my liquor better.

"We were talking about the Canaday girls?" I was fishing. He seemed to know it.

"You were. You were going on about the old man, the one who croaked." He turned and started arranging a display. Those candy-colored smokes came in a dozen flavors, maybe more. "You and Mack."

"I'm sorry." I tried for sheepish. He didn't turn. "I was pretty wasted last night, but yeah, I'm doing some work for the family." Nothing. "And, well, with the old man dying, I've run into some issues. I'm trying to get a handle on what's going on with them."

"Can't help you." He reached under the counter and pulled out another box, this one with a picture of an ice-cream sundae on the front. "I only knew them back in the day."

"I remember you said that." I did, vaguely. I looked at the package, at the melting ice cream on the front. "People really smoke these things?"

He nodded. "Some people. They're the next big thing, supposedly. E-cigs."

"E-cigs." I picked up the box and thought about Jill. I could see her going for a kiddie flavor like this. "One of his daughters smokes these."

"Huh." It's not good business to disparage customers. Randy didn't seem to care. "Not Judy, I bet."

"No, I was thinking of Jill." A memory tickled the edge of my mind. "You used to hang with Judith, right? I guess she was Judy back then?"

A nod, as he turned back to me. "Yeah, we had some fun."

"So you must have met the old man."

Another nod, this time accompanied by a snort of laughter.

"He must have been a hard ass." I thought about my father. He'd been gone before I started going wild, not that he would have cared much.

The big guy only shrugged. "He didn't have no truck with me," he said. "It was Judy's next boyfriend that made him crazy."

"Who was that?"

"I don't know." He went back to stacking cartons. "I'd gotten a new girl by then. I only heard about it when the old man came in here."

"Was he a smoker?"

"Yeah, like a chimney." Out of habit, Randy turned around. I bet that he could've grabbed Canaday's favorite carton without looking, but he stopped himself, putting both hands on the counter. "At least, back then. The first heart attack scared him, though. Scared him into quitting."

"How'd he quit?" I thought of Jill's electronic "smoke."

"Cold turkey." Randy's voice spoke of a grudging respect. "Just—stopped."

"You think he could've been using one of those e-cigarettes?" I thought back to what I knew of the old man's health. He hadn't been ill that long.

"Maybe," a shrug. "But I doubt it. He was pretty hard core. One of those 'I don't need a crutch' types."

"Huh." I didn't know what it meant, if anything. "Did Judith—Judy—smoke?"

"Not her." More respect. "Not Jackie either. Only their kid sister. She was always the daddy's girl."

I looked at him, wondering if he knew about the will. Wondering if I'd said anything in my cups. "I guess the rivalry goes way back." I was fishing again.

"Oh, yeah." He nodded energetically. "Jackie and Judy were always at each other's throats. Like cats and dogs. Judy wouldn't even stay at the old man's place when she visited, not once Jackie moved in."

"Did she before?" I didn't see Judith as the filial type. That seemed to be Jackie's role.

"I guess." He shrugged, big shoulders heaving up and down. "Or, no, I don't know. I don't think she's been back for at least a year. Maybe more."

That fit with everything I'd heard, and it made me wonder. What had I wanted to talk to this man about? Had I been that befuddled by the booze?

"What about Jill?" I was thinking about rivalries. About how siblings play things out.

He shrugged as he took the last box from me. "Jill was the baby." He placed it on the display, ice cream facing front. "She was spoiled. If she didn't get what she wanted, well, you know how girls can be. They're like cats, sometimes. You think they're all pretty and cute, but then they go for you."

Chapter Thirty-eight

Randy was right about one thing: Jill was determined to have her way. By the time I got home, she had left me a message.

"I'm going to talk to Dr. Sharpe about the kitten, Pru. It's bad enough that my sister is fighting me about the will. I won't have her fighting me about a kitten, too."

More power to her, I thought as I opened my fridge. As for me, my workday was done.

"Good. You can spell me." Wallis had come up behind me, as silently as a cat can. *"What's for dinner?"*

"Um, pizza?" I pulled the box out of the fridge, aware all the while of Wallis' eyes on me.

"I'd rather eat kibble." She turned to stalk off, which reminded me. *"Or something livelier…"*

"Wallis, where's the kitten? Why didn't you bring him out when Jill was here?" I turned around. She'd left. "Wallis?"

I wasn't worried, not really. Wallis may be short with me, but she'd never hurt an innocent kitten, would she?

"Innocent?" I could almost hear her sneer at that. *"And those chickens you eat…they're guilty of what?"*

"Wallis." I tore into the living room, where she lay sprawled on her side. Beside her, the kitten was trying to bathe.

"You missed a spot." Wallis murmured, eyes half-closed. In response, the kitten reached, straining, to lick the inside of his thigh, and fell over. Wallis raised her head ever so slightly, but she was looking at me. *"Innocent, indeed."*

"I get it." I stomped back to the kitchen. She could hear me, I was sure. "I'm not the only one who cares about the kitten." Wallis could have been talking about the kitten or about Jill. I couldn't tell and now didn't seem like the right time to debrief her. After all, Wallis would understand fighting for the lion's share. Or the lioness'.

What she wouldn't understand, I thought as I slid the cold pizza from the box, was why I was discouraging Creighton. Wallis might be beyond romance—the shelter where I found her had taken care of that. She was always and ever a pragmatist, though. Creighton gave me pleasure. He also brought us food. She wouldn't understand why I had to keep him at arm's length.

Right now, I wasn't sure either. I poked the cold cheese, then dug out a baking sheet and slipped two slices into the oven. A girl needs to eat something, and kibble wasn't an option for me.

I was still waiting for my dinner to lose its chill when the phone rang again. I like to think it was hunger that made me jump. After all, I told myself as I reached for the phone, it was probably only Jill again, calling to insinuate herself further into my life.

"Hey, Pru." A male voice. Not Creighton's. "Glad I caught you."

"Mack." I pulled the tray out of the oven. Those leftovers were never going to get any better.

"You okay?"

I took a bite. The pizza was still cold in the center.

"Yeah, I'm fine." I took my time answering. Proper chewing is important for good digestion.

"Good, that's good." If he noticed that I didn't return the question, he didn't comment on it. "I was wondering if you had plans tonight."

"I'm broke, Mack." I wasn't entirely. Jill had made sure of that, but it was a good excuse, simple and close to true.

"Yeah?" I took another bite, waiting for him to realize just how one-sided this conversation was. "I guess we got a little crazy, huh?"

"Look, Mack, if this is a social call, I'm not interested." The pizza wasn't that good, and I was getting impatient. "If it's not…"

"Okay, okay." I could almost hear him lick his lips. How much did he have to drink these days to sustain? "I'm sorry. Look, I heard that you were talking to Randy. Asking him questions."

"You heard?" I could picture the beefy tobacconist down at Happy's. He'd have put a far different spin on my afternoon visit, I was sure. "Never mind," I caught myself. I really didn't want to engage. "I don't need to know."

"No, Pru, hang on. Don't hang up." The man always could read me. "I eavesdropped, okay?"

My silence raised the question.

"Look, I'm staying with Randy. Staying in the back of the shop." A pause, but not that long. He'd already confessed to the worst. "It's convenient, and sometimes I help him out."

Translation: my ex was homeless, or would be if his drinking buddy hadn't offered him a place to crash. The fact that it was steps away from Happy's was probably a primary factor in Mack's decision to accept the tobacconist's charity.

"Mack." I searched for the words. I was sorry, truly. I also truly never wanted to hear from him again. If I could have helped him…but I'm a realist, no matter what Wallis might say.

"Look, Randy wasn't giving you the whole story, okay?" He rushed in before I could hang up. "What he was saying about the Canaday girls?"

"And I care, why?" He had piqued my curiosity, not that I thought he had anything of value to tell me.

"He did use to hang with Judith, back in the day. Okay?" Mack seemed to need some kind of affirmation. Maybe he had gotten used to people not listening to him.

"I gather she was kind of wild." It was the best I could do.

"Yeah, but not like you." I was about to hang up, when he caught himself. "Sorry, Pru. I was just— Anyway, that's all over now." I didn't bother agreeing to that. "But she dumped him."

"Bully for her." I didn't see why this mattered.

"And there was trouble. Big trouble, before she left," Mack said.

"Yeah, I heard." Poor Mack. He wanted to give me something. "I know her father didn't want her to go."

"Didn't—" I heard him cough. "Look, Pru, I don't know what you've heard, but I heard she was lucky to get away."

"Well, it all seemed to work out for her," I said. "And now, I've got dinner waiting." Another reheating couldn't hurt this pizza. Probably wouldn't help much either.

"Yeah, well, Pru, I thought you should know, you know?"

I nodded, then realized he couldn't see me. "Thanks, Mack. I appreciate it."

"Those girls, Pru. They never had anything on you."

Maybe it was the second reheating, something about the way the cheese had shrunk and begun to separate. More likely, it was Mack. Ten minutes later, I had tossed the leftovers and grabbed my jacket. The spring night had grown chilly, and I needed something a bit more nourishing than flabby scraps.

Hungry as I was, I began to feel better as soon as I hit the road. My blue baby handles like a dream—and without a hangover, I felt confident about letting her roar. There's no reason for 450 cubic inches, not when you're not hauling lumber or running guns. Then again, there's damned little reason for whiskey or spring fever, either. Talking to Mack had been curative, in its way. I'd felt bad for him. I'd even been a little shocked. Seeing how quickly and how far he had fallen. We'd been close once, maybe even closer than I was to Creighton. Now I couldn't save him, and he couldn't bring me down. And maybe—just maybe—that meant I could connect with someone else and not have it be the end of the world. As long as I kept some of my guard up. Creighton wasn't that smart. He wasn't a mind reader, like my cat.

I had the radio on, one of the college stations from over in Amherst. At this hour, the kids have gone home. Older students, or maybe its townies, take over, switching out the silly electro beats for music I can listen to. Some nights, it's jazz. Tonight it was blues, something slow and mellow. I turned the volume up as I drove, the roar of my engine bringing out the rich depth of the vocals. The singer was sexy. Sounded like her man was, too, and I let my foot sink, enjoying the way my car ate up the highway.

Enjoying the anticipation, too, even as I braked around a curve and turned off down a side road. Jim Creighton never struck me as a home owner. Then again, he never struck me as my type, until he did. Besides, Beauville didn't offer much by way of apartments, and as our resident detective, he probably knew too much about the local condo developments to want to rent out any of them, even the units that were going begging. No, he'd stayed in town and made good, after a fashion. Now he owned one of the new houses on the west side of town. Not fancy, not big like mine, but more efficient all around. I laughed to myself as I realized how apt that was, me with my history and a need for space. Creighton being all clean-cut. Maybe, I thought, I'd even share this little insight. It was harmless enough.

Of course, the problem with new developments is that they skimp on land. Builders know that buyers today want more space inside. They're willing to give up some foliage. Even privacy, if the price is right. So where my house is set back, that long driveway curving out toward the road, Jim's is right on it, pretty much, a short driveway leaving just enough space for two cars, side by side.

Both of which, I saw as I pulled up, were taken. Police business, I figured, as I idled out front, under the streetlight—another mod con that's lacking over on my side of town. Still, it made sense for a cop to live on one of the new "safer" streets. And so I waited. An office matter, I figured. Something to do with all that paperwork.

Like I've said, this is a small town. Most everybody knew about us, or thought they did. The people in his office knew better than to say anything, and the folks on my side of town I didn't care that much about. Still, like I'd been about to joke, I care about my privacy. Maybe it was my years in the city. Living cheek by jowl with a nine million others, you learn to put up walls. To cherish the freedom from interference. To ignore and be ignored.

Creighton's house did its best. I could see lights inside, but the blinds were drawn, and the streetlight in front of his house played havoc with what night vision I have. Still, I squinted at the windows. When I saw them move, I ducked. Like I said, I don't like people knowing too much about me.

I backed up then, sidling back out of the light of that lamp, back along the verge of the house next to Creighton's. Turned the engine off, and waited. It could still be a business call. I knew that Jim's job was as political as anything in town. Knew, too, that he took it home with him, too often. I'd felt it in the tension in his shoulders, in the set of his mouth. One of the reasons he liked me, I'd long suspected, was that I didn't push too much. Jim might want more from me, but he wasn't the sharing type. Not really.

There. A light. I looked up as the front door opened, spilling electric light onto the front stoop, and then ducked down again, grateful for my foresight in backing down past the property line. His staff might know about us. I didn't need them to know I'd made a booty call.

"Thanks." Through my open window, I heard Creighton's voice. "I'll call you." I didn't catch the answer, but soon enough I heard an engine start up, a gentle whirr of a late model in good shape as the driver backed out of the driveway. I slid down further in my seat as the car backed up beside me and paused. Yes, I felt like a fool, but there'd be no end to it if I popped up now. Besides, the driver must have been fishing for a phone or a cigarette, because in half a moment, it started off. I sat up just as the driver pulled by Creighton's doorway and under the streetlamp. Dark hair caught the light, reflecting blue highlights. The driver turned, then, the streetlamp outlining her profile. Judith Canaday. And as she disappeared into the dark night, I turned back and forth, torn between her and Creighton, who stood still on the doorstep, watching her go.

Chapter Thirty-nine

I was about to drive off. I mean, I didn't need a road map. But in the second that I lingered, watching Creighton watching her, he turned. Maybe he'd caught the movement as I'd sat back up. Maybe he's got some sensitivity of his own, honed by years of old-fashioned police work in our admittedly low-tech town.

Or maybe there was something between us. Whatever. Once he caught the movement he certainly recognized my GTO. He stood there, staring, and I stepped out of the car. I've never been one to avoid confrontation.

"That was quick." I walked up the driveway, keys still in hand. "Judith not the kind to cuddle afterward?"

"Pru." He didn't have to say any more.

"Sorry." I looked down at my keys, trying to remember what I was doing there. "None of my business."

"Come on, Pru." He reached one arm out to me. "Don't be like that."

I pocketed the keys and followed him in.

〉〉〉

As I'd expected, Creighton's larder was better stocked than my own. We hadn't talked yet, not much, but a half hour later, when I exited the bedroom, pulling on his old terrycloth robe, I found him grating cheese into a pan of eggs. By habit, I went to the cabinet behind him.

"Tabasco's on the table." He didn't even look up. "Want to get us some beers?"

"Sure thing." I grabbed two from the fridge. "So, are you going to tell me about it?"

He looked up, one eyebrow arched. "Pru, I don't know what kind of stamina you think I have but..."

"I get it." I handed him his beer. He'd earned it. "I mean, are you going to tell me what she came over to talk about?"

The eggs were done. At least, that seemed to be his excuse for turning away. "Pru, you know I don't talk about cases."

"Oh, so this is a case now?" I reached for my plate, grabbed some silverware and headed for the table. "And here I thought everything was pending, waiting for the final report from the medical examiner."

"It is that." Creighton filled his own plate and joined me. In a T-shirt and his old sweats, he looked almost disreputable. Between that and his willingness to respond to a little bit of fishing, I figured, I'd try again.

"But you wouldn't have any input into that, would you? Any bearing on a dispute about a will?" He looked down at his plate, intent on his food. I liked to think I'd made him work up an appetite. Hell, I was hungry, too. This was something different. "Jim?"

He responded by shoving a forkful of omelet into his mouth.

"It's the lab tests, right? They found something." I put down my own fork as the scenario became increasingly clear. "And Judith Canaday heard about it. She wants you to investigate."

"Not her call." His mouth was still pretty full, but I got that much. "I'm still waiting for the medical examiner's ruling."

"Wait, I'm missing something." He kept eating. When I stopped, he eyed my plate. I pushed it toward him as I worked over his words. "The blood tests. They came back?"

The briefest of nods as he reached for the salt.

"Is it possible that someone was sabotaging his care?" I thought of what Jill told me. Of what she knew. "Messing with his medications?"

"Pru." He scraped up the last of the eggs. "I love you, but I can't tell you anything, okay? It's an ongoing investigation—yeah, I'll give you that—but please, Pru, let's just leave it at that."

With that he stood, taking both our plates over to the sink. I sat there, drinking as he washed the plates and stacked them in the drainer. My mother would have loved him, it hit me, watching him work. When he was done, he dried his hands on a towel, looked over at me, and returned to the bedroom. I'd finished my beer by then, and so I followed. We didn't speak. With three little words, couched in his usual cop speak, Jim Creighton had already found a way to shut me up.

Chapter Forty

The next morning, I was in such a good mood I was even willing to talk to Jill Canaday. Driving over to Tracy Horlick's I almost welcomed the call. Creighton had told me enough to know that the feud between the sisters was escalating. If that meant I was getting rid of my pesky tail, my day would be perfect. If only I could figure out what to do with that kitten.

"Hi Pru, I hope I'm not calling too early." Damn, she sounded perky, too. "I was hoping to catch you before you left for the day."

"Sorry, Jill." I had the window open, the breeze running through my hair. "I'm already on the road. Early appointment." She didn't have to know I was on my way to walk a toy dog.

"What if I meet you at Mr. Wilkins'? I have to go by there this morning anyway, and…"

"I wasn't planning on—Hang on." Another call was coming through. A good excuse to get off the line. "I've got to take this, Jill."

I switched off without waiting for her response.

"Ms. Marlowe." Laurence Wilkins. "I wanted to know what time you'd be by today."

"Excuse me?" Damn, I'd meant to get someone over there. This would be an easy few hours' work for a good carpenter.

"The squirrels, Ms Marlowe. They're back." He paused. I didn't think he was hesitating. "When I originally called animal control for a reference, I wasn't sure about hiring an unlicensed woman for animal removal. It wasn't until I checked with the director of veterinary services over at County Animal Hospital that I decided to call you. I'm sure he would be interested to hear how his recommendation panned out."

I took a breath, counted to three. I didn't like this man, and I certainly did not want to go back to that sad and haunted nest. I don't respond well to threats. I did, however, have a professional reputation to maintain, as did Doc Sharpe. Beauville is a small town, and I owed it as much to Doc as to my own future earnings to make things right.

"I can be over there by noon, no problem." I tried to make it sound like part of the plan.

"I'll be here." He hung up first, a power play. Somehow I was quite sure he would be, and that Jill Canaday would be too.

Not that I was going to rush over. I could pull dominance, too, and besides, I did have other clients.

In her inimitable fashion, Tracy Horlick seemed to read my mood before I even opened my mouth.

"You're looking chipper," she said, as if that were a bad thing, eyeing me as she flipped a lighter until it caught. "Must be nice to have everyone at your beck and call."

"Excuse me?" I wasn't completely faking my ignorance. Creighton was not exactly chasing me.

"That Canaday girl." The old bag reared back, as if to escape her own cigarette smoke. "She's made you her new big sister, hasn't she?"

"I wouldn't say that." I couldn't figure how old Horlick knew about Jill Canaday's interest in me. Then again, I didn't question how old Horlick knew anything anymore. Easier to simply accept it—and try to use it. "And I don't know if that's a good thing."

Tracy Horlick's eyebrows might have been drawn on, badly, but they moved fast—rising almost to the door jam at the hint of gossip. "Really?"

"Well, it seems like she and her sisters are at odds." That was the most innocuous way I could think of phrasing it. "You must know about that."

I was fishing, and she knew it, those brows scuttling down again to gather in a scowl. "Maybe I do. Maybe not." She took a drag. "And maybe you should be careful who you're getting close to."

"So it's Jill who's being accused now?" That was more than I'd gotten from Creighton. That didn't mean it was true. "Last I heard, Judith was in the hot seat."

It was a gamble, but if I wanted to draw her out, I had to offer something.

"I don't know anything about that girl." Another drag, while I waited. At this rate, Horlick must be going through a pack an hour. "She left town like a bat out of— whatever. She hasn't been back here in years." Jill, then.

"Hey! Hey!" From inside the house, I could hear Growler.

"I think Bitsy wants his walk." I'd get as much from the bichon.

"Huh." With a noncommittal grunt, Tracy Horlick turned back inside. But instead of the dog's lead, she reached for a carton of cigarettes, sliding a fresh pack into her hand. "Hang on."

I did, while she opened the cellophane and carefully extracted a cigarette. There was something going on here, something I didn't quite understand. Horlick's habit was too intense for her to be taking her time like this.

"Hey! Here! Here! Here!" Sharp, eager barks certainly got my attention, if not hers.

"Mrs. Horlick?" For anyone else, I wouldn't have asked. Growler, however, deserved whatever I could get him.

"Hold your horses." She lit the new smoke, closing her eyes in satisfaction. "Both of you." She sighed audibly.

"Hey!" The little dog was growing hoarse. I could hear his claws scrabbling at the door.

"Why don't I just—" I reached for the lead, taking it off the coat hook by the door.

"Watch it!" Growler's voice surprised me, especially coming as Tracy Horlick turned.

"Do you mind?" I caught a glimpse of yellow-stained teeth.

"I just hate to keep him waiting." I showed my own. It was a submissive gesture. It worked. She blew the fresh smoke out of her nose and went to free the bichon from his basement prison.

"Dog in heaven." Growler was grumbling to himself as I snapped on the lead. *"Help us all."*

"You be careful where you take him." His person waved her Marlboro toward the street. "There's some crazy people out there. You never know what some of them will do."

"No sense, no sense at all." Growler was still muttering to himself as we turned the corner. I owed him an apology.

"I'm sorry," I said the words out loud, for added emphasis. "I thought she might know something about what's going on with the Canadays. I shouldn't have let her go on, though. It wasn't fair to you."

"Clueless." The black nose sniffed a tree trunk. Ever since the spring thaw, I'd been reminded of how intense scent could be to an animal like Growler. After the numbing cold, this was like doing shots. *"What is James up to?"*

The little tail went stiff, then wagged quickly, as Growler took in and catalogued the neighborhood information. In his way, I realized, the bichon wasn't that different from his person.

"What?" A snappy bark broke into my thoughts.

"Sorry." I was. "I meant that you also have a network, a way of picking up information."

"Pity you don't." The leather nose was back down in the dirt. I got a sense of an older German shepherd, a poodle—and a cat? *"Roberto, not again!"*

I had no answer to that, and besides, the dog deserved some private time. Instead, I followed after him until, his short legs flagging, he let me know it was time to return. By then, I was almost ready to face the rest of my day, not that a bit more information couldn't help.

"Hey, Growler, what do you think she meant—old smoke teeth—when she told me to be careful? I mean, I know she likes to make trouble, but does she really think Jill could be dangerous?"

"*You heard that, did you?*" The black button eyes stared up at me. "*Why don't you consider where her information comes from, walker lady? Why don't you consider the source?*"

Chapter Forty-one

No matter what Growler might think, I couldn't entirely discredit Tracy Horlick's words. After all, reading between the lines, Creighton seemed to take this new development seriously, and although I couldn't get him to talk, I knew he wouldn't mess around with a case. All of which meant that I didn't feel comfortable releasing that kitten yet—small animals can too easily get hurt in the crossfire.

I might be able to get something out of the lawyer, though. Especially if I could get back on his good side. With that in mind, I turned toward the center of town. Time to enlist some allies.

"Hey, Albert." I breezed into the animal control office, expecting to find him napping. The morning was warm, after all.

"Hey, Pru." The voice that greeted me came from the tiny alcove that served as a kitchenette. "Coffee?"

"Sure." I accepted with surprise. Albert was not only awake and offering me coffee, he was arranging what looked like donuts on a paper plate. "Are those —"

"From the coffee shop. Fresh this morning." He came toward me, but as I reached for one, he stepped back, keeping the pastries just out of my reach.

"Oh, how nice." I turned, just in time to see Jackie Canaday coming out of the office bathroom. She stopped short, and for a moment we both stared at each other.

"Would you, uh, like one?" With a smile I could see even under the beard, Albert offered Jackie the plate. Behind him, the kettle began to whistle.

"I'll get it," I said, stepping past the bearded man. I didn't know what was going on here. If I got out from between them, maybe I could figure it out.

"I'd have decaf, if you have it." Jackie called. She sounded better than she had on the phone, her voice a little less strained. "No milk."

"Not a problem." I wouldn't have trusted any milk in this fridge either. But I did find a jar of Sanka and stirred her up a mug. For Albert and myself, I went with the high-test. It was still instant, but at least we'd get something out of it.

"I'm so glad you could meet with me," Jackie had taken the one visitor's seat and faced Albert, who sat at his desk. Even that, I noticed as I brought over two of the mugs, was noticeably neater than the day before. One drawer did peek open about an inch, though, and I stared at it, hoping to hear another mind at work. "It's been such a crazy time," Jackie was saying.

"Shiny, bright..." A soft voice, deep from within the drawer. *"Shiny—what? Shiny, round. It's a button! Where is it?"*

"Pru?" I looked up. Both humans had turned toward me.

"Sorry." I hoisted my own coffee. "I guess I haven't had enough of this yet."

"I was asking about the kitten." Jackie definitely looked better today. More relaxed, in yoga pants and a cardigan that picked up the blue in her eyes. She held her mug on her lap as she smiled up at me. "I assume the kitten is still with you?"

"Yes." I didn't know what she'd said to Albert, or what he'd agreed to. My hairy colleague seemed overwhelmed by the presence of a female. "I've been in contact with your sister about him, in fact."

I didn't like the idea of relinquishing the kitten to Jill, not until I had a better sense of what she was up to. But I didn't trust this woman either.

The argument I was waiting for didn't materialize. Instead, she looked at me quizzically. "My sister?"

"Jill," I clarified. Of course, none of the sisters were talking to each other.

"Of course." She nodded. Whether they talked or not, she seemed to know her sister. "But that's not a permanent solution."

"Oh?" The instant was bitter. I drank more anyway. As Creighton had taught me, people love to talk. Give them silence…

"If you don't want it, you can give the kitten up." Except that Albert was the one who fell for it. "Pru can take the kitten over to County—"

"No, Albert, I can't." It was time to put an end to this nonsense. Partly because I was sick of it. A kitten is not a chess piece to be moved about in a surrogate battle. Partly because I was too distracted to let it continue. That quiet obsessing— *"shiny button, where did it go?"*—kept intruding itself on my thoughts. "If a family member may want to take the kitten somewhere down the line, then I see no reason to surrender it. As you well know, this is kitten season. The number of cats at County that will be euthanized—" I stopped. If there was anything wrong with the kitten. FVR. Anything. "But that's what you want, right?" I'd been so distracted. If I couldn't play on her better nature, maybe I could shame her.

"No, no, I don't." She put the mug on the edge of the desk and made a big show of looking contrite, turning the hem of her sweater back and forth. What it did was keep me from seeing her face. "I'm sorry." She looked up at Albert, who blinked. Those blue eyes still must have some force. "I was—at first, I was so overwhelmed. And when I heard the news…the lab report…"

She dropped the hem to fish around in her pocket for a tissue. I didn't see any tears, but the eyes that now blinked up at me were certainly large.

"You can't still blame the kitten for your father's death." I was past being polite. "That's like blaming gravity. Or age."

"No, I—I don't." She clipped the words, as if setting her jaw for a confrontation.

"I know you took care of him, but you must have known that he was ill." I, too, was through with pulling my punches. "And that he wasn't taking care of himself. Wasn't following the protocol for whatever medications he was on." I was saying too much, I knew it as the words came out. I had no right to know what was in the medical examiner's report. I didn't care. "He was a time bomb."

"He was lucky." Her voice had taken on a rough quality that surprised me. "Lucky he went when he did. Lucky that he didn't know."

"Pru—" Albert was rising from his desk. About to attempt some gesture of gallantry.

"His beloved youngest daughter," Jackie was saying, standing up to face me as she spoke. "His Jilly wasn't coming home to visit because she cared. All those visits? Sneaking into town on the sly? She thought I didn't know—but I found out. She was poisoning him," said Jackie, a look like that of an aggrieved chow on her long face. "Poison—only his heart gave out first."

Chapter Forty-two

"What?" I didn't care if I'd had the same thought. To hear it spoken out loud shocked me. "Now you're saying your baby sister killed him?"

"I know, you think I'm hysterical." She dabbed at her eyes. "First, the kitten and Judith, and then…But I knew, you see, I know—I lived with him, these last eight months. My father was a fighter. He was not going to just lie down and die."

"Jackie." I stepped toward her, reaching for her. "Please, calm down. I understand, it was a shock. But people die, even when we don't expect them to." I had my hands on her arms now, and I pressed the soft wool of the sweater, trying to get her to sit back down. "Believe me, I know."

"No, you don't understand. The lab…" The crying started in earnest now. "They're asking about his medication. Why—why else?" Her one tissue a sodden mess, Jackie pushed her hand into her pocket, stretching the soft wool as she searched for more.

"Albert?" I turned toward him, and he jumped back. That made room for me to reach around and open his desk drawer. I fished out a pile of paper towels, which seemed more to the point than any answer I could give. "Here." I handed them to Jackie.

"Thanks." She patted her eyes with the rough paper. "I'm sorry. I get…"

"No matter." I didn't need her going off again. This had to be what Creighton was talking about. What Judith had come over to tell him, which raised another question. "Have you talked to Judith?" That sounded too harsh. "Does she know about this?"

A small nod, then a swift shake of the head. "I don't know," she said, her words clipped. "If only I'd been there. I was out. You know that. We talked. I had to talk to someone. Mr. Wilkins. We've both been talking to him I guess so. I mean, we have to."

"I still don't understand." I didn't. Not anything about this family. "Why do you think poison—"

"Shiny!" I turned as I heard the cry. Jackie shrieked. Frank, released by my actions from Albert's desk, had launched himself over the desk and now landed in the visitor's lap, his agile black paws pulling at a button on her sweater.

"Frank!" Albert lunged for his pet, throwing his stout body over the desk, and knocking over the mug of coffee.

Jackie screamed again and jumped back, while the ferret—who had a much better sense of his person's agility or lack thereof—merely hopped back onto the desk, neatly sidestepping the flying mess that was Albert.

"Frank, how could you?" Albert pushed himself off and began rummaging for more paper towels.

"What is that?" Jackie had enough sense to turn to me for an answer.

"Frank's a ferret. They're perfectly safe," I said. Provided that you're not a worm or a grub, I was tempted to add. She was already enjoyably discombobulated. "He's Albert's pet," I added. Seeing as how together we had trained Albert to call the sleek masked ferret by his chosen name, rather than by the ignominious tag of "Bandit," I was tempted to reverse the order of possession. They were both so flustered, I doubt they'd have noticed.

"He wouldn't. Would you?" I turned from the flushed woman to the intense dark eyes of the ferret. He was staring at me, nose quivering. In his hands, he held—yes—a button. *"Get the order right…"*

"Frank." I held my hand out, palm up, and hoped neither of the other humans in the room were looking. Ferrets can be possessive, and they also have sharp teeth. What I was doing relied more on my special sensitivity than any rules of animal training.

"*Shiny.*" With a falling note as sad as a sigh, the mustelid placed the button in my hand. I took a moment to look it over: with its dome cap of worked metal, it was a pretty thing. "Sorry," I whispered quietly to Frank, as he, his tail low, slunk back into Albert's desk drawer.

"Here," I held it out to Jackie. "You wouldn't want to lose this."

"Oh, thank you." She dropped the wad of paper towels she'd been using to mop her thighs and reached for it. As she did, the thread in the shank—a thin wisp of white—fell to the floor. "This keeps falling off." She tucked it into the sweater pocket. "Even without that…that animal."

"You should probably use a thicker thread." The other buttons, I could see, were attached with the same wool as the sweater: a pretty sky blue. "Or maybe some of that yarn."

"I know. I ran out." She went back to patting at herself with the sodden paper.

"I'm so, so sorry." Albert was wringing his hands.

"Let me get some water." I grabbed the empty mug off the floor—at least it hadn't shattered. "He didn't get your sweater, did he?"

"No, well, maybe a little." I handed Albert's mug to him, motioning him toward the sink. "It's not a big deal." Jackie called after him. "I've had so much time on my hands, I've made dozens of these. Knitting was something to do while I sat with my dad."

The memory was too much for her. As I watched, her face collapsed in on itself, the blues eyes went wide and then scrunched up, as she pulled the sodden paper towels up to her mouth and started to wail.

"Jackie, it's okay." No, it wasn't. Her father was dead, and I suspected her life currently had no meaning without him to care for. I knew the formula, though. "You'll be okay."

The storm subsided as quickly as it began, and soon Jackie was simply sniffling into the wet, brown towels. Albert had returned with the water by this time, and she took it from him, sipping from it as she sniffed.

"Thanks." She looked at the desk and started to reach over to place the mug there, then thought better and held it in her lap. "I'm sorry. It's still so…" She started to play with the hem of her sweater again. I could see the coffee spot now, pale brown against the blue, right where the button had been torn off. She saw me looking and tucked the bottom of the sweater under itself, folding it up nervously as if the spot or the loose white thread were somehow her fault.

"Please, forget about it." I leaned back on the desk. "But could we go back to what you were saying before we were interrupted?"

I figured I had a minute or two at most. As soon as this woman had collected her wits, she would realize that not only was she wet and messy, but that she was confiding secrets to a total stranger. Hey, if it were me, I'd have been out of here long ago.

As it was, she nodded, pliable now that she was already wrung out. "He was so strong…If only I'd been there…" Jackie bit her lip."

"Maybe it's a good thing." She blinked up at me, and I tried to explain. "He might have—" I caught myself. "You might not have been able to do anything, but if you'd been there, the state wouldn't have requested an autopsy."

"But it's not fair." Her voice was shaky. "I was always there. Always." The neat roll of the sweater unfolded as Jackie raised her hands wide. "And she's been saying crazy things. She even said that I didn't need to leave. That I didn't …" The hands came in again, covering her face. "I can't."

"Pru." Albert's voice was low, a warning, and I could feel him straining to pass by me; his belly was warm and soft against my arm. What he wanted was to get to her, probably one of the more noble impulses he'd ever had—unless he simply saw her as vulnerable. Still, I held him back.

"What did the lab tests show, Jackie?" I repeated my question to make sure she understood. "What poison did you find?"

"Nothing's official. Not yet." She looked up at me, those blue eyes wide and clear. "These things—with time, they go away, you know. But now that they know what they're looking for, they'll find it. I looked it up—contine? Cotinine? She must have thought it would be gone."

I shook my head, confused. "This continine, it's a poison?"

"It's what you get." She swallowed and blinked. "It's what the body does with liquid nicotine."

◇◇◇

I couldn't come up with a response to that, not fast enough. And at the sight of both of us, me and Albert, staring at her open-mouthed, Jackie must have remembered where she was and who she was talking to. Gathering up the mess of paper towels, she looked around in vain for a waste basket. Finally, after what must have been thirty seconds of serious searching, she simply deposited them on Albert's desk, stood up, and walked out.

"Why'd you do that?" Albert was the first to recover, turning on me with unexpected vigor. "She just came in because of the kitten. I could have handled that. What are you doing here anyway, Pru? That lawyer called again, you know."

Wilkins. Jackie's insinuation had driven my errand out of my mind.

"That's what I'm here for, Albert." No sense in letting my erstwhile colleague see my lapse. "I need a carpenter. Someone who can do some work on Wilkins' house for me."

"Mack's looking for work." Albert was sulking now. "You can always call him."

"Someone who'll show up after lunch. Someone I won't have to hunt down at Happy's," I added, to make myself clear.

"Well, there's Dave Altschul. You know him." Albert was staring at his desk, so I waited, willing him to feel the pressure. "He did some work for the county last year."

Good enough. "And how do I find this Mr. Altschul?" Albert opened his mouth. "And don't tell me Happy's, Albert. I want someone I can call this morning."

"Hang on." Albert pulled a peeling wallet out of his back pocket and fished out what looked like a grocery receipt. Fumbling around for a stub of a pencil, he copied a number off of it onto the back of a state wildlife notice, and handed it to me.

"Looks familiar." I eyed the number. Albert's handwriting can be hieroglyphic at times. "Is that an eight?"

"Yeah." Albert checked and nodded. "That's the number for the smoke shop. You know, Randy's?" I did, but I waited for an explanation. "Dave doesn't have a phone at the moment. But he's a good worker and real reliable. Honest. Just—well, he takes his calls at Randy's."

"Great." I didn't remember the male population of Beauville as being quite so ragged. Still, I folded the flier and pocketed it. "I'll try him." I got up to leave then, when the thought hit me. Randy's sold those fake cigarettes. Maybe the burly proprietor would know if Jill had been in recently. If she'd bought something she shouldn't. "Maybe I'll just ask him," was all I said. "Thanks, Al."

With a nod, I turned toward the door and turned back. I didn't mind being hard on Albert. He needed training. Frank, though? The masked ferret was only being himself. Besides, he was a friend.

"Bye, Frank," I called softly. Silently, I willed my thoughts to him. *"Sorry about that, little fella."*

I guess I'd gone too far, though, because all I got was silence as I walked to the door. Silence, and then, just as I pushed my way outdoors, one quiet muttered word: *"button."*

Chapter Forty-three

As much as I wanted to interrogate the fat smoke shop owner, I had another appointment to keep. My plan was to do some damage control at Wilkins' house, see what was up with the squirrels, and then set him up with this carpenter, Dave. Not that I'd let the lawyer deal with the contractor himself. Anyone who hung out with Albert, I'd be happier wrangling myself before I let him loose on a client.

I girded myself for another onslaught as I pulled up at the lawyer's palatial home. Midday, and the birds were out in full force. The squirrels couldn't be far behind. But as I walked around the side of the big house, I found the area strangely quiet. Even as I pulled my ladder out from under the tarp and propped it against the wall, I didn't hear anything louder than a lust-crazed sparrow.

"Yo! Babe! Over here!" I realized I was chuckling as I ascended. Considering how I'd felt last time I was up here, it was a pleasant change. *"Check this out!"*

I almost turned to look before I caught myself. That glossy black neck plumage hadn't been freshly groomed for me. Besides, as much as I wanted to avoid the pain and loss that I had felt before, I knew I had to face it. Wallis would scoff at my hesitation—call it human weakness—but until I could relinquish my place on top of the food chain, I felt obligated to experience whatever my empathy would bring. True, this empathy was amplified by my sensitivity, but to deny it would be worse. I thought of Mack, numbing himself against the world. Of my mother, whose bitterness had turned inward. No, I'd rather take the punches, even if it meant being laughed at by my cat.

With that in mind, I reached out to touch the roof. My hand on the raw wood, where I had torn out part of the fascia, could pick up little. The *nom-nom* vibrations of a wood beetle, the distant hum of two moths. That sparrow, going on so, seemed to be drowning out any other higher animal. Either that, or my reluctance had kicked in, amping up my new resistance skills even when I consciously willed them away. Putting both hands up, I stared into the dark, torn crevice I had enlarged and tried again.

"Nest?" I tried the thought as a feeler, imagining twigs and grass. Warmth and a safe, dry space.

"Safe." That came back to me like an echo, bringing with it a wave of guilt. Yes, this had been safe, until I had come along. Unless…

I took a breath and steeled myself. I needed to know. *"Babies?"*

The answer, when it came was faint, more a memory than a thought. A keening cry in the darkness, *"gone."* I closed my eyes as the sadness washed over me. I didn't know where the mother was now. Behind me, in the trees, most likely, and whether she was watching me or she even picked up on my regret, I would probably never know. What I did have was something akin to closure. The loss was final and maybe—just maybe—it predated my interference with her world. Fishing my hammer out of my belt, I reattached the wire mesh. Whatever had happened in seasons past, whatever had happened here, this nest was gone.

"I hope you don't think that will be sufficient." The voice, coming from below, startled me.

"Mr. Wilkins." I turned enough to see him, scowling up at me. "I was going to come see you." First rule of training: every animal wants a response. By refusing to answer him directly, I was denying him satisfaction. I doubted he could be trained. Lawyers aren't as smart as most animals. It did, however, give me satisfaction to try.

"I fixed the mesh to prevent a re-infestation," I said calmly, as I descended the ladder. "You may have heard animals passing through, but they haven't nested again. And I've arranged with a contractor to repair the squirrel damage." I looked up at the fascia. Originally, I'd been willing to take the blame for some of the damage. Now, with the lawyer eyeing me like that, I realized I'd been acting out of misplaced guilt.

"You do realize that this whole panel is going to have to be replaced?" It was a rhetorical question, a technique I'd learned from Mack in his contracting days. "Rotten all through. I poked at it to see the extent of the rot. It's pretty clear that the squirrels chose your house because the wood was already so soft." I pointed with the hammer, another trick I'd learned from Mack. Lawyers—maybe all white-collar types—are secretly in awe of tools.

He started to protest and I barreled on.

"Not to worry. I'll work with the contractor. He's a carpenter, licensed, of course." I made a mental note to check that. "And we'll coordinate to make sure the nuisance animals don't return while he's working."

"I'd trust her." I turned to see Jill coming up behind me. "Pru really knows animals. She understands how they think." Standing beside me, the youngest Canaday seemed to tip the scales. With a gruff grunt, Laurence Wilkins nodded.

"Thanks." I turned to my uninvited ally. I wanted to ask her what she knew. Why she had phrased her support the way she had. But I couldn't, not with the lawyer standing right here.

Instead, I turned back to the client. "I'm sure you'll agree, Mr. Wilkins, that it's better to do the job right the first time, rather than have to go back and do it over."

That shut him up, at least temporarily. He backed off, literally, taking two steps back as I collapsed the ladder—and handed it to my new apprentice.

"When do you want to start?" Keeping her close, at least I could get some questions answered.

"I think I have." She laughed. A merry sound, but it set my teeth on edge.

"You know, you can't smoke around animals." I was feeling my way toward the question I really wanted to ask.

"I know that." She looked down at the ladder, as if it were going to be able to answer for her. I led her over to the tarp and together we covered it. "I told you, I quit."

"When?" She was hiding something. Something besides my ladder.

"I've been quitting the last five years," she laughed again, before she noticed that I hadn't joined in. "Seriously? When my dad had his first attack. That scared me. And I knew people who were doing the e-cigs, then. I know it's a crutch, but, hey, whatever works, right? I'm hardly smoking them anymore."

I raised my eyebrows at that, but kept silent. People tell themselves what they need to believe. And I had questions of my own. "So, your dad ever smoke those?"

"Dad, no?" She shook her head. "When he quit, he went cold turkey."

"He ever fall off the wagon?" Another shake. "Maybe he was tempted, and you told him about the e-cigs?" A more vigorous shake. "No, like I said, I only started with these after he had his first heart attack. He couldn't—they wouldn't have been safe for him."

"Safe." I kept my face blank, waiting.

"Nicotine raises the heart rate." She sounded so earnest. "Breathing, you name it."

"It's also a poison, but it wouldn't have to go that far, would it?" I was trying it out. Seeing how it felt. "Not with someone like your dad. Someone who already had a bum heart."

"What? You think…." If she was acting, she was good. As the implication dawned on her, I could see the color draining from her face. "My sister—what, no." She turned to the lawyer. "Larry, tell her!"

Larry? I stopped. What happened to Mr. Wilkins? My mind jumped back to that first day at Wilkins' office. The way the sheltie greeted her…

"Tell her what?" The man in question interrupted my thoughts. "Ms. Marlowe, if you're going to attack Ms. Canaday—"

"Wait." I put my hand up, calling for quiet. Turned from my client back to Jill. *"I'm* not attacking anyone. I'm not the one—"

"Please." Wilkins coughed a little. Cleared his throat. "I believe I have some insight into this situation. Jill, do you mind?" He motioned and I followed him away from the house. "Jackie Canaday is a very volatile woman," he said, his voice low. "Very—and very unfair to her youngest sister. At times it seems best to accommodate her."

"So I gather." I looked at him. Tried to read him. "Why did Jackie come to see you that morning? The morning her father died?"

"Ms. Marlowe, please." He did his best to look affronted. "There are some things I cannot talk about."

I waited. This had gone beyond protocol.

"I'd rather Jill not hear about this. You understand, of course?" I didn't, but he took my silence for assent. "She called me panicked. She was making wild accusations—saying horrible things about her sisters. I thought it best to accommodate her. To contain any damage she might do." He looked over to where Jill was waiting. "She has always resented her younger sisters, and I was afraid she would misread things. Lash out, so I cleared my morning for her. Clearly, my efforts didn't suffice."

"You don't think she did something…" The timing was awfully neat.

"No." He was shaking his head. "I am confident that David's death was from natural causes. I'd seen him only a day or two before, you know. I could tell he was growing weaker."

"His daughters don't seem to think that."

"His daughters are guided by what they want to see." He glanced over at Jill, who was waiting by the ladder. "If anybody is casting aspersions now, it may be that those parties are simply seeking to deflect attention. Not necessarily from any misdeeds, but in order to further their own interests, whatever they might be."

I nodded. "People can be nasty." I thought of that squirrel nest. Of what I had done for money. "Come on, Jill." I motioned to the waiting girl. "If you're still up for it, we've got work to do."

Chapter Forty-four

Call me crazy, but taking Jill with me seemed the sensible option. I didn't know what was going on, but I knew something was off. Was she innocent, smeared by her older sisters in an attempt to get her inheritance? Probably. Could she have hastened her father's death, either by accident or intent? Yeah, that was a possibility, too. Would I learn more by watching her than by running away? I didn't need any special senses to figure that one out. Besides, she was still my best bet for housing that kitten.

"Wow, this is a great car." She settled into the passenger seat of my baby-blue baby, apparently willing to let bygones be bygones. I'd suggested she leave her Mini at Wilkins'. It would mean an extra trip at the end of the day, but I wanted to be in the driver's seat. Besides, you can tell a lot about a person by the way she reacts to your wheels—and to your driving. Gushing about my car wasn't bad. But considering what had just transpired, it was a little odd. I held my tongue as I pulled onto the road. That's when I'd see what she was really made of.

"What do you know about squirrels?" I threw that out as I accelerated into a turn.

"Um, two litters a year?" Her hand went up, but she forced it down before she could brace herself on the dashboard.

I smiled. "Right." The girl had nerve. "Do you know the law on nuisance animals?"

I ran her through her paces as I drove back into town. She had read the literature, and she was good under pressure. But as I neared what passes for a main street in Beauville, I found myself wondering. How much of the good-girl front was an act? Was the toughness I was witnessing the real Jill Canaday?

Our first stop was at a regular's. Old Meryl Sandburg did her best, but her Siamese often got the best of her. I made a weekly visit, ostensibly to trim the hefty feline's claws. In reality, I would do a quick assessment—make sure the tiny octogenarian was still up to living on her own, if cohabiting with a twenty-pound yowler qualified. Once a month, I brought litter and food by, too, telling her it was part of the service. No sense in infringing on anyone's dignity.

I gave Jill the rundown as we pulled up to the neat bungalow. The crocuses of a few weeks ago had already given way to tulips and hyacinths, dotting the small front yard with bursts of red and blue. Either Meryl was doing better now that the weather had warmed up, or others in the community had the same instincts I did.

"Good afternoon, Mrs. Sandburg." I called as I let myself in the unlocked door. "Hi, Princess."

"Oh, Pru, good to see you." The wizened face turned up to me with a smile, pale eyes blinking. I smiled back. It was hard not to, even for me, and immediately dropped down into a crouch.

"Princess?" The seal-point pushed her coffee-colored head into my hand. I knew, because she had told me in no uncertain terms, that her full name—her *real* name—was both long and Thai, reflecting her exalted lineage. Queen Raja was my best translation of it. In a model act of noblesse oblige, however, she accepted the name her person had bestowed on her. The old lady might not have been completely aware of the transaction, but her feline companion accepted the familiar moniker as an honorific. As she aged and grew more to resemble an ottoman than the sleek heartbreaker of her youth, the blue-eyed cat was even growing fond of the term.

"Where shall I put this?" I'd left Jill to lug in the twenty-pound bag of kibble.

"I'll take it from here." I stowed the sack, Mrs. Sandburg's kitchen being as familiar to me as my own, and pulled out a bag of loose catnip. The Queen—"Princess"—eyed the baggie with interest. "Nails first, Princess." We made eye contact. She accepted my terms.

"Mrs. Sandburg, this is Jill Canaday." I turned to make the introductions once I had stored the bag under the counter. "She's considering studying animal behavior." That was a bit of an exaggeration, but it covered the bases.

"I knew your father, dear." The old lady had come up to my assistant and taken her hand between both of hers. "I'm so sorry."

"I'm going to show her how I clip Princess' claws." Disengaging Jill, I directed her over to the sofa. Princess had followed me, an air of sufferance on her chocolate face, and I rewarded her with a small pinch of the catnip. She responded by lolling on her back, which made it easier for me to scoop her up.

"Notice how I cradle the cat's body," I said, once I had Princess on my lap. "If she feels secure, she's less likely to struggle."

"Royalty become used to being groomed." The thought, more a passing observation than a comment, made me smile. The big cat was already stoned.

"Then you press gently on the paw pad to make the cat extend her claw." Princess politely obliged.

"You have such a way with her." Meryl Sandburg clasped her hands together, watching.

"She really does, doesn't she?" Jill said. Princess kicked—I'd looked up a little too fast.

"Is everything okay?" The old lady's voice quavered.

"Yes, we're fine here." *Aren't we?* I focused on the cat, but found myself wondering: Was Meryl Sandburg as good at manipulating me as I was this paw? Was this one of the female wiles my mother had so completely rejected by the time I was coming along?

"What is that scent?" Princess was distracted, which was good. I took the opportunity to move her to Jill's lap. Her highness

accepted the shift with regal indifference, as I took up her other front paw.

"Again, you gently press the pad." I demonstrated, as the cat's leather nose twitched toward me, taking careful stock of my shirt.

"She must smell the squirrels." Jill chimed in. Turning to the old lady, she explained. "Pru was removing some problem animals over at—"

I had to stop her. Talking about other clients is never a good idea, and talking about pest animals an even worse one. Too many people associate unwanted animals of any kind with vermin and uncleanliness.

"Jill, please—" I reached over, put my free hand on her arm. "Privacy is—"

I didn't get to finish. "Squirrels, oh my." The old lady exclaimed, her voice rising. "Can't you use poison?"

"What?" Jill whipped around—too fast for me to remind her that I still held a paw.

"Mrowr!" Half-squeal, half-hiss, the cat drew back in protest.

"Whoop!" Meryl threw up her hands in alarm, further startling Princess, who pulled her paw—claw still extended—through my hand as she jumped.

"Pru!" Jill was by my side in a moment, a tissue in her hand. "Are you all right?"

"I'm fine." I took the tissue and pressed it into my palm. Princess was on the floor, glowering. "I must have touched the quick."

"My poor Princess!" Mrs. Sandburg was attempting to lower herself to her knees.

"Mrs. Sandburg, please let me." I stood, but Jill was ahead of me. With both arms around the old lady's shoulders, she guided her back to her chair. "I'm sure Pru didn't really hurt her."

"I'm sorry about that." I smiled, making a fist. I didn't need her to see how the tissue had already turned red with blood. "My bad."

She blinked at me, and for a moment I wondered if the excitement had been too much for her.

"I wonder about you, Pru," she said, at the same moment patting Jill's hand. "Perhaps you're getting a little, well, old for all of this?"

"Nonsense." I kept my smile on, as a tactical measure, until, down on the floor she could no longer see my face. "Princess?"

There was nothing ambiguous about the hiss that answered me. But although the tubby Siamese was the one under the end table, I knew I was the one who'd been cornered. Under any other circumstance, the thing to do would be to leave. To let the animal calm down before proceeding. Right now, the way Meryl Sandburg was cozying up to Jill? I didn't dare.

Luckily, I do have an edge.

"Princess—Princess Raja—I am so sorry." Although animals don't necessarily understand me, I trusted that my intent, and also my respect, would come through. *"I am here to serve you. To groom."*

I reached for the catnip, but we were beyond that. I tried to picture a cat with a kitten. Something calming and natural. Wallis with the kitten.

Another hiss. Well, Wallis wasn't the most maternal cat. And females do tend to be territorial rivals, much like—I thought with a flash of regret—our own species.

"Why?" The cat was calming down. The question might be vague, but it was better than that spitting hiss.

"She was startled." I tried to re-create how Meryl Sandburg's voice had sounded. How she had yelped. *"They both were."* I didn't know what else I could tell her. Wallis and I communicate easily, having had years of practice. Besides, as she likes to remind me, she is an exceptionally intelligent creature.

"And I am not?" As I watched, Princess sat up from her angry crouch and eyed me.

"You are regal and I wait to serve you." In a gesture common to both our species, I lowered my eyes to the ground.

"You may." As calm as if nothing had ever happened, Princess stepped out from under the table, brushing against me as she passed. My offering had been accepted.

"Let's try that again, shall we?" With another smile, a little more natural this time, I pulled the hefty beast onto my lap. And although Meryl continued to fuss, I made sure to focus on the feline until all four paws were done. Jill, I couldn't help but notice, was doing her best with the old lady, cooing and petting her as if she were the one with the claws.

"Thank you." With careful steps, the old woman saw us to the door. I had cleaned the litter box and refilled Princess' food and water dishes by then, as the old lady clung to Jill's arm. "I do hope you'll come around again." She was addressing Jill, I realized. "Some people simply understand how things ought to be done."

My mother, particularly toward the end, had railed against what she called "the good folk of Beauville." I was beginning to understand why.

"What happened back there?" I asked as we made our way back to the car.

"Gosh, Pru." She looked over at me, eyes wide. "I'm sorry. I guess you spooked me, grabbing my arm like that. I thought that, you know, with the catnip and all…"

"Catnip isn't a sedative. Some cats barely respond to it." I grumbled as I unlocked the car. My hand was throbbing and her affectation of wide-eyed innocence wasn't making it feel any better. "And you can't go talking about other clients that way. They trust us. They let us into their houses."

"Got it." She climbed into the passenger seat. "I thought, maybe, because Mr. Wilkins is such a big deal in town, it would sound good. You know."

I looked over at her as the engine roared to life. "Meryl Sandburg is a long-standing client," I said. "I don't have to sell her."

Jill wisely didn't respond to that, and as I drove away, I had to ask myself if what I'd said was true. Maybe the cat had acted on her own, responding to something I hadn't caught. Or maybe it was me. The old lady seemed ready enough to believe the worst of me—and the best of my new young acolyte. I didn't think that Wilkins' name carried that much weight. Though clearly he meant a lot to Jill Canaday, enough to totally absorb her. Unless it was the mention of poison that had caused her to bear down—startling the cat and completely redirecting the conversation.

Chapter Forty-five

I had a few more calls to make, but Jill didn't protest when I drove her back to her car. The silence had grown awkward by then, and I'd have taken twice the clawing Princess had given me to be able to go back and question the regal feline.

Since I couldn't, I was merely wasting my time. And by the time I started back home, I realized I still hadn't called Dave, the carpenter. I wasn't too worried about securing his services. Beauville wasn't a hotbed of construction activity, not since the recession anyway. Still, if I had any hope of staying in Wilkins' good graces, I should at least be able to report that a repair was on the way.

I still hadn't figured out what to do with Ernesto, either, but at least he seemed to be in good spirits. He'd made himself apparent immediately on my return home, nearly tripping me as I walked into the kitchen with two bags of groceries.

"Watch it!" I'd stumbled sideways as the little furball scooted away.

"Finally." Wallis sauntered in soon after, watching with interest as I removed a dozen eggs and a package of bacon. *"Cook much?"*

"I know, Wallis." I'd never felt the call toward homemaking. But until my money situation improved, rotisserie chicken was too much of a luxury.

"I can…" She brushed up against me, a solid warmth against my shin. *"Contribute…"* The thought ended in a purr, as I got a glimpse of spring fledglings, still soft with down.

"Thanks, but we can manage." I'm never sure how serious Wallis is about her hunting. She is, after all, a housecat. I know better than to offend her by expressing this out loud, however. "Look, I'll make some eggs as soon as I reach this carpenter, okay?" She didn't answer either.

Trying not to take it personally, I fished out the scrap of paper Albert had given me. Randy's. Well, it was a small town.

"Hey, Pru." I could picture the big man behind the counter. I pictured him with a smile. A greasy smile. "What's up?"

"This isn't a social call." I heard the acid in my tone and worked to counter it. "I've got a job for a buddy of yours. Dave Altschul." I paused and waited. More silence. "He's a carpenter, Albert says?"

"Yeah, yeah, Dave does all kinds of stuff." A slight noise— almost a hiss—and I realized he'd slid his hand over the receiver. "No, he's not here now."

"Do you know when he'll be back?" I wanted to ask him about Jill, but not over the phone. I couldn't tell who the man was talking to or who was in his shop. Better to stick with asking about the carpenter. There couldn't be that many people offering paying work around here.

"Not sure," said Randy, after a brief pause. Another silence, while I considered driving over there. "You can probably find him at Happy's though."

"Great." I hung up. So much for Albert's recommendation, although in truth most of Beauville did end up at Happy's, the blue-collar Beauville, anyway. "Wallis?" I looked around for my cat. She had clearly heard all she needed and had disappeared.

›››

It wasn't even dark by the time I got to Happy's, not that it mattered much to the crew at the bar. Three men, all grizzled, were facing the wall as I walked in. Only one looked up.

"Mack." It was an acknowledgment, rather than a greeting, and he squinted up at me as the door swung closed.

"Pru." He started to stand and appeared to think better of it. I'd bet he'd been here a while.

I waved off Happy as he came over. "I'm looking for some-one," I said to the room in general. "Dave Altschul?" Nothing. "I've got a job for him?"

Some low muttering could be heard in the back. Whether from surprise or relief, I couldn't tell. I turned to my onetime beau. "Mack, do you know him?"

"What's this about, Pru?" He talked over the drinker between us as if he couldn't hear. Maybe he couldn't. "This have something to do with those Canaday girls?"

"What's it to you?" Seeing Mack, worn and legless with drink, was making me mean.

"You know your business." He turned back toward the bar. He'd heard it too. "It's just…"

The drinker between us got up. As he headed for the restroom, I came over. "What?" It was as close as I'd come to apologizing.

He nodded. Non-apology accepted. "Those girls are bad news, Pru. I don't think you knew them back in the day…"

I shook my head. Judith had been a year or two behind me. Jackie was older. Jill not even a blip on my screen before I left town.

"You looking for me?" I turned. A burly redhead, his face dusted with freckles, stood facing me. Behind him, the bearded stool warmer. "Something about a job?"

"You're Dave?" I wondered at his timing. Surely, my voice had carried to the back of the bar.

He nodded. "You work with Albert?"

"Sort of." If that were how I'd pass muster, I'd take it. "So you're available for a carpentry job."

"Yeah, sure." He looked at me, taking in my worn jeans, the flannel shirt I'd donned once again as the spring afternoon grew cool. "What's it pay?"

"I'll negotiate that with the client." I kicked myself for not thinking of this earlier. "But it will pay top rate, if you can get to it immediately."

"I'll see if I can clear my schedule." He was smiling now. "Why don't you tell me about it?"

I followed him over to the far side of the bar, where I filled him on the damage. I hadn't told him who the client was, but he'd nodded at the address.

"The Wilkins place," he said. "I know it."

"You do the addition?" I didn't want to say the work was shoddy.

"Me? No." He shook his head, laughing. "I'd have done a better job. At a better price, too."

I liked this guy, so far. "I gather some of his neighbors agree with that."

"Or they're just stingy." He looked up at me, a smile teasing the corner of his mouth. He knew I was checking his credentials. "I did old man Canaday's gutters a few years back. Man, he was on me about every nail."

"Well, I'll be project-managing this job," I said. "But we'll start with some trust."

He nodded, accepting my terms. "How about I come around tomorrow, after work, and take a look at it?" he said, once I was done. "I could be there three, three-thirty."

"Sure." I hadn't realized he had other work. That also spoke well of him. "But do you have any other way I could get in touch with you?"

He looked at me, confused.

"Albert just gave me the number for Randy's. Said you were staying there. And Randy, well, he sent me here."

"Albert." The tone said it all as he held his hand out. I handed him my phone and he punched in a number. "Not that Randy's any better."

"Speak of the devil." As Dave had been speaking, the door had opened behind him, letting in the last of the summer twilight as well as the hefty smoke shop proprietor with Albert close behind him.

"You found him." Randy came up to us, beaming. "This little lady was looking for you all over, Dave."

I raised my eyebrows. That was warning enough for Albert, who took his friend's arm. Randy, however, wasn't to be stopped.

"Said she had a *job* for you." He emphasized the word with a leer.

"We've talked." I cut him off. "But come to think of it, I've got some questions for you, too."

"Oh?" The fat man threw one leg over a stool and tried to slide onto the seat. The move was supposed to look smooth. Instead, I was reminded of a dog trying to wipe its butt on the ground.

"Yeah, about the Canaday girls." Mack had settled back onto his stool by then. Now his head jerked up and just as quickly looked away.

"You must have been catching up on old times this week, huh?" I watched Randy, watched the smile falter. "Big chance to provide some comfort, huh?"

"Yeah, uh, well…." The leer was gone now, as Randy looked around at the other men. "That wouldn't, uh, that wouldn't have been right."

"Oh, come on," I was pushing. "Not even good old Judy?"

"What? No." He said it a little fast. Shook his head like he was nervous.

I thought of Albert, of the scene I had interrupted at his office. "'Cause Albert here hasn't been wasting any time." I paused, trying the idea on for size. "He was hitting on Jackie, when she came in to talk to him about their dad's cat."

"No, I wasn't." Albert doesn't usually speak up for himself, so it was a surprise to hear his voice as he jumped between us. "I was helping her figure out what to do."

"Really?" My question was for Albert, but I was watching Randy. "'Cause I was wondering about Jill, too. She must be the age Judy was when you were seeing her. Huh, Randy? And I hear she's been coming into the store."

"What? No." Randy shook his head. He was staring at Albert. Albert took a step back. "I mean, yeah, sure, I see her sometimes, but you can't think….She drops in when she's in town."

"Does she?" The voice, at my shoulder, was soft. Still, I jumped.

"Jim." Even in the dim light of the bar, he looked a little brighter and certainly more clean than any of the other men. "I didn't see you come in." I'd have noticed if the front door had opened up again, I was sure.

"Couldn't help but overhear the conversation," Creighton said, taking a hit off a beer bottle. So he had been here all along. "And when Dave came up to talk to you, I thought I'd join in."

"I had some questions." I turned toward him, my back stiff. Every man there knew we were lovers. If they expected to see some kind of interplay—if they expected me to back down— they had another thing coming. "I happen to know that Jill Canaday smokes those e-cigarettes."

"They call them 'vapes,' Pru." He took another drink, empty-ing the bottle. "And I know it, too. And to head off your next question, she didn't see her dad the day he died." He reached past me to put the bottle on the bar. "She got in just about the time they were calling him at the hospital."

So he was asking. Checking on Jill's whereabouts. On her— the word sprang into my mind—alibi. I wanted to know more, but not here. Not now. Not with a half-dozen hairy woodsmen staring at us as if we were the evening's entertainment.

"Well, if I'm going to work tomorrow, I'd better call it a night. I've got things to do," said Dave, breaking into what was becom-ing an awkward silence. "See you tomorrow, Pru. Three-thirty at the latest." Putting his own bottle on the bar, he sauntered out.

"See you." I kept my eyes on Creighton, gauging my next move.

"You might want to call it a night as well." He leaned in, softening his voice with a smile.

"And you?" I heard the hoarse note in my voice and cursed silently. I hadn't meant that, or not only. And I certainly didn't need to stoke the salacious interests of the men around us. Sure, I wanted Creighton. I can't stand that close to him and not, but I was more interested in what his plans were. Jim Creighton is not the kind of man to hang around at Happy's. Not without a reason.

"I think I'll have another drink with Randy here." He nodded to the bartender and another bottle appeared. "We've got some catching up to do."

I could have sworn I heard the big man swallow. "Be right back," he hurriedly excused himself, leaving his own beer on the bar.

I watched the shopkeeper as he trundled toward the back of the bar. Randy hadn't been straight with me about his connection to the Canaday girls. Some of that might be bluster. But if Creighton wanted to question him that meant there was more going on. If my favorite cop came over afterward, and something in his smile suggested that this was likely, I'd do my best to get it out of him. By any means necessary.

With as much dignity as I could muster, I nodded to the assembled crew and turned to go. I heard some rustling behind me as the men rearranged themselves around the bar—and around Creighton, who had suddenly become the center of gravity. What I didn't hear were any calls for me to stay. This was men's stuff—drinking and, in the case of my beau, talking. Largely, I suspected, about the women who had been, and maybe still were, so instrumental in their lives.

Who those women were was on my mind as I walked to my car. Jackie seemed pretty simple to me—the good girl. The one who gave up her life to care for her father after her mother's early death. What I didn't know was why. Had she wanted the role, the chance to step up and make herself invaluable? Or had she been forced into it by circumstance and a demanding father?

Judith was the wild one. Like me, she had chafed at the restrictions of a small town. Having a stern father, a lawyer no less, probably hadn't helped. She'd gotten away, and by the looks of it, she wasn't coming back to stay.

That left Jill. The baby. Clearly, David Canaday had been gentler on her than on either of her sisters. Maybe that was because he was aging, and she was the last one at home. Maybe there was something else going on—a resemblance to the girls' departed mother. A certain softness in her nature that had been absent in her sisters. Or maybe the baby of the family was simply better at playing their surviving parent. When I thought of the way she had second-guessed me, I knew I had to consider that as a possibility as well.

But not tonight. I confess, when I'd first seen Creighton at Happy's I'd wondered about his motives. I kind of liked the idea that he might be checking up on me, even if I knew I was going to have to shake him off at some point. But the cast of his questions had made it clear that he was there on business—and that he'd checked at least one person's whereabouts during the time that David Canaday had fallen ill. That meant that there might be something to Jackie's accusations. Something in the final autopsy report. I didn't know what he'd tell me. He can be as close-lipped as I am. But after a day with Jill, I might be able to trade information. At any rate, I looked forward to making the attempt.

When I got to my car, I saw a scrap of paper had been slid under the wiper. It was starting to rain, and so I grabbed it. I didn't need mush on my windshield. After so many years in the city, I was used to fliers everywhere. Chinese restaurants, iPhone repair services, you name it. But as I peeled the dimpled paper off the glass, I saw it wasn't a professional printing job.

It was a note. Block print, with blue ink that was already beginning to run. I glanced at it as I ducked into my car. Had I taken someone's space? Not likely on this half-deserted commercial strip. More likely someone wanted to sell me something—or buy my car. Tossing it onto the passenger seat, I briefly wondered how much I could get for my baby-blue baby. How much cheaper a more gas-efficient car would be to drive. No, some temptations are not worth a girl's time.

The rain was coming down harder now, and I was grateful to be inside. With wet sluicing down my windshield, I pushed my hair out of my eyes, seeing the blue on my fingers. Probably on my face, too, I thought, as I glanced again at the passenger seat.

SHE DIDNT DO IT, the note read. *SHE WAS HELP.*

Chapter Forty-six

Great. I sat there blinking at the damp paper, wishing I had left it to disintegrate in the rain. "'She didn't do it'?" I read, looking for more—or at least the missing apostrophe. "'She was help'?"

It seemed pretty clear: "She" was Jill. I'd been asking about the youngest Canaday girl, after all. Creighton had come in just as I was getting into it with Randy, and what he said pretty much cleared her. Unless...Help? That could explain the timing, demolishing Jill's alibi for good. But why leave this note for me and not the cop who was investigating? Why leave a note at all?

I checked the back of the paper—there was nothing else. For all I knew, the scrap might been left on my car by mistake. Or been part of a longer message

Leaving the paper on the seat, I ducked back into the rain. My wipers had been running for at least a minute by then, and when I lifted the driver's side wiper I saw a bit of paste. Dyed yellow with pollen, caked down from the motion of the wiper, it didn't come up easily. Still, I managed to pry it out, and took it back into the relative shelter of my car. White—paper probably—mixed with that pollen and what looked like the corpses of several insects. The rain that dripped from my forelock onto the sodden mess didn't make it any clearer. If something else had been written, it was gone.

I turned back to the original note, which was beginning to curl on the leather passenger seat. Between the rain and my cavalier handling of it, I was lucky the scrap of paper was still legible. But as I reached for it, I paused—wondering, for a moment, if I should be doing something, anything, with the truncated missive.

No, I finally decided. This was a note, not a bloody weapon. A semi-literate one, at best. And it had been left for me. Besides, as much as I might respect Jim Creighton, I was under no illusions about our small town's forensic resources.

Maybe if I could figure out who sent it, I'd hand it over. Maybe if I could figure out what it really meant, or why it had been left for me out here, in the rain.

Beauville isn't much for nightlife. Unless you want to drive to Amherst, Happy's is pretty much it. On a night like this the crowd was pretty settled. From where I sat, I could see the front door, but I didn't expect it to open up again till someone ran out of money. Or Creighton had gotten what he needed. And so I was left to wonder who had known I was here.

Randy, for one. The big man had sent me to the bar when I called. He knew the family—knew at least one of the women intimately—and he had excused himself before I left. Then again, he'd come up to me inside. If he had something to say to me, I couldn't see why he wouldn't say it. Who was there to hear? Who would disagree?

Albert knew my car, that was for sure. He'd been drinking, but he could easily have excused himself while I was talking to Randy or to Creighton. On the pretext of hitting the head, it wasn't impossible that he had snuck out the back.

Dave the carpenter was also a possibility. He had left before I had, and he knew the Canadays, too. He might have heard about my car from Albert, or a dozen other sources. But if he had something to say to me, wouldn't he just have waited till tomorrow? The one thing I didn't get from the note was any sense of urgency. If there was, it was certainly lost on me.

That left Mack. There was something up with my ex, something besides regret. He'd not been happy that I was working with the Canaday girls, though if that was because of them or because it threw me in closer with Jim Creighton, I couldn't be sure. Knowing Mack, his concern might have been completely self-centered. He knew that we were over. Didn't stop him from hoping—or from playing an angle.

I fingered the damp page, considering my options. For all I knew, it was a meaningless rant. A misguided memo tucked under my wiper by mistake. Ten more minutes, and the note would have been illegible anyway. Wiping my hands one more time on my jeans, I squinted out at the rain, and drove myself home.

> > >

"*Wet.*" Wallis didn't even try to hide her disdain when I entered the kitchen, dripping. "*Just like a kitten.*"

"Thanks, Wallis." I reached for a towel to dry my hair, then thought better of it. Odds were, Creighton would be over later. I'd had a hard day.

Ten minutes later, I was soaking in the tub. My old house had its drawbacks. Heating it to a livable temperature had nearly ruined me over the winter. But it had a few good points as well, and this was one of them. A claw-foot tub, deep enough for me to sink into, long enough for me to stretch my legs. A tumbler of bourbon perched on the edge completed the luxury, a way for me to warm myself inside and out—and prepare for the evening ahead.

Wallis, of course, thought I was crazy. But she perched on the toilet to watch me anyway. I closed my eyes and tried to ignore her censorious stare as I took another sip.

"*You…humans.*" The scorn dripped off her like rain. "*With your…soap.*"

"And how are you, Wallis?" I didn't want to fight. I wanted to drink, and so I did. "How's the kitten?"

"*Exactly.*" She shuffled a bit. I suspected that the presence of so much water made her nervous. "*At least he's learning to bathe himself.*"

"Thanks, Wallis." I thought of when I'd picked up Ernesto, only a few days before. I'd bathed him. Washed off the tea—or whatever—that had splashed him. I remembered how he'd sneezed. How he'd recoiled from…something. "Mint smells like catnip to you, doesn't it?"

"Mint?" She regarded me quizzically, and I tried to conjure a memory. A stand of cat mint—a close relative of catnip—that had grown wild out back where I'd sometimes caught her, in late summer, rolling around.

"Ah yes." The rumble of a purr. *"Don't waste that on a kitten."*

"You and I, Wallis." I raised my glass. "We may be more alike than you think."

"Huh." Wallis stood up and looked at the bathroom door. I'd offended her, finally. *"Don't be silly."* She jumped to the floor. *"I'm beyond being shocked by anything you do. You may, however, want to know that you've got company."*

Sure enough, a few seconds after she stalked off downstairs, I heard a car pull up. I smiled to myself and finished the bourbon. This evening was playing out exactly as I'd hoped.

"Come in," I yelled. The bathroom was at the top of the stairs. My voice would carry to the door below. "It's unlocked!"

I closed my eyes again and leaned back. Stretched my legs, letting one foot peek above the bubbles. Creighton would know where to find me. I heard the door open. Of course, he might want to pour himself a drink first.

"I'm up here." I called down. A girl gets impatient.

"Pru?" I sat up with a splash, the warm buzz of bourbon and bath shocked out of me. The voice, from the foot of the stairs, was not that of Jim Creighton. It was female. Jackie Canaday was in my house.

Chapter Forty-seven

"Told you you had company." Wallis slid by me without pausing.

"Thanks a lot," I couldn't help muttering, even as my guest stared at me, wide-eyed.

I'd hustled down only a moment before, grabbing first for a towel and then my old robe. "Just a minute!" I had yelled, suddenly feeling quite vulnerable.

"Thank you." Her voice had risen up to me, sounding a bit tentative at the greeting.

"Sorry about that," I rushed to explain once I made my way downstairs. I'd made myself decent as quickly as I could, but Jackie had still had time to wander into the kitchen. She turned as I spoke. "I was expecting— I wasn't expecting company."

She blushed and turned away. "I'm surprised that you left your door unlocked," she said. "I mean, considering some of the things that go on here."

"Must have been an oversight." Hell, she'd left her own front door open the day her father died. I'd apologized reflexively, and now I was getting cranky. "So, what brings you over to my side of town?"

It was late, especially for Beauville standards. As much as I wanted her gone, I also wanted to know.

"Oh, it's probably nothing." She walked over to the table. "May I?"

I nodded. I'd already invited her in.

She pulled out a chair and sat, heavily. "Thank you." She seemed to be waiting, so I took the other seat.

"Yes?" I don't do hostess.

"The kitten," she said at last. "I came over to see the kitten."

"Your father's kitten?" I was tempted to look around. Surely Wallis was listening in. Instead, I kept my eyes on my house guest. "You came over here tonight to see the kitten?"

She nodded, a little too vigorously. "I know it's late. I'm so sorry. I've been so busy. There's just been so much to do." She started digging around in her bag. By the time she came up with a tissue, she had calmed down enough to explain. "I know that I overreacted at first. That much— that much is clear. And since it was a present for my father, I thought, well, since both my sisters will be leaving town…"

"I'm not sure Jill will be." I thought about what the youngest Canaday had told me. "She's planning on at least staying the summer."

"Oh, is she?" That seemed to throw her. "I've been so distracted. But at any rate, she will undoubtedly be going back to school in the fall, and I'm sure that a kitten would be too much trouble to take with her."

"Wait." I stopped her. "You came over here at night to tell me you'd reconsidered taking your father's kitten?" She nodded, eyes wide. "Look, Jackie, this is something that you and your sister are going to have to work out between you, okay?"

"Oh, okay." She stood up as if to leave. "I really should get going." She turned away from me, away from the table. "Oh!"

Wallis was sitting there, eyeing her with that cool green gaze.

"This isn't…" Jackie's hands fluttered up to her chest. "I'm sorry, this isn't…"

"No." I took a step over, to put myself between the woman and the cat. "This is my cat, Wallis." Something was wrong here.

"Of course."

"She's afraid." Wallis was slightly amused, I thought. *"She's afraid to touch me."*

"She won't hurt you, you know." I ignored Wallis' silent protest and reached to pick her up. "Here."

One hand reached out, and I thought Jackie was going to pet Wallis' head. But as her hand came near, Wallis tilted her head up. Going to sniff her, I thought, but Jackie withdrew as if my aging tabby had been a tiger growling.

"That's all right." She clasped her hands in front of her. "Well, I won't bother you anymore."

"Put me down." Wallis twisted in my grip in case her message was unclear, and I released her. She trotted away as I walked Jackie back to the front door.

"There's one thing." I waited. Whatever she said, I figured, was the real reason she had come. "It's about my sister…"

I nodded. Of course, the accusations were beginning to pile up.

"I have some concerns." She bit a lip that already looked scraped and raw. "There are some inconsistencies in her story."

"Inconsistencies." If she was finally going to accuse her baby sister of poisoning their father, she was going to have to say it out loud. Jill, I was learning, wasn't the goody two-shoes I'd originally thought, but I had no reason to believe she was a killer.

"Some, well, some legal issues." As I stood there, I felt the brush of fur against my bare ankle. A question, like a feeler, reached into my brain. I held it off, focusing on the woman in front of me, keeping my silence. Waiting.

"I don't know if you should trust her, Ms. Marlowe," my visitor said at last. "I don't know if you can, you see."

I nodded. This was what I'd expected. But even as I waited for the rest to come out, I saw a flash of light. Headlights. A car had pulled into my driveway and was making its way up to my house. Creighton. Jackie had to leave.

"I understand there's some tension in the family." I opened the door and put my hand on her upper arm. I'd push her if I had to, but it seemed she was moving. "And I gather that Jill is the focus of it."

That was the blandest way I could put it. I didn't care about being kind, I simply wanted her gone. But I'd clearly said the wrong thing, because she turned to face me, the timid pliability gone.

"I'm sure you and she can work this out." I was pushing her now, softly, but steadily.

"Jill? I'm not talking about Jill." The brush against my foot. The kitten. I lifted my foot, hoping that this would suffice to block the curious kitten from lumbering out my front door. The car in the driveway went dark. Surely, Creighton would see that I was escorting a visitor out. I willed him to wait, for privacy's sake.

"I'm talking about Judith." Jackie was staring at me now. "She'll say anything. You can't trust her, Ms. Marlowe. You can't."

I didn't respond. I didn't have to. Jim had come up behind her, quiet as a cat.

"Miss Canaday," he said, his voice soft and calm. She turned and jumped. He nodded, acknowledging her.

"Detective." She blinked at him, gathering herself, and for a moment I thought she was going to engage him. That he was here at her request.

"Ms. Canaday here was just telling me about her sister," I said, keeping my eyes on Jackie. "Telling me about how Judith is out to get Jill. Next she was going to say something about poison, I'm sure. About how it was really Judith who poisoned their father."

"I wasn't—" Jackie's eyes dropped as she caught herself. "Officer, you know the history, even if Ms. Marlowe doesn't."

"I know she was never charged," said Creighton. I couldn't help it. I looked up at him then and swallowed. This was a whole new can of beans.

"Jim?" He shook his head. Turned to Jackie, who looked sickly white in this light.

"Look, Ms. Canaday, there's no point in dredging up old history. Or in spreading rumors." He shot me a glance. "And pending means just that. Pending. When there is something definite, Ms. Canaday, you'll be among the first to know. And now," he stepped aside from the doorway, "I think we should all call it a night."

She looked from Creighton back to me and then at him again. "Don't forget," she said, her voice strained. I stood there silent, taking the full force of her gaze until she crumbled, looking down at her feet as she stepped back out through that door and headed for her car.

"Charged?" Creighton had my full attention now. "What was that about?"

"Ancient history." He shook his head. "When Laurence Wilkins' wife died, her family made a fuss."

"Sounds familiar."

He grunted. "She'd been ill even longer. Congestive heart failure. Judith was her aide. She practically lived over there, the last few months. I always thought she got a raw deal."

I raised my eyebrows. "She won your support, huh?"

"My sympathy, Pru."

A movement at my feet alerted me to the kitten as Creighton walked into the kitchen. I heard the bottle of bourbon opening, the liquid warmth tumbling into a glass, as I lifted the little beast.

"*Why won't he play with me?*" The kitten's fur was feather soft against my face.

"*He's tired.*" I willed the thought back. "*They're all tired.*"

"Interesting company you keep." His voice was tired. I turned to see him, drink in hand, brushing through the accumulation of papers on the table.

"She dropped by while I was in the bath." I closed the door with my foot and followed him in. The kitten squirmed in my grasp. "Unannounced," I added as he sipped my bourbon.

"She come by to drop this off?" With one finger, he brushed the newspaper aside, revealing the note beneath.

"*Don't leave!*" The kitten was struggling now, I could feel him yearning—not toward the door, but toward the window. I could see Jackie's taillights as she disappeared down the street.

"Wait, she—?" I caught myself in time. "Where's Wallis?" I needed an interpreter, fast.

"I don't think she got out." Jim was still drinking, but his attention was on the paper in front of him, dry now and dimpled. "I was careful. So, she came by to leave you this?"

I looked down at the note. I had brought it in and left it here. She had seen it. She must have. Unless—had it been underneath the paper when I first came downstairs? When I had gone up to bathe?

"What? No, Jim." I read it again, the words taking on a newly ominous cast. "SHE DIDNT DO IT. SHE WAS HELP."

The window now showed only dark, and the kitten settled in my grasp. *"Play with me?"* he cried. *"Don't leave."* Jackie had asked about the kitten, but hadn't even bothered to pick him up.

Chapter Forty-eight

Creighton didn't believe me, or not entirely. I'd given up trying to dissimulate at that point. "Someone left it on my windshield at Happy's. Maybe it was Jackie."

"Interesting." He looked at it, poking at the edge. "Could be nothing. Just someone trying to get to you."

"I don't understand." I'd poured myself more bourbon by then, my surprise visitor had already ruined my good bathtime buzz. "Why would anyone?"

"You tend to get in the way, Pru." A look, not quite a smile. "You ask a lot of questions and stick your nose in where it's not wanted."

I didn't deny it. "But—this? What does it even mean?"

Another look, with even less smile. "You're involved with Jill Canaday. You're doing work for her lawyer."

"Her lawyer. I thought Wilkins represented the family—"

Creighton held up a hand to stop me. "He does, or he did. He represented old man Canaday, anyway, and it seems he's the executor of the will. But I gather Jill has hired him specifically."

"To…" I left it open. He didn't answer, so I spelled it out. "Why does a newly rich college girl need a lawyer?"

He raised his eyebrows. That was a warning. I was getting into his business here. "Because of the money?" Nothing. "Because of what her sisters are saying?"

"Pru, you don't know," he said. He was shaking his head, sad now that the drink had taken the edge off, I thought. "Families are complicated. There are old grudges…"

"Tell me about it," I said, when it became clear he wasn't going to. "I don't know how my mother and I managed to talk at all toward the end. But nobody accused me of finishing her off."

As I was talking, I was watching my beau. Something about the way he nodded let me know I'd hit on it.

"Does Wilkins do criminal cases?" I kept my voice low, even, hoping that I wouldn't alert Creighton.

"Pru." The smile at the side of his mouth let me know he heard what I was asking. "Why would you be asking about criminal cases when there haven't been any charges?"

He was looking at the note again, one finger pushing the note back and forth as he stared at the ink, at the paper. I waited for him to say something more. To say anything, but his mouth was set, firm. Closed. I could see lines around that mouth. Others forming around his eyes. Fatigue was wearing out the boy scout in him. Didn't make him any less handsome, though. Not in my book, and when he turned toward me, I let my questions go.

"Come on." I took his hand. The evening hadn't gone as I'd expected. Didn't mean it couldn't still be salvaged. Not at all.

"Button?" As we climbed the stairs, I heard the kitten cry. *"Why won't he play with me anymore?"*

Chapter Forty-nine

"If you expect me to babysit, you really ought to quit upsetting the creature." Wallis was in the kitchen the next morning. She had given me and Creighton our privacy, declining to join me even after he left some hours before dawn. *"I can't keep mopping up after humans."*

"What did I do, Wallis?" I was feeling mellow, but the strange interactions of the night before hung over me. "I don't know why Ernesto suddenly became so homesick."

"Homesick, she says." Wallis proceeded to wash. *"Doesn't listen. Doesn't care."*

"That's not fair." I had the coffee set up to brew. I didn't want another creature in my life to shut me out. "What am I not listening to?"

"Oh, maybe me." The sound of her voice was nearly drowned out by the lap lap lap of her rough tongue. *"Maybe our tiny houseguest."*

"Wallis, I wish you'd just tell me what I'm missing." Even mellow, I have my limits. "And can you not do that while we're talking?"

"Hungover, are we?" The washing didn't stop, but she did pause for a moment as the kitten came into the room. *"Why don't you ask him yourself?"*

I looked down at Ernesto. He looked up at me. He looked good. I had to give Wallis credit. The bedraggled mite I'd brought home a week before had begun to fill out, his fur taking on the glossy sheen of a well-groomed cat. Maybe I'd been too harsh to my longtime companion.

"You think?" The thought came to me over the swipe of tongue on fur.

"Well, kitten. What is it you want to tell me?"

"Lonely." The desperation of the night before had faded. The longing was still there.

"Isn't Wallis good company?" I caught my cat's sudden startled jerk and quickly amended my words. "Aren't I?"

"He played with me, with the button." The face that looked at me seemed to imbue this simple act with great importance. *"He's gone."*

With the unselfconscious ease of the young, Ernesto curled up and fell asleep.

"Well, that certainly cleared things up." I looked around. "Wallis?" My cat was gone.

〉〉〉

Tracy Horlick was not much less cryptic.

"I hear they're still investigating," she said. The light in her eyes could have been a taunt. Then again, it could also have been the reflection of her glowing red butt.

"Really?" I wasn't in the mood.

"Cause of death." She paused, waiting for me to respond. She took another drag. Behind her, in the house, I heard a sharp yip. Growler. "Makes you wonder," she added, ignoring the cries of her pet.

"These things take time." I wasn't going to rise to the bait if I could help it. Not that I didn't sympathize with Growler. "Lab tests and all that."

"Not when it's simple." Her words came out with the smoke. "Not when it's a natural death."

I nodded, not wanting to get into it.

"I heard that the youngest girl uses those electronic cigarettes." She took a big drag on her own decidedly old-school butt. "They're poison, you know."

"There's no—" I stopped myself. So much for not getting dragged into Tracy Horlick's mire. From inside the house, I heard a sharp bark. "There's no evidence of anything amiss."

"I knew it." Tipping the ash off into the shrubbery, she turned into the house. A moment later, I heard the scrambling of claws as the bichon raced out of the basement. "He's completely under her thumb," she was muttering, as I bent to clip on the fluffy white dog's lead.

So she knew where I was getting my information from. I wasn't going to tell her how wrong she was about me and Creighton.

Chapter Fifty

"Ready to boogie, Bitsy?" I silently apologized for using that awful name.

"About time!" With a yip, he acknowledged me. *"Jerome, really..."* Black leather nose quivering, Growler took in the neighborhood news. *"But he's a—he's a raccoon!"*

Trying to give the little guy some privacy, I stared off into the distance. Growler's life was more circumscribed than many, living as he did with such a harridan. Why she had a pet, when she usually kept him locked in the basement, was beyond me.

"The social angle, old Smoke Teeth." The words broke through and I turned away. *"No! No!"* A series of sharp barks brought me back. *"I'm talking to you, walker lady."*

To anyone else, we must have made a pair. The tiny white dog barking up at me as I, mouth agape, bent over to listen.

"I'm sorry, what?"

"She got me to go out with." A little chuff accented his words. *"To sniff about."*

"Of course." Poor guy. Bad enough to belong to such a person. Worse to have to be a prop for her forays. "And then she got tired of you?" It wasn't kind, but it was honest.

Another bark. *"No!"* I didn't press. I did, however, find myself wondering. I'd accepted that it was common knowledge about the autopsy. The Canaday girls' increasingly public sniping would have made that clear. But the idea of nicotine poisoning? Could Jackie be spreading that rumor?

"Breeders, huh." With a short snort, Growler lifted his leg, leaving his own mark where so many of his peers had before. *"Led around like...like...."*

The button eyes looked up at me, and I finished the thought: "Like so many house pets?"

"Huh." Another chuff. *"Exactly."*

"He's completely under her thumb." Tracy Horlick's words came back to me. Maybe she hadn't been talking about Creighton. About me. I stopped and looked down at the little dog.

"Growler," I said, looking into those wide dark eyes. "Are you saying that the gossip is being started by a woman?"

The white tail started wagging.

"It's Judith, isn't it?" Creighton had said charges had been dropped. To Tracy Horlick—hell, to half of Beauville—that wouldn't matter. No wonder the middle Canaday girl had left town, risking her father's displeasure. Growler's comments, what he had been saying about his witch of a person, all came back.

"Judith is using Randy at the smoke shop to spread rumors about her baby sister," I said, as Growler started to whine, his canine misogyny winning out. "She wants everyone to suspect Jill."

I thought of the note. Of the timing. "But why not just have him tell me? I was asking..." Of course, Albert. The bearded wonder had been almost courtly to Jackie—and then done his best to deny it. "And if she can implicate Jackie, too, so much the better."

Judith Canaday was after it all.

Chapter Fifty-one

I was beginning to understand why Creighton had kept me out of it. Had done his best to keep things quiet—keep things under wraps while the investigation proceeded. Bad enough the lab was taking its time, the town of Beauville had already begun a trial—and one of its own was in the dock. If anyone else heard about that note, Jackie would be suspected too. My guy had taken it with him, and I made a mental note to tell him about Judith's visit to the medicine cabinet at her father's house as well. Aspirin for a headache, indeed.

I needed to wash my hands of the lot of them. Imagined how Wallis would react, her single-minded focus on a thorough cleanse. But, I still wanted my own questions answered as I drove over to Wilkins' place that afternoon. To start with, I wanted to know what had gone on with Wilkins' late wife and what role Judith had played. Maybe this had nothing to do with Jill Canaday. Maybe this was about Judith and her dad and a particularly bad, old habit. But maybe I had been cleaning cages with a murderer.

"Hey, Pru." Dave, the carpenter, was waiting for me as I got out of my car. Leaning against a battered blue pick-up, with a tool kit by his feet, he nodded toward the house as I walked up to meet him.

"Dave." Glad as I was to see him, I couldn't help wondering. He knew these people, had worked for David Canaday. What if he'd been the one to put the note on my windshield? What if I had it all wrong? "Follow me," was all I said, as I started walking around the house.

He fell in step beside me. "I already checked it out. Saw what you did up there." A smile caught at the side of his mouth. "Some squirrels, huh?"

"There was a nest situation." I kept my voice neutral. He was looking at me, that smile still twitching at the corners of his mouth. "The wood was rotted away."

"Well, it's gone now." While I waited, he went back to his truck, returning with an aluminum ladder that he deftly placed against the side of the house.

I bit back the urge to respond and instead watched as he climbed up and took some measurements.

"Okay, I can do this by Friday," he said, once he'd climbed down. "Assuming the weather holds. You want me to leave the gate up here?"

"There's no point." The sad, sinking feeling swelled up inside me again. "I can probably take it down now, leave the mesh."

"Suit yourself." He pocketed the measuring tape. "I need to take some notes."

As he walked back to his truck, I climbed up to the ruined corner. The wood crumbled at my touch now, its rot dried out by the air and the sun, but I let my hand rest there. Waited for the emotions to flood through me.

"Nest…home…gone." The thoughts were faint, memories most likely. Though whether they were echoes left in the dark space by that bereaved mother, or phantoms conjured out of my own guilt, I couldn't tell.

"I'm sorry." Hand flat against the ruined wood, I tried to concentrate, to picture a nest with young ones safely inside. All I saw was black. *"I was at fault."*

"Gone…" I had an image of another nest. Older, and a sudden attack—

"Miss Marlowe?" I looked down. Dave was still by his truck. "Hello?"

The window. I turned to see Laurence Wilkins, inside his office, staring up at me. "Hello," I said.

"May I ask what you're doing?" From up here, his brow looked furrowed. It could have been the angle.

"Doing a last check for signs of animal infestation." That was true, after a fashion. The image lingered like a nightmare. I had to shake it off. "Dave, the carpenter, has already made some measurements."

"And is eavesdropping part of your 'last check'?" There was no mistaking the sarcasm in his voice now.

"What? No." I smiled, a submissive gesture to de-escalate. I needed to focus. I had things I wanted to know. I'd been trying to figure out a way to ask Wilkins about his late wife, before I'd been distracted. Any chance of that disappeared, however, as he retreated back into the room. In his place, I saw a familiar face staring up at me. Jill Canaday, eyes wide.

"Hi, Jill." I couldn't pretend I didn't see her, not when she was staring up at me. "Sorry to interrupt."

"It's—it's fine." She didn't sound fine. "May I talk to you—in private?"

"Suit yourself." She disappeared and I dismounted the ladder. Dave was by the base by then, looking at me funny.

"Sorry." I was apologizing to everyone today. "Thought I'd take a last look around."

"I gather." He wasn't even trying to hide the smile anymore.

"Hello." Laurence Wilkins used the word like a wedge, coming up between us. Jill, coming up behind him, hung back.

"Laurence Wilkins, Dave Altschul." I made the introductions. "Dave says he can probably start work this week." Always build some extra time in with the customer. That way, nobody gets bent out of shape.

"Pru?" Jill's voice was soft, but the request was clear in her voice as she gestured toward the front of the house. I nodded and followed, leaving the lawyer and the contractor to sort out the details.

"What is it?" My voice stayed even, my face still.

"You don't know?"

I shook my head. A non-denial denial.

She sighed heavily, gazing off at the side of the building. The negotiations must have been ongoing. Between a local carpenter and a lawyer, I wouldn't have put money on who would come out ahead.

"It's about my dad."

I nodded, waiting. "We've just heard the news. There's going to be a report — a final ruling from the medical examiner about my father. They're saying that his death wasn't natural." She paused and licked her lips. "That it wasn't even accidental."

So it was official. "Nicotine?"

"I don't know." She took a breath. "They're saying that the cause isn't clear—or that it's overdetermined?" She seemed unsure of the word. "At any rate, they're saying 'unnatural means.' Do you know what that means?"

"Yeah." I looked at her. Despite everything I was learning about her, she still seemed younger than her years. Maybe she was scared. Maybe it was an act. "It means that it's a good thing you're talking to your lawyer, Jill. It means the authorities are going to investigate his death for possible foul play—even murder."

Chapter Fifty-two

"Jim, you could have told me that the old guy was murdered." I'd driven over to the town cop shop straight from Wilkins'. Found my beau in his office and cut through any small talk. "That I was hanging out with a suspect in a patricide. Maybe two."

"Hang on, Pru." He pushed his chair back and looked up at me. It was true, I was leaning over his desk. He didn't look threatened. Amused, rather, as he stared up at me. "I don't know where you're getting your information."

"Jill Canaday. The only one in that family who smokes. Or uses those stupid e-cigarettes, I should say." She had been vague on the details. Didn't matter, the outline of the case against her was clear. "Unless it was Judith, who I have reason to believe was behind the note."

"Did you just deputize yourself?" Creighton was grinning now. "Or, no, become a forensic expert?"

"That note was left for me, Jim." I pulled out his one guest chair and plopped into it. "Look, I think Randy from the smoke shop wrote it. He told me he hadn't kept up with the Canadays, but I'm pretty sure he's lying. I think he could tell you about Jill, about her bad habits. Maybe something about Judith too. Like if there was anything in her father's downstairs medicine cabinet that shouldn't have been."

"Maybe he could, Pru." He leaned back further. Damn, he was looking relaxed. "But nobody is saying that. At least, nobody who works in this office."

I waited. He could be close-mouthed. He is a cop. But he'd already started talking. And, besides, he seemed to be in a good mood.

"Jill Canaday is not a suspect, Pru." He sat up. "We're not even sure we're looking at a homicide."

"I thought…" I paused to remember what Jill had told me. "Something about unnatural causes of death."

Creighton shook his head, his smile disappearing. "The man was a mess. The state police lab had their hands full with him."

"I figured they weren't taking their time for fun."

"They are backed up," said Creighton. "But now they have someone out from Boston. He's good, but maybe too good."

"How's that?" It wasn't just that Jim was talking to me. This was interesting.

"He found everything. Seems like the guy was a heart attack waiting to happen."

"I knew he was sick—"

"He didn't." Creighton shook his head again. "At least, he didn't act like it. He was taking painkillers. Using something for his cough. Everything he wasn't supposed to take, he was taking. I'm almost surprised to hear that he wasn't shooting heroin. But, no, there wasn't anything that jumped out, nothing that shouldn't have been in his system. Truth is, if this guy hadn't joined the lab, we'd probably have chalked this up to human error. As it is, well, the DA wants me to look into it."

"So there *are* going to be charges?"

"There's going to be an investigation." Creighton held my gaze. "That's different."

"And Jill?"

"I don't see how she could have played into it. She wasn't in town when it happened."

I thought of the note. "Unless she had help."

"More likely someone trying to stir up trouble." Creighton looked at me. "You really don't like her, do you?"

"It's not that." I paused. "I don't think. Things are funny around her. Around all three of them. You know?"

"Why don't you tell me?" He was in cop mode. I didn't care. I needed to think this out.

"They're all so different—all three of them. And, well, I feel like all of them have something to hide…" It wasn't until I said it that I realized how true that was. As soon as the words were out of my mouth, though, I regretted it.

"What do you mean?" Jim sat up.

"I—" I was tempted to say "nothing." I knew my beau too well for that. What I could do was try to trade. "Why don't you tell me what you're looking for?"

"Pru." He was shaking his head. "Believe it or not, this is my job."

"I don't want anything taken out of context…"

His eyes narrowed. I could see him weighing his choices. Rather to my surprise, he started speaking again. "Look, there are abnormalities in his blood tests. Nothing that couldn't be explained away by carelessness or human error but…"

I nodded. I got it. "You're waiting to hear how the DA comes down."

"Not everything is black or white, Pru." His voice was gentle. "There aren't always simple answers."

"Tell me about it," I muttered as I left.

> > >

"Hey, Pru!" Albert hailed me as I checked my messages. I tried to ignore him, but he kept waving and calling as I strode across the foyer that the police department shared with animal control.

I'd not planned on dropping into his office. Doc Sharpe had finally gotten back to me, letting me know he'd had a cancellation that afternoon. I would barely have time to go pick up the kitten and get to his office. If the good vet was squeezing us in, I could at least respect his schedule. But Albert was at the door now, panting from his exertions.

"Albert." I didn't pity him exactly. I also didn't want to be the cause of his coronary. "Your ladder. I'm sorry. I'll bring it back tomorrow."

"It's not that, Pru." His eyes darted into the cop shop. "Can you…" His head jerked back two times—a third.

"You okay?" If this man was having a seizure, I wasn't sure what I'd do.

"Yeah, yeah." He looked around. "I wanted to talk. You know, in private."

"Got it." I followed him back into his office but refused a seat. If this were about a woman, I'd be off in a flash. "What's up, Al?"

"You know, um, that I respect you, right?" I gave him the deadeye. That usually makes him cut to the chase. "I mean, this isn't from me."

He'd begun fiddling with the papers on his desk. I needed to intervene.

"Albert, I've got an appointment." I turned to leave when another voice—softer but no less urgent—called me back.

"Shiny." Frank. I craned my neck but could see no sign of the ferret. *"Want it, want it all…"*

"Is Frank there?" Albert didn't blink at my non sequitur. Instead, he opened a drawer and the masked face popped up. *"Shiny?"* The black nose quivered in anticipation.

I shook my head and formed a silent thought. *"Sorry,"* I tried to meet his button eyes. *"What are you seeking? Is Albert treating you well?"* I wasn't sure what exactly I would do if Albert ever mistreated his pet. That I would do something was a given.

"Watch out for yourself." With a nod of his own, he dove back into the desk. *"Here somewhere…mine…to eat!"*

"Uh, Pru?" Albert may have missed the entire exchange. It had, however, given him time to collect his thoughts, paltry as they might be. "It's that lawyer."

"Great." I knew what he was going to say before he formed the words. "He complain about me?"

"Yeah." Albert hung his head, as if he'd been the one who'd been yelled at. Maybe, I thought, remembering Wilkins' high-handed way, he had been. "He's pretty mad."

"I wouldn't let him get to you, Albert." I thought back to our last encounter. Everybody had said that David Canaday was the tough one. Well, maybe the late lawyer's partner had a mean streak of his own. "I did the job, and he has no cause to complain. Not to you, anyway. You can tell him that, if he calls again."

"*Shiny.*" The muted voice inside the desk was happy now. Frank had found whatever it was he had wanted. "*Just had to dig for it. Had to dig.*"

With a nod to the human, and a silent shout-out to the ferret, I took my leave.

Chapter Fifty-three

"So how is this little fellow?" No matter how many years Doc Sharpe has put in as a vet, he still talks like that. I'd taken the kitten out of his box and placed him on the table in front of the white-haired vet. Not that age mattered. Doc Sharpe looked as thrilled as a little boy about the puffball before him. "Are we feisty? Are we fun?"

"He's feisty all right." I kept one hand on the kitten while Doc Sharpe looked in his ears. I used my other to push his paws back down—the swinging stethoscope was too tempting a target.

"Hmmm." He slid the stethoscope down the kitten's side, settling on his belly. "Sounds good. How's he been doing?"

"Good." I gave him the basics—food, litter usage. "We had some sneezing at first, and I was wondering about FVR. But that seems to have stopped. There is one thing." I bit my lip. I'm not a suspicious person, but I still hated to bring it up. "The day Judith gave him to her father. The day I first saw him? He was shaking and he vomited. He's too young to have a hairball, and I was worried."

Doc Sharpe looked up at me then. I could read my own concerns on his face. "You didn't bring him in?"

"I didn't want to risk it." I looked around. "Not when you have so many kittens here." He knew what I meant. Distemper spreads like wildfire. "Wallis has had her shots, so…." He understood. "And then, well, he seemed to recover. I was hoping it was something he ate."

"Could be." The vet turned his back on us, leaving me holding the kitten. I knew that was a sign of his trust in me. Clearly, I could control a kitten. Most people could. But with lawsuits on the rise, I also know he would never leave an animal unattended with any other pet owner—or caregiver, which is what I was. It was also, I thought, a way for him to gather his thoughts in relative privacy.

When he turned around, his face was blank. "You were thinking of the greater good?"

It was a leading question. "Maybe," I said. "Or maybe I just didn't want it to be anything." Now was the time, if there was ever going to be one. "Doc, I—"

He looked up at me, his pale eyes watery and tired behind those glasses.

"I meant to tell you," I licked my lips. Caught myself doing it, too. "The kitten has had his first FVRCPC," I said.

"He has?" Those eyes might be tired, but they didn't miss a thing.

"Yes." I reached to move the kitten. Ducked my head. "That's one reason I was concerned, you see. I thought maybe he had a reaction." I was over explaining. Talking too much. Time to shut up.

The silence was palpable. Even Ernesto seemed to sense it, squirming under my hand.

"How long ago?" Doc broke the silence, placing the hypodermic back on the tray.

"Three days." I knew he was thinking of the virus' incubation period. Of the risks I'd exposed the shelter to, simply by bringing him in. But he could do the math.

"Well," he said. I watched as the truth put new creases in his forehead. "If he didn't have FVR, then that should take care of it. Too soon for the booster, though. Rabies?"

I hadn't realized I was holding my breath until then. "Good idea," was all I said. "Can't be too careful."

Ernesto mewed softly, as Doc put the combo vaccine aside and readied the rabies shot. When he was done I put the kitten back in his carrier. "I'll have Jill disinfect this room when she comes by later."

"She's really helping out?" Clearly, he trusted the youngest Canaday girl to be more thorough than Pammy when it counted.

"That she is, and she's a natural." He pulled off his gloves and deposited them in the trash. "Not like you, Pru," he added quickly. "But she has a feel for animals. Clearly loves them. If this kitten is going to end up in her care…" He shook his head.

"We'll give him two full weeks." I finished the thought. That was the standard protocol for distemper, long enough for the virus to manifest. If he didn't sicken by then, he would most likely be fine. "After I bring him in for his booster, I'll release him. If she still wants him," I said.

He looked up. "I can't imagine she won't. She's already told me she'll be here for the summer, at least. I gather she's considering staying here. Helping to put her father's estate in order."

"Does that include his work with the Friends of County?" As soon as I asked, I realized this must still be a sore spot. The vet's face paled as he shook his head. "I'm sorry, what is it?" I asked.

"Only the usual." With one finger, he pushed his glasses back up his lumpy nose. "Too few resources and too many commitments."

"Might things be looking up now?" I am far from a pollyanna. Something about the old Yankee, though, made me want to give him hope. Maybe it was that he'd overlooked my theft of the hospital's drugs. Maybe it was simply that he was kind. "Considering our biggest enemy is gone?"

"You would think, Pru. You would think."

"Well, maybe Jill will be a positive influence. I know she's working with the family lawyer." I wasn't going to gossip. I still didn't know what exactly was going on. "But things change." For all I knew, she'd be locked up in two weeks. For all I knew, I could be, too.

Chapter Fifty-four

"We're home!" I made too much of a fuss coming in. I was worried about the kitten. About Doc Sharpe—and my own career. The Canadays were trouble, no two ways about it, and I had already heard more than I wanted.

"More than you wanted?" Wallis greeted me with a gentle pass-by and watched as I unlatched the door to the carrier. *"Has Ernesto finally started using complete sentences?"*

"Wallis, I thought you could read my thoughts," I said. I didn't want to enunciate what my fears were. I told myself I wanted to spare the kitten. The truth was probably more selfish.

"With ease." Wallis came forward, sniffing the kitten. *"I'm not the one with the stunted senses, you know."* Quickly, as if she didn't want me to see, her tongue darted out, knocking the kitten over with a thorough swipe. *"I'm not the one who doesn't take in what's right in front of her."*

"I know, Wallis." There was nothing to it but to admit it. "You're right."

"Clueless." With a bat of her paw, she set the kitten scurrying off and turned to follow. *"Thinks that every child is her responsibility. Thinks that every kill is, too."*

"But Ernesto isn't…" I paused. This was too cold-blooded, even for Wallis. Unless she meant the squirrel…

"Not the sense of that kitten." And with that she left the room.

◇ ◇ ◇

Wallis had left me with a lot to think about, but I didn't need her to point out the obvious. If I was going to extricate myself from this family, I had to get ready for Ernesto to leave us. And that meant checking out Jill—and Jackie—Canaday's home. If I had missed something—a geranium, even some peeling paint—I'd be in a better position to know what had made the kitten so sick that day. What his prognosis was. I reached for my phone and then thought better of it. The Canadays felt no qualms about dropping in on me unannounced. Who knew what I'd find if I did the same? I reached for my keys instead. If Jill was going to cohabit with her oldest sister, I needed to make sure neither of them would be a potential threat to the kitten. A surprise visit was in order.

"Ms. Marlowe." Jackie answered her door wearing jeans and that same blue sweater. "Did we have an appointment?"

"No." I looked at her. She looked different. Better, I thought, despite the casual clothes. More relaxed. "I wanted to have a look around."

"A look around?" Her voice ratcheted up an octave. So much for more relaxed.

"If you don't mind." I stepped in. The kitchen looked the same. So did the living room when I got to it. Minus the dead body on the floor, of course. "Do you have any houseplants?"

"What? No." She paused, clasping her hands together. "My father—he thought they were clutter."

"I see." I didn't. Not really. "So he must have been thrilled about getting a kitten."

"Judith didn't—" More hand clasping. "She didn't know him like I did. She wasn't around that often."

"I gather." I was done wasting sympathy on this family. "You didn't stay around to meet the kitten the other night. His name is Ernesto, by the way."

"Oh." She swallowed. I waited. "I guess I was a little…when Detective Creighton came by, I realized that perhaps I should have waited. Should have made an appointment."

She was right, she should have. I still didn't buy it. I thought about the note. She had to have seen it. What had it meant to her?

"Did you have any help?" I was watching her. Looking to see if she'd react to the phrasing of the letter. "So you didn't have to do everything alone?"

Her face was impassive, pale and drawn. Her fingers, how-ever, were active, rolling the edge of her sweater back and forth. Kneading again or—no, I was thinking of the motion like a cat would. She was rubbing her hands together as if washing them. A nervous reaction. She saw me looking and tucked them under the hem of her sweater. The same blue sweater I had seen her in before. Or not quite. Something was different.

It hit me. "You got the spot out," I said, pointing.

"What? Oh, yes. Yes, I did." She grabbed at the edge of her sweater, rolling it up as if I'd said the opposite.

"I'm sorry." I shook my head, confused. "I shouldn't have said anything. Only, it's such a nice sweater, and it's handmade, right?"

"Yes, I knit." She cleared her throat. "Knitted. I used to have all this free time."

"Of course." I remembered those hours by a bedside. "Your father."

"Well, yes." Jackie looked away, blushing. The hem of that sweater wasn't long going to survive the way she was rolling and pulling at it. Already that bottom button, the one with the rounded metal top, looked ready to pop off.

The button. Wait. With a top like that, it would roll back and forth. Make a little noise as its embossed top defined tight circles on a hardwood floor.

"You knit for your father." I remembered the way he lay there, clutching his chest. Clutching at his vest. His hand-knit vest. "The vest he was wearing."

"Yes." Her eyes darted forward, meeting mine. "They—I didn't get it back."

"No, you wouldn't." The EMTs or someone in the emer-gency room. Someone would have cut it off. The man was dead, but they'd had to try. I pictured it now: argyle, the blue wool diamonds a little lopsided. At the time, I'd thought it odd that such a tightly wound man had worn a loud vest. That the slight distortion in the pattern had been caused by those last frantic struggles. "That vest didn't have buttons, did it?"

She shook her head, confusion wrinkling her brow.

"The button. The one on the floor. The one—" I saw it again in my mind—"the one the kitten was playing with. It came from your sweater. From this one."

"Oh." She dropped the hem as if it were hot, both hands rising in a flutter. "Maybe. They come off all the time."

"I don't think so." I was remembering the brown spot on the sweater. The tea spilled on the floor—and on the kitten. The blush, the averted eyes. The way her face now scrunched up as if to fold in on itself. They all made sense. "You said you hadn't met the kitten. Hadn't seen him—even though you called me to come take care of him. But you had. You clearly had. You oversold your lie, Jackie." I paused as it all became clear. "Your lie that you weren't there."

She was sniffling. The tears beginning to slide down her cheeks. "I think you were there. That your father grabbed for you as he choked. That he tore the button off your sweater as he fell. I think you watched him die."

"No!" She was crying now, big gulping sobs. Her face behind her hands. This was my cue to comfort her. To reach out to her like the big sister I'd never had. But I'm not that type of person. Instead, I watched and waited until the storm began to subside. The sobs became hiccups. And, finally, the hands came down.

"You did." My voice was calm. There was no point in revealing the anger burning inside me. By all accounts, David Canaday had been a terror. By all accounts…"Did you kill him?"

"What? No!" The speed with which she answered, as well as the sudden change in tone, made me look at her anew. "No way."

"No?" I thought of the painkillers in the medicine cabinet. The inhaler. "You didn't help him along?"

"I—" She stopped, shook her head. "No. I'll confess, I wasn't always the most patient. My dad could be—He was…" She bit her lip. "He was a bastard, okay? And at some point, I quit arguing with him. I even told him—" Here she stopped to laugh, a cold exhalation that could have been part cough. "That it was his funeral. But no."

While she was talking, the door behind her opened. Jill stepped in. Now the youngest Canaday girl stood behind her sister, stunned.

"That morning, I had a million things to do. I had his party to get ready for. I wanted to clean. And he—well, he was being himself. Insisting that I double check the guest list. Make sure his beloved ex-partner was going to be there. He had an announcement to make. Something with his will, I had no doubt. Though we've already heard what the big surprise there was.

"I just wanted to get him his breakfast. Get out and do my errands. Have some time for myself. He'd already rejected the eggs I made. His stomach was always bothering him. I just wanted to go out, so I made him some herbal tea. And he was on me about how it tasted. Did I put the honey in it? Did I squish the leaves up in the little tea ball correctly? And then he…he started coughing, and he vomited a little, and he—"

"He grabbed for you." I filled in the blank. "He grabbed for you as he fell."

She nodded, her face crumpling up on itself again. "I only wanted to go out." She took a big breath. "And so I did."

I looked at her, then up at her sister. Jill stood frozen in place, mouth open slightly. It was a lot to take in. A lot to confess. I wondered if there would be more. If Jill would be the one to get it from her. Or Creighton.

The younger woman stepped forward. This was her house, too. Her family. I waited, curious as to how she would approach her sister. What she would say and how.

"Jackie?" Her voice was calm. Shock, I figured. It would be a lot to take in. "What are you talking about?" Her sister turned to look at her, and I saw the resemblance again, beyond the sagging jawline, the tear-swollen eyes. "Dad hated herbal tea."

Chapter Fifty-five

In the history of non sequiturs, it wasn't much. It did call me to attention, as quickly as a high-pitched whistle would to a dog. Even Jackie sat up straighter, as the implications sank in.

"Wait." I raised my hand for silence. "The day your father died, he was drinking something unusual for him? Something new?"

"No. No, he wasn't." Jackie shook the idea off. "You don't know, Jill. You haven't been around much. Dad was changing. He was getting out more."

Jill raised her eyebrows. I'd never seen her directly rebut her oldest sister, but those brows were saying something.

"Okay, so maybe he hadn't changed that much." Jackie got it. "But he was trying new things. Laurence Wilkins was getting him to."

"He was?" Jill sounded so surprised that I almost forgot she was on friendly terms with her father's former partner.

Jackie was nodding. "They had lunch every week, over at Mr. Wilkins'. I guess he got Dad to try this new tea."

"I didn't think things were that great between them…" Jill sounded thoughtful, though I couldn't tell if she was questioning the friendship or her sister's veracity.

"Oh?" I looked at the younger woman.

"I know they were partners, but they weren't…Dad could be—" She shrugged. "You know, he was getting crankier with age."

Something was brewing here. Something besides tea. It was time for me to step in.

"Did Wilkins give your father this tea?" The two sisters stared at each other. Then both started to speak.

"You can't think—"

"He's had it every day."

"Wait a minute." I put my hands up, calling for quiet. "First things first, I doubt this had anything to do with your father's death. Nothing showed in the toxicology reports. Nothing that they didn't expect anyway. But just to be on the safe side, why don't we find that tea and we can bring it to Detective Creighton for testing."

"Sure." Jackie might still be sniffling, but the confession—such as it was—had been good for her. She seemed positively sprightly as she led us back into the kitchen and over to the cabinet. "It's not here." She looked around at us. "I must have used it up, when we had people over. Someone always wants to avoid caffeine. But that just proves that there wasn't anything wrong with it."

"Of course not." Now it was Jill's turn to be defensive. "Isn't it clear that Jackie will say anything?" This was directed to me. "Larry wouldn't—"

"Larry?" Jackie was as shocked as I'd been. "So now he's 'Larry'? Is that where you've been every night?"

"Pru, you can't believe—" Jill tried to ignore her sister. Jackie didn't give her a chance.

"Jill, he's twice your age. More. He's Dad's age."

"Hey, look." I broke in. This was none of my business. It was also beside the point. "What you two do is your own business. But Jackie? You've got to tell Detective Creighton what happened. There are other cases that he could be working on."

"I can't believe you let Dad die." Jill wasn't letting go. "You just stood there and watched ..."

"*I* can't believe you're involved with his partner." Jackie was ratcheting up the volume.

"Ex-partner." Jill was standing up for herself. "Larry was always constrained by Dad anyway. Dad was so old-fashioned."

"Jill, there's a lot you don't know." Jackie wasn't giving up. "About Mr. Wilkins, when Judith worked for him…"

"No." Jill shook her sister off. "I know what she was accused of. It isn't true. Mrs. Wilkins was always sick, from when I was a little girl."

"Jill—" Jackie wasn't about to let this go. "I'm not saying she hurt anybody. I know what everyone said, but—"

"Look, Larry has told me all about it, okay?" Jill's face had gone white. "He's told me everything. It's ancient history."

"From what I hear, she was never charged with any wrongdoing." I turned from one woman to the other. "Never formally charged—but basically run out of town. If there's any more to the story, one of you has got to tell me."

The silence was so thick, I could have cut it with my knife. And in that moment, I pitied Judith. No wonder she had lashed out—first at Jill and then at Jackie. Neither bothered to defend her.

"Call Detective Creighton," I said, finally. These Canaday girls were making me sick. "Tell him everything. If you won't, I will. And believe me, it will sound better coming from you."

Chapter Fifty-six

If the Canadays were examples of how sisters turned out, I was glad to be an only. The dynamics at least kept me occupied as I drove back over to Wilkins' place—to what I trusted would be a much simpler kind of interaction.

"Hey, Pru." Dave was leaning into his truck when I pulled up. He straightened up with a toolbox in his hands. "I was finishing up for the day."

"Pru." I turned. Mack was standing there, a takeout hot cup in his hand.

"Mack." I swung back to Dave for an explanation.

"This kind of work," he said, "I need someone to hold the other end of the board."

I nodded. Carpentry can call for an extra hand. I didn't like that my referral had hired my ex, but I shouldn't have been surprised. They were friends, and Beauville was a small town. Hey, maybe this would be good for Mack. Get him back into working mode. I didn't like the look of that cup, though. Mack didn't used to like coffee that much.

"I'll go get the tarp," said Mack. Still holding the cup, he turned and walked back around the house.

"I gather there's some bad blood between you two." Dave was leaning back into the truck bed, securing the toolbox, I figured.

It wasn't a question, but I answered anyway. "I'm not crazy about having him work on a job like this." I nodded toward the house. "Wilkins is a lawyer. He's a real stickler for details, too."

"Don't worry, Pru." He surfaced again. "I can run a job. And nobody—not even your lawyer-client—is entirely one thing or another. Mack is trying. He really is." He looked back toward where my ex had disappeared and rubbed his chin. "He deserves a second chance."

I opened my mouth, and then shut it. Dave had a point. He also had taken a job on virtually no notice.

He was watching me now. "Wanna see what I've done?"

"Yeah." I followed him around to where Mack was folding a canvas tarp. Up near the roofline, I could see new wood, neatly attached. Part of it—over by the window—was already painted.

"You think you'll finish tomorrow?" I pointed to the raw wood.

"Weather permitting," said Dave.

"Hey," I interrupted. Mack was pouring out the contents of his cup.

"What? I'm watering the plants." He shook the rest of the takeout cup into the flower bed. "They need something after what our ladders did."

"I'm not sure they need what you drink."

"It's Dunkin, Pru. A regular—cream and three." He shook his head sadly. "Want to smell my breath?"

I shook my head, but as he carried off the folded tarp—and the empty cup—I stepped over to the spiky leaves and got a whiff. More cream than coffee, sweet as candy. It brought me back to when I used to keep half-and-half in the fridge for Mack. When that was how he started his day.

"Dave was going to leave the tarp down." Mack had come back for his tools. "I was the one who pointed out that it was killing the plants."

I looked at my ex. It was odd hearing him trying to score points. But Dave seemed to accept it.

"I don't have an eye for these things," he was saying. "But Mack here says that they're already budding."

I looked over at the bedraggled greenery. Neither the tarp nor the ladder had done those pointy leaves any favors. Plants in New England, though, they've got to learn to deal or they don't survive.

"One good rain, they'll spring back, I bet." I kicked at a bruised leaf. My mother had flowers like these. I remembered spikes of flowers, pink and purple. "So you think one more day?"

He nodded. "As long as Mack is available to help me."

I smiled. He was making a point, too. So, yeah, I'd let him. As long as the job got done to the client's satisfaction. Who was I to begrudge my ex some honest labor?

"May I help you?" Laurence Wilkins appeared at the corner of the house, the sheltie close by his side. "Is there some problem out here?"

"Not at all, sir." Dave hesitated a moment before that final syllable. It did the trick, however. The lawyer smiled, almost imperceptibly. "Just cleaning up and Ms. Marlowe here came by to check on how we were doing."

"Good, good." The sheltie took us in. Three people represent an irresistible herding opportunity to a sheltie, and as I watched, she began to circle around us.

"What's he doing?" Mack looked back as her low spotted back passed close behind him, the black leather nose sniffing at the ladder that was still leaning against the wall.

"She," I corrected. "She's herding us."

Wilkins nodded. "It's her training." I didn't bother to set him right.

"No, girl!" he called as the dog waded deeper into the foliage by the house. "Come here."

"This is my job." I heard her reply. *"I need them closer."*

"She's fine." I interceded. "She's doing her job."

"Her job?" Dave looked amused. "Don't tell me she's going to take over my gig now."

"Come here!" Wilkins' voice was getting louder.

"She could do all our jobs." I joked, to lighten the mood. "Honestly, Mr. Wilkins, she's not bothering anything."

"Biscuit!" The dog looked up, and I felt rather than saw the confusion on the slender doggy face.

"*This is what I do,*" her brown eyes were sad. "*You do what you need to do.*"

"May I take her for a walk?" I don't usually offer my services for free. I wasn't going to let him bully the dog.

"What? Oh, no." He snapped his fingers, and with a doggy sigh, Sheila made her way over to heel beside him. "That's what we were about to do."

"You might try tossing some tennis balls." I can't help it. I don't like to see an animal suffer from lack of stimulation. "Let her round them up."

"I'll keep that in mind," he said, as they walked away.

"What's his problem?" Mack sidled up to me as I watched Wilkins and the dog.

I shook my head. "He doesn't understand her." Mack was pretty much out of my life before my transformation. He knew what I did for a living though. "A dog like that, she gets bored, she's going to get into trouble."

"Sounds like someone I know." His voice was low.

I shot him a look. He was working for me, more or less. I did not need Dave or his other pals thinking I was fair game. But he backed up, hands up in the air.

"I meant that Canaday girl!"

Judith, of course. They all knew her from Randy. Besides, it was easier to accept his excuse than argue, especially since Dave was coming over again.

"Well, I'll leave you guys to it." I addressed the carpenter. "Call me if you need me."

Chapter Fifty-seven

It wasn't that I didn't trust Jackie Canaday. I didn't, but that wasn't the point. It's human nature to avoid unpleasant tasks, and admitting to an officer of the law that you lied about the death of a family member is what most of us would call unpleasant.

I did, however, want this all resolved. Thanks to that kitten, I'd gotten involved in their affairs. The sooner these were all ironed out, the faster I could be on my way. With, ideally, a check for my time and troubles.

"Hey, Jim." I got his voice mail as I drove. "Wanted to see if Jackie Canaday checked in with you. Turns out she's got quite a story to tell."

I left it at that. If the woman had any brains, she'd have called him. Hell, if she'd had any brains she would admitted that she'd been there and saved herself—her family—the ordeal of the extended autopsy. If not, my message would be enough to get Creighton to reach out. It wasn't, I reminded myself again, my problem.

I was almost home when my phone rang. Jill Canaday, I saw with a glance. Doubtless wanting to complain about her sister. Doubtless trying to draw me back in again. I let it go to voice mail, feeling more free than I had in weeks. It was nearly five. Cocktail hour. In the next day or two, Judith would fly back to L.A., and Laurence Wilkins' house would be made whole again. Tonight, I'd write up a final invoice that I would deliver personally. And in two weeks, all things being equal, I'd deliver up the kitten, healthy and hale, to Jill. Or to Jackie. Whoever had won that particular catfight.

"Hey, Wallis." I called out as I walked into my house. "Ernesto. I'm home!"

I threw my jacket over a chair and saw a flash of fur. "Sorry, were you sleeping there?"

"I was…waiting." Her eyes were flashing, her tail lashing back and forth. *"You've got to do something about that kitten."*

"Oh, hell." Something was wrong. I could tell. "Where is he?"

"Where else?" I followed her as she led me to my bedroom where Ernesto was curled, fast asleep on my pillow.

"Wallis?" I turned to her. I'd picked up discomfort. That something was wrong.

"Look." Her whiskers, as well as her Egyptian nose, pointed, and I saw it. An old catnip mouse I'd gotten Wallis, back in the day. Now it lay, half-eviscerated, on the comforter.

I laughed with relief. "I'm sorry, Wallis. I'll get you a new one."

"No, you silly. Look!" I wasn't sure what I was supposed to be seeing. Ernesto was sleeping normally. He looked peaceful. Healthy. I sat on the bed and placed my hand on his fur. His heartbeat felt steady and calm.

"Christ." Wallis' use of profanity was unnerving. *"Don't you have a phone to answer?"* She grabbed the dismembered toy and jumped to the floor just as my cell rang.

"Hello?" I didn't recognize the number.

"Pru, thank God!" The voice, however, was familiar. Jill— even more breathless than usual. "I've been trying to reach you."

"I just got home." I waited, as Wallis batted at the toy. If Jill was expecting me to invite her over, she could think again.

"Can you come over? I'm at Larry's." I closed my eyes. Willed myself not to lose my temper. "It's Biscuit."

"Jill…" I took a breath. If Jill told me about the dog acting out, I would explain how to handle it. That poor animal was probably bored out of her mind. If she'd begun barking incessantly or wouldn't stop herding Jill, it wasn't my fault.

"She collapsed. Panting." A pause, during which I could hear Jill's own breath. "I think she's really sick."

"Wait, what happened?" I looked up at the clock. "I was there less than forty minutes ago."

"I know." Jill had the grace to sound a little ashamed. "I was in the house. My sister was coming over and I didn't want her to—I didn't want to see her. I heard you when Larry took Biscuit out for her walk."

I thought back. The little dog had been herself. Curious, eager. Ready to play.

"Jackie got here just as Larry came back." Jill was still talking. "I waited until they'd gone into his office and I—I wanted to let Biscuit out some more. He didn't really take her for a long walk. I filled her bowl and went to call her, and that's when I found her."

"Found her?" Wallis, alerted by my tone, was staring at me.

"She's collapsed. Just lying there, all hunched up. And her breathing—Pru, it doesn't sound good."

"Jill, listen to me." I tried to recall everything I knew about the sheltie. Thought about her love for treats—for sweets. "Is there any chance she could have eaten chocolate?"

"What? No, there's no chocolate in the house. I wouldn't.... Oh, Pru."

She started to wail again. I had to think fast. If I were there, I would have grabbed her face. Made her look at me. Made her focus. All I could do now was use my command voice—pitched low, a little louder, trying to get through. "She may have eaten something else—something she shouldn't. Has she vomited?"

"I don't know, Pru. I don't know!" This wasn't working.

"Do you think you can make her vomit?" I thought of my own animal emergency kit. "Do you have any ipecac or any other emetic?"

"I don't know!" She was wailing. "I'm at Larry's and he's gone out and, Pru—she's shaking!"

"Jill!" I yelled to get her attention—this girlishness was no longer cute—as I made some quick calculations. "Look, you've got to take her to County and quickly. I'll call Doc Sharpe and tell him you're on your way. And, Jill? Hurry."

While Wallis watched, lashing her tail, I called Doc Sharpe. When Pammy picked up and offered to take a message, I may have been less than polite.

"Pru, you don't have to bark at me." She giggled at her own weak joke.

"Pammy, this is an emergency."

"For emergencies, we recommend taking the ill or injured animal over to Amherst…"

"Pammy!" I yelled loudly enough so that Wallis gave me a perturbed look. "I know the script, but I can't. This is serious."

"Well, I don't know what to tell you Pru." A pause, during which I heard her pop her gum. Xylitol—the sweetener in sugar-free gum—was another sweet canine poison. The possibilities were endless. "Doc Sharpe's left already. I'm only here because he told me I had to clean the cages."

"He left?" Doc Sharpe practically lived at County. "Never mind." I didn't have time to get into it. The man was allowed to have a life. I also didn't have much choice. Jill would already be on the road, and County was better stocked than I was. Cursing my poverty—I was always telling myself to put together an animal emergency kit, or at least get some activated charcoal—I gave Pammy some quick directions. She started to sputter and protest, but I was in alpha mode.

"Just do it, Pammy." I didn't have time for another Jill Canaday.

"Jeez," she whined a bit, but at least she heard me. "You don't have to yell."

Before I could take off, however, I had to figure out what was going on with Ernesto. "Wallis, what is it? What am I missing?"

"Just go, Pru." Wallis was looking at me, her green eyes holding my gaze. *"He's sleeping."* She didn't add that he would be okay. Cats are pragmatic and, like all animals, realists. She was giving me permission, and with a nod I took it.

Jill was racing up the walk to County when I pulled up,

burning rubber as I screeched to the curb. "It's closed!" She was sobbing, the dog in her arms limp. "It's closed."

"Come with me." Leading her around to the side entrance, I pounded on the door. Not even six, and the place was locked tight. Pammy, still motivated by my outburst, opened it relatively quickly and stood back as I barged inside. "This way."

Switching on lights as we went, I led Jill—and a curious Pammy—into the first examining room, where I motioned for Jill to lay the sheltie on the table. "Hold her, please." I needn't have bothered—the dog lay still. Her tongue lolled out of her half-open mouth, her eyes dull. Affecting a calm I didn't feel, I placed one hand on the sheltie's silky fur. I could feel her heart racing. It felt irregular, but my own pulse was going so fast, I couldn't be sure.

"Sheila?" I focused on her soft warmth, hoping to get through. As I did, I pictured the house, the garden. The torn leaf clusters under the ladder.

"There were squirrels there." Her voice was weak. *"I heard them."*

"Good girl." I wasn't sure who I was talking to, but both Jill and Pammy stood to attention. On the table, Sheila wagged her tail once and then let it lay limp. It was both heartening and heartbreaking. I had to act fast.

"Pammy, you have the hydrogen peroxide?" For once, the ditzy assistant seemed to have followed my instructions, and it was the work of a minute to fill a syringe. "The basin?"

She held it out. This was the scary part. Hydrogen peroxide will usually make an animal urp up whatever has made her sick, but not always. I had helped Doc Sharpe insert a stomach tube to give activated charcoal, but that was iffy—especially without a qualified assistant—and if the sickness or poison was of a different sort, then making the poor dog vomit might actually be counterproductive. I wasn't prepared to intubate if Sheila stopped breathing. I wasn't entirely sure what had poisoned her—or if, indeed, it was poison.

"Jill, I'm kind of flying by the seat of my pants here." I held up the syringe. "This may not work."

"We have to try it." She sounded confident, and for a moment I believed her.

"Your boyfriend may not agree." I wasn't going to not act. I was, however, suddenly aware of the potential penalty for killing a lawyer's pet. "I mean, if I'm wrong, and Sheila's gotten into some kind of caustic chemical or she chokes…"

"Pru, please. Just do it!" Another limp wag of the tail. And so I did. With Jill holding the dog upright, and Pammy holding the basin, I injected a large syringe of the fizzing, bubbling solution down the sheltie's throat.

I withdrew the syringe. We waited. At least the dog was still breathing. I hadn't choked her.

"Is she gonna…" Before Pammy could finish, the dog on the table lurched. I held my breath. If Sheila went into convulsions, there was precious little I could do. But then, with a second lurch and a kind of choking bark, the sheltie heaved, spewing foam and what looked like green vegetable matter past the basin and onto Pammy herself.

"Can I put this down now?" Pammy held out the empty basin.

"Yes, thanks." For all her prissiness, the ditzy blonde aide had been a brick. I turned to pull a handful of paper towels from the dispenser for her. As she wiped herself down, I knelt to clean up the mess on the floor.

"Look!"

I jumped up, terrified. Jill was still holding the little sheltie. But now, instead of laying, limp, in her arms, the little dog was struggling to her feet, her claws scrabbling against the metal of the table.

"You saved her!" Pammy hugged me.

"*We* saved her." I hugged the assistant back, ignoring her damp jacket. "Good work, folks."

"Thank you, Pru." Jill's face glowed as she beamed at me.

That's when I realized that something was wrong. Now I'm not a big one for hero worship, but it wasn't just the younger woman's wide dark eyes that were making me uncomfortable.

"Tell me again what happened," I finished mopping up the floor, more to make my questions sound like they weren't important than because I wanted to do Pammy's job for her. "Starting with after I left."

"After you left?" I reached for the basin and wiped it down. Rinsed the syringe and put it aside to be sterilized.

"I told you." Jill sounded exhausted. She had reason to be, but I had my reasons. "Larry took Biscuit for a walk, and I guess he ran into Jackie. Maybe that was why the walk was so short." She paused, and I followed up, peering at her over my shoulder.

"Did you see them? Do you know if Jackie had any interaction with the dog?"

"What? No." Jill was shaking her head. "If you're thinking that my sister…"

"I'm not saying anything." I wasn't. There are a lot of things that could sicken a dog. "I mean, it sounds like your boyfriend wasn't the most careful of caregivers."

It was a low blow. It was also the truth, and I was sick of pretending. Jill flushed. Pammy, meanwhile, had gone mooneyed. She might not know the details, but she knew a soap opera when she heard one.

"No way, uh uh." Jill wasn't getting mad at me. Not yet. "He's just busy. He doesn't know animals. Doesn't connect with them like you or I do…" She paused, and I waited. Something had occurred to her.

"Larry Wilkins is your boyfriend?" Pammy couldn't resist. I cursed her silently.

"He's a friend, okay?" Jill was on the defensive now, but something in Pammy's little moue of disapproval made me take note. "And he's not a—a dog poisoner."

"Okay." I ceded the point for the moment. "Then what do you think happened?"

She bit her lip, which made her look even younger than her years. "Maybe she got into the garbage?"

It was possible. But even as Jill spoke, another possibility was dawning on me. That Jill had sickened the dog. Maybe to cast blame on her sister or her lover. Or maybe—and this thought made my skin crawl—to get closer to me. Munchausen's by proxy, with a pet. I stepped over to the table to check on the poor dog.

"How are you doing, girl?" I stroked her head as I asked, by all appearances simply another affectionate human. Silently, focusing in on those soulful eyes, I asked another question. *"What happened to you?"*

"Sweet..." She was still weak, exhausted by her ordeal. Even as her thoughts reached me, I could feel how tired she was. How much she wanted to sleep. *"I'm a good girl..."*

"Yes, you are, Sheila." I cupped her head in my hands. "You're a very good girl."

"I had to..." The doggie consciousness was slipping away.

"You did it again." Jill interrupted us. I could have slapped her. Instead, I fixed a smile on my face and turned to her.

"What are you talking about?" I asked.

"The way you talk to her." A chill started up my spine as I realized my mistake. "Pru," Jill was asking, "why do you call our dog Sheila?"

Chapter Fifty-eight

"Just seems like the right name for her," I said. I could feel a flush rising up my cheeks. Anger, more than embarrassment. So I went on offense. "I mean, Biscuit? Really?"

"I guess." She kept eyeing me. But by then, the examining room was back together. And Pammy, at any rate, was eager to get going.

"You think I can still charge Doc for the OT?" She had her keys in hand.

"I'll ask him," I promised her as I rummaged around in the cabinet. "I know the financial situation—" I paused, remembering. "Hey, Jill, where does Larry stand on the Friends of County?"

She looked at me blankly as I handed her a cardboard carrying case. It was the kind we give out when people adopt cats or rabbits, but Sheila was small enough to fit—at least for the ride home.

"Your father," I explained as I lifted the snoozing sheltie into the box. "He was on the board, and he was pretty consistently against raising expenses. Even for behavioral training. But maybe you have some influence?"

"Oh, I don't know about that." She was blushing now, too. Pammy, who was pointedly holding the door to the exam room open, raised her eyebrows to me over the other girl's back. Clearly, the blonde assistant had some thoughts about the May-December romance. And about the need to leave. "Larry's been a big supporter of my work. I mean, the work I want to do," Jill was saying to the floor. "He's been after me to get more involved."

"He could put his money where his mouth is." I pointed out, as I ushered her into the hall. "Take your father's place on the board."

"He's actually been encouraging me to take his place," she said. "But he already knows all about it, and there's a lot of paperwork."

"Doesn't seem that complicated." I followed her to her car as Pammy locked up. "I'm sure you could do it."

"Thanks. Maybe I'll take a look." That blush again as she looked up at me. I helped her slide Sheila's carrier into the back seat.

"I want you to keep an eye on her." I adjusted a seatbelt around the box. "Any more trouble breathing, any seizures, anything like that, you call me." She nodded vigorously, as I reached out one more time, trying to make contact with the exhausted dog. "And call Doc Sharpe first thing tomorrow. You should have him give Biscuit a thorough going-over."

"Will do, boss." I turned, breaking contact with Sheila, but Jill seemed to be all smiles. "But I think I'm going to start calling her Sheila. It just seems right."

Chapter Fifty-nine

I was too tired for anything serious after that. But too wired to call it a night, I started driving and found myself downtown—if you can call anywhere in Beauville that. I'd pulled up behind Happy's before I'd realized where I was.

"Beer." I corrected the barman as he reached for the bourbon. One thing I didn't need tonight was to get a load on.

"On the wagon, huh?" Mack. I should have known. He emerged from the depths of the bar, bottle in hand. "Me, too."

"I don't think beer counts." I reached for my own bottle and raised it in greeting. Mack did the same, and rested his on the bar without taking a drink. That might have cost him, I couldn't tell for sure, but he'd made his point.

"Not when I'm working." He read my look. "Now that I'm working again."

"Good for you." I looked past him. Happy's is dark at the best of times. Call it design, call it evolution. People don't come here to be seen. "You here with Dave?"

"You looking for him?" He eyed me, curious. I didn't deign to answer. "No, just some of the guys," he said finally. "Join us if you want." With a shrug, he was gone, leaving me feeling oddly alone.

Happy's. This was my place as much as Mack's, only now I felt like a stranger. It wasn't gender. I'd always been one of the few women who hung out here. I'd always been able to hold my own. More likely it was Creighton. Everyone knew I was with a cop, and that made everyone wary. Even, I figured, my ex.

Only I wasn't. Not tonight. In fact, not for the last couple of nights. My choice, I figured. I could have called him. Gone home and waited. Not that either option would free me of the basic underlying problem. I cared for Creighton. We had something—something he'd called "love." But if he ever found out the truth, if he ever really got to know me, that would all disappear.

I took a pull from my bottle then, closing my eyes as the cold beer ran down my throat. Craving the faint buzz that would take the edge off the day, off the loneliness that could never really end. Drinking for the feel of it. It wasn't that I didn't understand where Mack was coming from. I did. Too much, maybe. That was why I'd asked for a beer. That was why I'd waited till now to drink it.

"Want another?" I swallowed with a start. Randy, from the smoke shop, was standing before me, a little too close. Something about his smile told me that he could see my thirst.

"No, thanks." I put the bottle down on the bar. It was, I realized, empty. Happy brought over another. "I can get my own."

"I like a woman who can drink." I hadn't asked. He didn't make it seem like a compliment. "My girl, now, she'd be a lot happier if she could put it down like you just did. A lot less uptight."

"Your girl?" I smiled, wondering when Judith was going to break the news. Maybe she'd just take off without telling him. "You and the Canaday girl still an item?"

"Yeah, well, kind of. Again." He looked at the floor, then at the bar. "Hey, Happy, we need another round."

"She blew you off, huh?" I couldn't really blame him for trying. Judith was a looker, and her time in L.A. had taught her how to make the most of what she had. Randy, on the other hand, had only gotten fat and sad.

"No way," he said, with something like a laugh. "We might even get married now. Now that her father is out of the way. Hey, barkeep!"

"What's your hurry?" The barman came over, grumbling, two beers in hand. He placed them on the bar and leaned over, arms apart, like he was daring Randy to take them. Randy broke quickly, pulling some crumpled bills out of his pocket. I nodded, taking it all in. You have to be pretty bad not to have a tab at Happy's. Maybe it was more than self-control that had Randy and Mack drinking PBRs tonight.

"You're lucky we still come here." Randy barked. He'd seen me watching.

"Like you have anyplace else to go." The barman counted the bills and turned away. "You good?" This was to me.

"Yeah, I'm good." I pulled a bill out of my wallet and slid it across the bar. Waited until the wizened barman had it firmly in hand, and then I turned. Unlike Randy and Mack, I did have someplace else to go.

〉〉〉

"You're home." Wallis greeted me at the door.

"Yeah, I'm sorry, Wallis." I tossed my keys on the table. "I should have come right home. I was just—"

"Ernesto's fine. He always was." She followed me into the kitchen. *"You, however, look like a fledgling someone's been practicing on."*

"I feel like it." Rather than explain, I reached for the Maker's Mark. I was home, I was safe. I didn't have anyone else waiting for me.

"I'm not sure that's what you need." A healthy swallow, and still those green eyes looked sharp.

"Maybe not, Wallis." Another swallow as I kicked off my boots and headed up to bed. "But it is what I can get."

Chapter Sixty

The next morning opened bright and sunny, and as soon as I'd walked Growler I headed over to County. Doc Sharpe was back at work—Jill had texted me—but I wanted to see for myself how Sheila was doing. Besides, I realized, I might have to explain myself to the vet.

I found him in the same examining room we'd used the night before. Jill was standing, observing, as the vet examined the little dog. They both glanced up as I came in. Jill looked anxious, and I suspected she hadn't slept. Doc Sharpe, as usual, was unreadable, his face as set as New Hampshire granite.

"Morning." He nodded to me as I squirted some Purell onto my hands. Seeing as how I'd been way outside the bounds last night, today I was playing strictly by the book.

"Good work last night, Pru." I needn't have worried. The old Yankee didn't hand out praise lightly. "You may have saved this little gal's life."

In truth, Sheila looked like a different dog. Standing, alert, on the same examining table where she had slumped the evening before, she looked around curiously as Doc Sharpe moved his stethoscope over her compact torso.

"Treats?" The sheltie was a little confused by the attention. *"Good dog?"*

"Good dog," I replied out loud. "And thanks, Doc. I'm glad to hear it." I wanted to ask about his absence. About why he'd left early yesterday, but my questions could wait.

"Yes, yes." He nodded, pursing his mouth. "She sounds good."

Putting the stethoscope away, he took the dog's jaws in his hand. Out of habit I reached to steady her, but Jill was there first, holding the dog still as Doc Sharpe opened her mouth.

"Some irritation," he said after a minute or so. "That's to be expected."

"It is?" Jill knitted her brow.

"The emetic." The vet moved from Sheila's mouth to her ears. "No, I'd say she ate something that didn't agree with her. And your fast thinking, Pru, got it out before it could do any lasting harm."

"I'm glad." I didn't expect the flood of relief that washed over me. Jill, meanwhile, looked like she was going to collapse. "Are you okay?" I asked her.

"Yeah, it's just…" I took her place by the dog, as she collapsed against the cabinet. "It was stressful." She looked up at the vet. "Pru told me I should stay up to watch her, and I did."

Doc Sharpe looked at me, his raised eyebrows asking the question.

"I said you should be alert to any changes." It wasn't my fault if the girl overreacted. "But I'm glad she's okay."

Jill nodded. She still looked distracted, though, and I was getting the sense that it wasn't fatigue.

"Was Larry upset?" I could sense Doc Sharpe's surprise at my use of the lawyer's first name, but I kept my eyes on the girl.

"No, not about…" Jill bit her lip. "Not about Sheila. That's what we're calling her now, Doc. He seemed angry that I took her here without him."

"He must feel responsible." Doc Sharpe chimed in. "This is his dog."

"Maybe." Jill didn't seem convinced. "Hey," her voice perked up, eager to change the subject. "I know it's silly, but…"

"But what?" I didn't have time to wait her out.

"I offered her some of her favorite treats—sweet potato, with peanut butter. They're sweet, you know? But she didn't want them."

Curious. *Sweet*, Sheila had said to me. Doc Sharpe, however, was already responding. "I wouldn't worry too much. She's had a scare. Might still have a raw tum, you know. I'd say she's in fine shape, all things considered." The vet clearly thought the subject was closed. "And if you don't mind?"

"Not at all." I was used to cleaning up after exams. "I hope you're feeling better," I added as the vet washed his hands and forearms, up to the elbow.

"What? Oh, I'm fine." He was rinsing, in water hot enough to steam.

"I thought, because you left earlier than usual last night…" This was awkward. The vet was allowed to have a private life.

"Business, Pru." He pulled a wad of towels from the dispenser. "Damned business."

That was harsh language from him, and so I stepped back. "Fair enough, Doc."

"I'm sorry, Pru." He had the grace to look embarrassed. "I just—bah!—money."

"If I can be of any help…"

"You already are." He turned from me to Jill. "And now I'm afraid I've got another appointment. You take good care of that dog now. And stick with Pru here. You can learn a lot from her."

With that he left us, and I lowered Sheila to the floor as Jill hooked the lead onto her collar. No need to carry the sheltie today.

"What's wrong, Jill?" Now that we were alone, I wanted to get to the bottom of this. "This isn't just about staying up to watch the dog."

"No." She wasn't looking at me. Sheila was aware of her attention and wagged her tail. "I'm just—I wish you hadn't mentioned Larry, that's all."

"You had his dog." I pointed out the obvious. "It's clear that you two are at least friends."

She nodded, sadly, Sheila watching her every move. "It's not him," Jill said finally, and I remembered the day before.

"Do you really think I'd carry tales to Jackie?" Jill had been hiding. That may have been what allowed Sheila to eat whatever had endangered her life.

"It's not you," Jill said. "She's got this boyfriend now."

I shook my head, confused.

"He's friends with that guy, the one who's doing the work on Larry's house?"

Of course. Beauville isn't that big. If Jackie was seeing any member of the working class—or even the non-working class— odds were, he drank at Happy's.

"You think Dave or Mack will tell her you were there?" I didn't want to make this hard on her. I did want her to face reality. "You are an adult, Jill."

"It's complicated." She made to leave, but as she reached for the door, she turned back toward me one more time. "I'm trying to do something. Un-do some of the damage my dad did, and I don't want anyone—I don't even want Larry to know, you know?"

"I think so." I didn't, but I had an idea. Something besides the various mind trips he'd played on all three of his daughters. Before she could pass out of the door, I dropped down, ostensibly to pet the animal I had saved. "I know that Sheila is in good hands with you," I said. Silently, I entreated the dog. *"What is going on?"* I asked. *"What do you sense?"*

"I knew," said the dog, her dark eyes meeting mine. *"I knew all along."*

Chapter Sixty-one

I hung around after Jill left, hoping to get more out of Doc, all the while mulling over the sheltie's words. I'd known animals to endanger themselves in defense of others—their people or their young—but Sheila hadn't been fighting off an intruder. Thoughts of her age came to mind again. Cognitive dysfunction can take many forms.

While I waited, I put on a coat and gloves. Those enclosures Pammy hadn't cleaned the night before weren't going to get better with age.

"Want a hand?" I was surprised to see Pammy in the cat room. I'd have thought she would gladly have forgotten the ostensible reason for her overtime the night before.

"Yeah, sure." She handed me a spray bottle, while she gingerly poured the contents of a litterbox into a plastic garbage bag. The two cats she'd displaced—young females, recovering from surgery—paced nervously in an empty cage, and I tried to send calming thoughts their way.

"Here, let me." Holding it with her fingertips like that, she was as likely to drop the bag as fill it. Besides, the faster done, the sooner those cats would be back in somewhat familiar surroundings. "My clothes are all doggy anyway."

"Thanks." She hung back as I emptied the tray. "Hey, that was exciting last night, wasn't it?"

"That's one word for it." *I knew all along...*I sprayed the tray—we use a mild bleach solution—and set it aside while I looked for more litter. Pammy jumped to get it for me, wrestling the heavy box up to the counter. More agitation from the cats.

"We were, like, heroes." I looked up. Pammy's eyes were as wide as ever, but there was something else—an element of animation, maybe—that made her pretty cheeks even pinker than usual. "You were, anyway. You saved that poor dog's life."

"It was a team effort." I rinsed off the tray and handed it to Pammy to be dried. She was trying, and Doc Sharpe still had to work with her. Besides, positive reinforcement is as good a training tool as any treat. "You were really good. Very calm."

She mewed like a kitten at the unexpected praise. If only I had something that would provoke the same reaction in these cats.

"What do you think of that girl—Jill? Why is she involved with that old letch?" Good old Pammy.

"All I know is she was caring for the dog, Pammy." I refilled the tray and put it back in the enclosure.

"She wasn't doing a very good job." The aide leaned in, her voice sinking to a conspiratorial whisper. "Letting the dog eat leaves like that."

"Speaking of, I'm going to look for Doc Sharpe now." I peeled off the gloves and handed them to her, the rebuff clear in my voice. The vet might still be busy, but I'd wait. Pammy's rosebud lips started pouting, even as I headed toward the door. Well, aversion training worked, too.

As I waited outside Doc Sharpe's consultation room, I found myself musing over what Pammy had said. Catnip was a leaf, too. It wouldn't have calmed those young females down, but it would've made them happier—assuming they were both among the sixty percent or so of felines who respond to the herb. Odds were, a pinch would have had at least one of the two lolling around and that might have calmed her companion.

But Pammy had been speaking about the other couple. She was right; it was an odd match-up. Wilkins was single, and Jill was above the age of consent. But if he was going to go for a younger woman, why hadn't he moved on Judith when she'd been practically living in his house? Unless, it hit me, he had.

"Doc?" The door had opened, but it only disgorged an older woman. A cat adoption, I was betting, as she silently brushed by me. Stereotypes exist for a reason, though Wilkins' late wife had been a dog person. Had adopted Sheila.

If Wilkins and Judith had been having an affair…

The vet looked up at me, startled.

"Pru, you're still here." He blinked, his eyes small and watery behind his glasses. "Did we have another appointment?"

"No, just touching base." He'd been a rock. He also had years of experience on me. "What do you think was up with that sheltie?"

"Who knows?" He shrugged and shook his head, as if to dismiss the craziness of all species. "By the way, how's that kitten?" I didn't know why he was distracted, but I was betting it had to do with his absence yesterday evening. "You said you were worried about the vaccine?"

"He had a bit of a reaction." The vet froze at my words. "He was off his food, a little lethargic."

"Pru." He was looking over his glasses at me now. "You know, if it's distemper, you should do the humane thing."

"I know, Doc." I did. I also knew I had an edge, not that I could explain Wallis' insight to the vet. "But I really think this was just a reaction."

"He's eating again?" Doc Sharpe was not going to be put off by generalities.

"He's better." I tried to sound confident. After all, Wallis must know what she was talking about. "So, you want me to get an adoption kit ready?" I needed to change the subject.

"Excuse me?"

"The woman—the one who just left?" I smiled, thinking of the two cats who had just been spayed. My money was on the big gray. She'd match well with the silver-haired matron.

"Ms. Kirk was not here about a cat."

"Oh." I waited, only slightly surprised. Melissa Wilkins had opted for a dog, too. "A dog, then?"

"No." The vet stepped out of the doorway, pulling the door shut behind him. "Ms. Kirk was here on a different matter entirely." He must have seen the look on my face, because he stopped and turned toward me. "Some things are private, Pru."

I nodded as he turned again and walked down the hall. The woman had been sixty if a day, but she'd had the same rimless glasses as the vet and a neat silver pageboy. Doc Sharpe had been widowed for as long as I could remember. Besides, it was spring.

"You shouldn't be bugging him, you know." I turned. Pammy had come up behind me rather quietly. She still had the gloves on from cleaning, and a sour look was scrunching her well-plucked brows together. "If there's any extra work, you know he'll give it to you anyway."

"I know that," I heard myself snap. I didn't like being surprised. "I was offering to help. I thought—"

"You're just as nosy as anyone else." She was pulling the gloves off. "And if you want to help, you can do the small animal cages. It's getting busy out front. And we have snakes." She pursed her mouth in distaste—though whether for me or the legless reptiles was anybody's guess—and held the gloves out for me to take. It was an unnecessary gesture. Protocol would have me donning fresh gloves when I changed rooms anyway.

"I'll take care of it." I took the gloves. At least I could dispose of them properly. Pammy had been a help last night, and the small mammals and lizards deserved someone to care for them, too. "And Pammy, about last night? That is the best of what we do. Thanks for helping."

She looked away, the pink coming back into her cheeks. And I went to clean more cages, feeling like at last I'd done something right.

Forty minutes later, I was waving to Pammy and heading out. The parking lot was nearly full, the sun shining off an increasing number of late-model cars. Beauville was changing, it occurred to me, as I walked over to where my vintage baby waited. It was still early for the bulk of the tourists, which meant that many of these cars belonged to year-rounders. Maybe that would be good for the town, I thought. More work for the likes of Dave and even Mack. More work for me. And maybe—it hit me, as I stopped short—more options for all of us.

Suddenly, I saw Doc Sharpe. He'd been leaning over a car window. Talking, I could see, to that same woman who had been in his office not an hour before. Had he been gone all this time? I didn't think so—not with the crowd I'd seen hovering around Pammy's desk. More likely, his visitor had come back, perhaps hoping to snare him for lunch.

As I watched, he started walking toward me—and she drove away. No lunch date today, I gathered. And since he had seen me, I waved.

"Looks like your friend was hoping to spirit you away," I said.

It was the wrong thing. Doc Sharpe was old school and intensely private, and his bushy brows furrowed. "Pru, it's not what you think."

"Doc, it's none of my business, I know." I had overstepped, and I was ready to admit it. "I'm just—well, it's nice to see you getting out. Being social."

"Ms. Kirk is not a social contact." He was looking at me strangely. "I would not mix my social life and work, Pru."

"I'm sorry, I—" I wasn't sure how to explain.

"It's nothing." He waved my apology away. "There's no way you could know. I haven't wanted you to know. But you have a right. Pru, Ms. Kirk is a forensic accountant. County may be going bankrupt."

Chapter Sixty-two

Once he started, Doc spilled it all, explaining that the money problems of the big animal hospital were worse than I had known. Not just in their severity, but also in their duration.

County had been hemorrhaging money for the last few years, the vet explained. There had been some irregularities that the gray-haired accountant was doing her best to track. Expenses had spiked. As he talked, I began to understand the struggle he'd been through—the fatigue, the pressure. All of it hidden under that gruff Yankee exterior. Yes, County still had municipal funding, but much of that had gone into an endowment—and that endowment had been shrinking slowly, rather than paying the dividends that were supposed to keep it—us—afloat.

"I'll keep going as long as I can, Pru," he'd said at last, once more rubbing his tired eyes. "But, I confess, that's why I've been urging you to—well, one reason…"

With a gruff pat on the shoulder, he had walked off, leaving me stunned. Animals will mask an illness. Hide a weakness as long as they can. I know that and expect it. But old Doc Sharpe? He had caught me by surprise.

I drove off, my mind reeling. I'd never taken Doc for the profligate type—it went against everything the old Yankee stood for—and had to wonder what else was going on. What else…or who else. When the call came in from Jill, I ignored it. Sheila was okay, and I had more important things to think about than mentoring the youngest Canaday. At the very least, if County closed I didn't need the competition.

That call did get me thinking though. Thinking that what I had to do was to cement my position with my few paying clients. Odds were, I'd run into Jill soon enough anyway. I'd planned on dropping by Wilkins' place later that afternoon. Given the weather, Dave and Mack would be finishing their painting. If I were there, I could inspect their work and dun the lawyer for a check. I was kicking myself now for starting work without a deposit. In this economy, nobody was safe. And trusting a lawyer? Well, more and more, I was learning that was never a good idea. From now on, I'd get cash up front.

With a sinking feeling in the pit of my stomach, I ran through the rest of the day's calls. If I was distracted, I did my best not to show it. I didn't need another fiasco like I'd had with Meryl Sandburg and Princess. It was close to six by the time I headed back downtown. Close to closing time, and I needed to talk to Albert.

My dark mood a stark contrast to what had become a beautiful spring day, my driving was probably a bit more aggressive than usual. I told myself I needed to get there before the animal control officer left for the day, but I was using the car to let off steam. I caught myself when I heard a grackle exclaim—not that those flashy gawpers are models of calm—but I still got there in record time and managed to slip inside the building without running into Creighton. Jackie should have told him what had happened by now. If not, well, I really had no dog in that particular family fight. Only one tiny kitten.

Frank greeted me as I walked into the animal control office, dashing across the floor to sniff at my leg.

"Hey, Frank." I squatted to be closer to eye level. "What's up?" I was speaking in a whisper, but soon realized I didn't have to. A soft snore emanating from the area of Albert's beard revealed why his mustelid companion had the run of the place.

"Looking for the sweet!" Frank wasn't always hungry, but the search for prey was a major part of his life. *"Something tasty to chew on."*

"You raiding Albert's snack drawer again?" For all his flaws, the fat man did share with his pet. Not always willingly, but he did.

"*Sweets....*" The black eyes held mine as the leathery nose twitched. "*Not good for you. Not good at all.*"

Despite everything, I had to smile. Whether Frank had picked this up from Albert or from some other dieting human, it surely had little bearing on his lithe and muscular body.

"What!" Albert woke with a snort, and I rose, silently asking the ferret's pardon.

"Hey, Albert." I walked over to the desk. I might envy Albert's job security right now but not the mess before me. A mess not entirely of his making. "What's up?"

"Not much. Heard you came by Happy's last night." He pulled himself up in his chair and brushed some crumbs off his chin. "Heard you had a run-in with Randy."

"Hardly a run-in." No, I didn't want Albert's job, but the notices piled up before him could mean work for me.

"Heard you were pretty tough on his girlfriend, too."

"Who, Judith?" I spotted a flyer about raccoons, but it was just a reminder about their protected nesting season. Another one, from what I could read upside down, seemed to cover new trapping regulations.

"In his dreams, maybe." Albert laughed. At least, I assumed it was supposed to be a laugh. Considering his success rate with women, I didn't want to encourage him. Besides, I was here for a reason.

"Hey, Al." I pulled one leaflet free from the pile. Nuisance animals. "I'm wondering if you have any more work you don't want to do. Anything like the Wilkins job."

"I don't know, Pru." He sounded a little sheepish. "I mean, Wilkins still isn't happy with what you did over there. I thought you were going to make nice?"

"I don't 'make nice.'" I had to brazen this one out. "I got rid of his squirrels. Even set him up with Dave, who's rebuilt the side of his house for him."

"Well, he called to complain again. Said you were still poking your nose in where you shouldn't." Albert looked up, blinking. "He even said you tried to poison his dog?"

"I? What?" This was too much. "I saved his dog's life, Albert. I mean, come on."

"I told him that didn't sound like you." Somehow, I doubted Albert would speak up for me to anyone. Not that he didn't like me, but that his ability to stand up to another person—particularly an angry lawyer—was minimal at best. "But, you know, he's a big deal in this town."

"Jeez…" I thought about Jill's call. If the Canaday girl had blamed the incident on me, she was going to have a lot of explaining to do. Then again—I caught my breath—it was possible that her boyfriend may have misinterpreted. Maybe that call—the one I hadn't taken—had been to warn me. "Look, Albert, Wilkins has got it all wrong. And I am going to straighten it out, okay? Just don't go giving my referrals to anyone else just yet."

"Sweet!" As I stormed out of the office, I heard Frank—still on the prowl—behind me.

"Pru, it's me." I started to play back Jill's voice mail as soon as I stepped out of the office. I didn't know how I'd gotten into this predicament. That Wilkins was angry at me for tearing a hole in his house, I understood. That he had caught me eavesdropping—even if I hadn't intended to—was another strike against me. But poisoning his dog? No way I was taking the rap for that. Saving Sheila was one of the few things I'd done right recently.

"There's something I need to talk to you about." Damn right, lady, I thought, and waited for her to get to it. "It's about Larry—Larry Wilkins."

"Pru?" I spun around, startled, to see Creighton standing behind me. Of course, I'd been standing in front of the shared building, oblivious to whoever might be watching.

"Jim." I hung up my phone, unwilling to explain. "I was just in with Albert."

"I gather." He tilted his head, his smile taking on a funny angle. "Thought you might drop in on me after."

"Had a call." I held up the phone as evidence. "Something with a client."

He nodded. "I won't keep you. Just got a call myself that I thought might interest you."

I waited. He wanted to be asked, but old habits die hard.

After about a minute he chuckled, softly, as if I'd said something funny. Then, shaking his head, he explained. "All that fuss about David Canaday? All the sniping? It wasn't anything."

"But, wait—" I thought about Jackie. About the nicotine. About the tea.

"The medical examiner has finally weighed in," he said. "I shouldn't even be sharing this with you, only I know you've been dragged into this by his daughters. The ruling is that his death was accident or misadventure, but without a finding of fault. It seems he took too much of one of his medications. So, well, I guess I can't say 'no harm,' since the guy died. But it's no foul. I'm not going to be investigating. It's a good thing we didn't hold up the funeral, huh?"

"Jim, hang on." I stepped toward him, trying to figure out what was wrong. "Did Jackie talk to you? She was going to."

He shook his head. "No, she hasn't called. But, Pru, it doesn't matter."

"No, wait," I said. "It should matter. She saw him die. She watched, and she didn't help him. And then she lied about it to you—to everyone." I swallowed, my mouth suddenly dry. "I figured it out. I got her to confess. She said she would tell you."

"Pru, it's over." His voice was gentle now. A little sad. "None of that matters anymore. There's not going to be an investigation. Not by me. Not by you. No more drama. It's over."

"Over?" I wasn't sure, but I thought he was talking about more than the case.

"Good-bye, Pru." And with that he turned and walked back inside.

Chapter Sixty-three

I was in no mood to hear Jill's whining excuses after that. Nor was I about to start drinking this early in the day. Not in Beauville, anyway, where Happy's was the only reliable outlet—for both alcohol and, it seemed, gossip. No, I wanted someone to blame for all the various troubles I'd had lately, and I knew who. Driving a little too fast for the road, I got to Larry Wilkins' house in no time flat.

"Hey, Pru." Dave Altschul was standing out front, the paint on his shirt and jeans explaining his presence there. "I was going to call you."

"What's the problem?" I eyed the carpenter. He might appear more together than Randy or Mack, but he was another of the late-night Happy's crowd.

"No problem." He sounded a little hurt. "Just that we're done. I was going to leave an invoice for Wilkins, but I thought you might want to be the one to give it to him."

"Sorry, yeah." Flustered, I brushed my hair back from my face. I'd forgotten my original reason for coming here. "I can do that."

"Okay, then." He walked past me to the cab of his truck and pulled out a clipboard. Detaching the top sheet, he handed me a surprisingly professional-looking invoice. "Here you go."

I folded it in half. "I'll take care of it immediately."

"Thanks." He was looking at me funny, so I waited. "You know, Mack's trying, Pru. He did good work for me."

"Whatever." I walked away, embarrassed, and rang the lawyer's doorbell.

"Mr. Wilkins?" He opened the door almost immediately. Over his shoulder, I saw Jill holding Sheila's leash. For some reason, she was shaking her head. "I wanted to touch base with you. I believe our work on your house is now complete."

"Really." It was a statement, rather than a question.

"Would you like to check it out?" As I made the offer, I realized I myself had not. Well, Dave was still around, in case anything needed to be done.

"Give me a minute." He walked off into the other room, and Jill ran up to me.

"What are you doing?" She reached for my hands. "Didn't you get my message?"

"Yeah, I got it." I was still holding the invoice, which was getting crushed. "I also spoke with Detective Creighton." I waited. She shook her head. "The medical examiner's report? He's not going to be investigating your father's death."

"Excuse me?" Larry Wilkins had come back and was shrugging on a jacket. "Is she bothering you, Jill?"

"No, no, not at all." Jill dropped my hands and looked away, flustered. Sheila looked up at her. I could sense her confusion.

"I heard the good news," I said, to lighten the atmosphere. "I gather the investigation into Mr. Canaday's death is going to be closed."

"Well, that is good news." He looked over at his girlfriend as he ushered me out the door. "You have to excuse Jill," he said, the moment we were outside. "She's still taking it very hard. She didn't get to say good-bye, you know."

"I know that her sisters haven't made these last few weeks easy," I added. "For you, either."

"Simply the usual." He led the way around to the side. "It's my job to ease the transition for my clients."

I laughed. "I'm sure that if David Canaday had known how much trouble his will was going to cause..." I paused. Maybe the old man had known. Maybe it had been intentional.

Wilkins smiled, a dry, thin smile. "I was thinking of Jill, to be honest."

"Of course." I wasn't surprised, not really. Jill probably inherited his services with the lion's share of the estate. What I wasn't sure about was the ethics of their involvement. "You don't represent Jill's sisters, I would imagine?"

"No, no." He stared up at the roof. So did I. Dave's repair showed up the shoddy nature of the addition. It was solid. That nest was history, like other nests from years before. "Not anymore." Wilkins' voice cut into my thoughts. "So, tell me, if the squirrels come back, will the carpentry work also be covered under the guarantee?" He smiled, looking a bit sheepish now. "I probably should have asked."

"You should have." I sounded snippy. Somehow, I didn't see Laurence Wilkins forgetting to nail down a point. "And, no, it's not. What is covered is the removal of the nuisance animals. For one year," I added for good measure. Those babies—that keening cry—they had been kept alive in the mother's memory. "So tell me, is your work time-limited too?"

His eyebrows went up. "Are you questioning me?"

"I'm wondering about all the animosity between the sisters." I was working up to asking him about Judith. About his wife, when the thought struck me. Something about the passing of time. The persistence of memory. "I'm wondering if it pre-dates the will."

"I've been close to the Canaday family for years." Perfect lawyer doublespeak. In the back of my mind, I remembered him telling me, "I watched these girls grow up."

He hadn't answered my question, but I let it slide. Judith had been cleared, after all. And now the investigation into David Canaday was being closed. I needed to focus on saving my own career, and so as we stood in the bright sunshine I pointed out where Dave and Mack had repaired the edge of the roof. Already the paint was drying. Soon the patch would be indistinguishable from the older construction.

When I was done, I handed him the invoice. He hesitated before taking it—a split second that made me wonder again about the quality of that addition. But then he uttered the magic words—"Why don't I write you a check?"—and I relaxed, following him back inside.

"Pru." Jill was waiting in the hall.

"Jill." Wilkins nodded toward her. "Ms. Marlowe and I have some business to finish up."

He opened the door to his office and walked in, but before I could, Jill grabbed my arm. "When you're done," she said, her voice low, before letting go.

"Something wrong?" The lawyer didn't sound particularly concerned.

"No." I followed him into the office. Whatever Jill was on about, I'd find out later. Right now, I was so close to getting paid, I could smell it.

"Shall I make this out to Pru Marlowe," he paused. "Or to cash?"

"Are you suggesting I'm not going to pay taxes?" For a lawyer, Wilkins was, well, squirrelly about money.

"Not at all, not at all." With a fast scribble, he filled out the check, which he handed to me.

"Thank you." I checked—he'd signed—folded it and put it in my pocket. "Now, I don't expect you'll have any problems. But if you hear anything…."

"You'll be the first to know."

I lingered a few minutes once I was outside. Jill wasn't anywhere in sight, however, and I'd had a trying day. She'd never had any trouble finding me before. If she wanted to talk, she knew my number.

Chapter Sixty-four

When I heard the doorbell a few hours later, I wasn't unhappy. If Creighton were willing to let things slide back to their usual state, I would take that. In fact, as I went to answer it, drink in hand, I realized a smile was spreading across my face. The combination of the hour and the slight formality—he hadn't bothered to ring the door in a while—held great promise for a new détente.

"Jill." I didn't bother to hide my disappointment.

"Pru, I'm sorry." She looked around, as if she could see anything in the dark. "Are you busy?"

"Uh, no." I'm not usually indecisive. I'm not usually surprised, either. Blame the bourbon. The ten seconds it took to readjust were enough. Jill Canaday was in my house and closing the door behind her.

"Jill, hang on here," I moved to stop her. "You can't just barge in."

"Pru, I've got no choice." Leaning back on the door, she looked up at me, eyes wide. "I don't know where else to go."

"Seems to me you have several options." I was big enough to throw her out. It wouldn't be pretty, though, and I'd rather talk her into leaving. "You've got your sister's house, which by all accounts is big enough to take you in. You've got your lawyer boyfriend's house…" I was going to add something about Doc Sharpe. Hell, even he had seemed to fall under the youngest

Canaday girl's spell, when she leaned in and grabbed me, nearly spilling my drink.

"That's just it, Pru. I don't have a place of my own. I don't have any privacy—and I need to think things through."

"Well, I hate to break it to you." I reached up to pull her hand off my arm. She had a strong grip. "But my place is not your new hidey hole. I've got my own life to worry about."

"But don't you see? Didn't you get my message? That's what I'm talking about." Her eyes were wide and wild. "Life and… well…death."

"Hang on." What was going on with this girl? I did know she was probably not safe out on the road. And that much as I might regret it, I'd feel responsible if anything happened to her. "Let's go into the kitchen."

Wallis had made herself scarce by then, and I kind of envied her. Still, I got Jill seated and started the coffee. No way was I wasting good bourbon on this girl.

"Spill." I leaned back on the stove, arms crossed. She had disconcerted me, grabbing my arm. Especially with the buzz I had on, I wanted physical distance between us.

"It's—you know about the medical examiner's report?"

I nodded, fixing my eyes on her face. Looking for the lie.

"It said that my dad's death was accidental, right?" Another nod. This was history. "Because I was looking through his papers and—I don't know. I've been driving around, trying to work it out. That's what I wanted to talk over with you. Maybe I'm losing it."

"You've been through a lot." I wasn't disagreeing, just giving her an out. As if on cue, Wallis arrived with Ernesto in tow.

"I guess." Jill's eyes dropped to the kitten. "Oh, he wants to play."

Wallis glanced up at me as Jill bent over Ernesto. "Yeah, he always does," I said. Wallis was staring at me, in her eyes the command: *"Listen!"*

"At least he's—" I stopped, catching myself. I couldn't tell Jill that the kitten had been obsessing about a button since I'd taken him in. "I think he's looking for a toy." A weak recovery, but the best I could do.

"What a little precious." Jill seemed grateful for the distraction.

"He left." The kitten, lamenting the loss of his playmate, his silent "voice" mournful and low. But more than that. Insistent. Demanding to be heard. *"He left."*

I was listening. I didn't know what for. Maybe I was hearing old man Canaday's final eulogy, I thought, fatigue and whiskey playing up the melancholy.

Only something wasn't sitting right. Something my buzzed brain couldn't quite work out. David Canaday couldn't have been the lost playmate. Canaday had pulled the button off his daughter's sweater in his death throes. Then he had fallen. He was gone. Jackie had then fled—Jackie who "always" locked her door. All that commotion would have sent the kitten into hiding. So who came back to kick that button, kick it once and back again? It wasn't me. I'd been too careful, backing out of the house that day. Someone had set it rolling, intentionally or not, once Ernesto had emerged. Someone had spurred the kitten's urge to play. To hunt. To kill.

"Jill?" I worked to keep my voice calm. "Who else has the keys to your father's house?"

"We all do." Jill was holding up a finger for the kitten to bat. "I mean, me and my sisters."

She glanced up at me, and I turned, to hide my face. To reach for the mugs. No, I realized. Creighton had checked out Jill's alibi. She had only arrived that morning. Would Judith? Unless...

"Would there be a set of keys with your father's papers?" Jackie had called the lawyer as her father lay gasping out his life. Even if she hadn't explained everything, she would have sounded panicked. Desperate to get out of the house. And he would have known it was time.

"I don't know. But, Pru? I read something—I saw—" I heard a gasp as the truth hit her, too. "No!"

I ignored her, focusing instead on pouring a hefty shot in each mug. We'd need it, I knew, as I tried to organize my thoughts. As I considered what to say next. Something about trust misplaced. About being young. Something that would soften the blow.

I didn't get to. And nothing softened the blow that bashed me first into the cabinet and then, as I stumbled and grabbed at the counter, to the floor.

Chapter Sixty-five

I woke confused, a child again. Unsure where I was. Frightened. Where was my mother? Where was…?

A wave of nausea roused me, urging me first to my knees and then, struggling, to my feet. I ran for the bathroom without thinking, only realizing once I was on my knees again, heaving, that it was the bathroom on the second floor. I'd woken in my old bedroom with no idea how I had gotten there. But while I washed my mouth out, the illusion of childhood illness—and the childish search for comfort—dissipated, leaving me sore and spitting mad.

"Jill!" I roared, my head aching from the effort, as I stumbled from the bathroom out to the landing. "Jill Canaday!" I didn't know what the girlish pretender was up to, but as I sank down against the wall, my head swimming, I knew I had let myself be had. Despite the smoking. Despite the affair with her father's partner. Despite all the warnings I had gotten, her innocent act had finally taken me in. She had attacked me in my own home. She must have—I remembered being in my kitchen. I remembered talking to her, putting two and two together—but I had no idea why.

"Jill!" I yelled again. I was still dizzy, still nauseous. I'd been hit hard. I wanted retribution—and some answers. "Where the hell are you?"

"Pru!" The voice that answered was not that of the youngest Canaday girl. Nor was it entirely in my head. A loud meow

reached me from downstairs, turning in my mind to a discernible voice. *"Pru!"*

"Wallis?" I made myself stand, but the remnants of the bourbon and the blow to my head could not be so easily shaken off. Only a hand to the wall kept me upright.

"Pru..." The voice was fainter now, fuzzy.

"Wallis!" I yelled, trying to find my balance. I'd been wrong—wrong about everything. I'd begun to believe that Jill was truly innocent, manipulated by Wilkins and almost framed by Jackie, back when her scared and desperate oldest sister thought she would surely take the blame for their father's death. But now—this...I had no idea what the crazed girl would do. "Wallis?"

"Get out, Pru!" The voice was faint, and I whipped my head around, desperate to hear. To see. Big mistake. I stumbled. Found myself on hands and knees. I gulped in air and coughed. Breathed and coughed again. There was something else beside my aching head going on here. There was smoke.

Forcing myself to calm down, I crawled to the head of the stairs. I could see it from here, the white wisps climbing from the old house's first floor. Had I left the oven on? Had Jill been smoking when she came in? Damn that girl with her fake cigarettes. There was nothing honest about her.

Not that she mattered now. I was letting myself be distracted. Nodding out, while the smell of smoke grew stronger. I needed to get downstairs. To see what was on fire. I could handle this if I just...

No, I couldn't stand. The attempt made me dizzy. Made the world swirl and retreat. I sat hard, catching my breath. Ignoring the smoke creeping up the stairwell.

"Get out!" Wallis. She must be trapped, too. Calling to me. Her only friend. And I—I couldn't risk it. Couldn't try standing again. I laughed, a dry choking rattle. Stuck at the top of my own stairs. Helpless as a child.

"Prudence Marlowe." The memory came to me, clear as day. "You're a young lady, not an animal."

Me, on these stairs. Sliding down on my behind. My mother at the foot, hands on her hips. Scolding.

"A young lady…" How fast I'd go. How much fun.

The memory jolted me. Swinging my legs around to hang before me, I started down. One bump, two. I stopped. Another bump and my head would explode. Twenty-odd years had past since I'd scooted down this way. Twenty-five since I had an eight-year-old's flexibility. No matter. Smoke. Head throbbing, I pushed myself off. One step. Thump. One more step. Thump.

The smoke grew thicker. The jostling too much for my tired brain. Halfway down, I stopped again. I couldn't. "I'm sorry, Wallis." I mouthed the words, even as I leaned against the wall. "I'm sorry."

"Pru." The reply was soft. Wasn't what I expected. "My little animal." My cheek against the cool, flat wall, I could see her. My mother. Only now she wasn't yelling. Wasn't even angry. I saw her at the base of the stairs, looking up at me. She was smiling. With a final push, I made my way down.

"Pru!" The front door burst open, light and air pouring in, blessed air. Creighton was shouting. Running to me, calling my name as he carried me out the door. Already I could hear the sirens. The fire trucks arriving. He held me to his chest. "Pru."

"Jim." I buried my face in him, breathing in his solid warmth. And then I pushed away. "Where is she? I don't know where—"

"It's okay." He held me as I staggered. "We got her. The first ambulance took her—she hit her head. Took in a lot of smoke, but she's okay. Jill's going to be okay."

"Not Jill…" I didn't have the words. I whipped around. Woozy, flailing. "Wallis!" Grabin Jim's arm. "She's in there with the kitten. Save her, Jim. You've got to save Wallis."

"Pru. The firefighters…I can't." His face looked so sad, I turned away. Saw the streams of water hosing down my sad old house. The smoke billowing out.

"Babies…nest…"

I sank to the ground, buried my face in my hands. He was here. He was safe, but he couldn't save…*I* couldn't save the one other being I cared for. The one who understood me. Who understood.

"What?" A gentle pressure against my thigh—a soft thud—as Wallis dropped Ernesto, blinking and a little confused, into my lap. *"I couldn't carry you, too. That's what the big guy is for."*

Chapter Sixty-six

The house was saved. As much as I might complain about Beauville, the response had been swift, and by midnight the fire was out. Sure, I had a ton of water damage—my mother's old couch had finally bitten the dust—but the basic structure was sound. If I chose to restore it, that was.

"We could go back to the city." Wallis, sitting on an ottoman, tilted her head as she broached the question.

"We could." I agreed. I had refused to be taken to the hospital. Refused to be parted from my pet or the kitten. Through sheer orneriness and the intervention of a certain cop, I was finally released from the EMTs' care. Now I was bundled into Creighton's big armchair, wrapped in a blanket and drinking sweet, milky tea, liberally laced with brandy.

"We could what?" Jim emerged from the kitchen with a plate of toast.

"Just thinking out loud." I smiled up at him. The adrenaline had worn off, leaving me exhausted but also more clearheaded than I'd been in days. Being with Creighton helped. With Creighton and my cats.

Wallis went back to washing Ernesto. "You never want to tell me what's going on with an investigation, I get that." I began to put my thoughts in order. "But usually you give me something, Jim."

He shook his head, chuckling softly. "Sometimes it's not that complicated, Pru. Sometimes, there's just nothing to tell."

"Then why was everyone talking about this? Old lady Horlick. The guys at Happy's. I mean, everybody thought, well, where there's smoke…" I caught myself.

Randy—he'd been the one to spread the gossip. The one person everyone spoke to. With the smoke shop as his base, he'd started the rumors—gotten people talking about Jill, about how she could have poisoned her father. Not because of Judith—that romance was done and gone. But for Jackie. After all those months of casual abuse, of hoping her father would die and leave her. After watching him collapse, she had been scared, scared and guilty, and she had pressured her boyfriend into spreading lies. Vicious, desperate lies.

And the note? *SHE DIDNT DO IT. SHE WAS HELP* That hadn't been a last-ditch attempt to tie Judith in with Jill. I could see now—the scrawled writing, the bad grammar—that note was all Randy. He might have been wheedled into helping his panicked girlfriend by spreading a few lies, but he couldn't stand seeing her little sister railroaded into a murder rap. "She was helping," I bet he meant to write. Maybe he didn't have time. Maybe the paper had ripped awkwardly. Or maybe the man was as semi-literate as he seemed.

"I can see the wheels turning, Pru." Creighton took the chair opposite. Managed to put his feet up on the ottoman without discomfiting Wallis too much. "But we don't really know what's happened yet. Maybe once Jill wakes up…" He pointed to my cup. "Drink your tea."

I sipped, feeling the warmth blend with the fatigue in my body. Feeling it lull me into sleep. It was sweet, sweeter than I would usually like, but this was good. Something Sheila would like. Like catnip to Wallis…

Something was bothering me. Hinting around the edge of my tired brain. Catnip. Which gave Wallis a pleasant buzz, but which—yes, now I remembered—Ernesto seemed immune to. Cats, kittens especially, might react aversely to the herb at first, but most loved it. Unless it had no effect at all on them. But Ernesto had sneezed…

It meant nothing. So many things could make a kitten sneeze. FRV. An upper respiratory infection. Dust. Or an irritating plant. Something like those leaves that Sheila had ingested. Spiky and dark green.

I closed my eyes and the memories flooded over me. The hot tea. My house. Home. I remembered flowers from my mother's garden. Stalks of cup-shaped blossoms, purple and pink, above such spiky leaves. Foxglove, which re-seeded itself and spread. Digitalis. The source of life-saving medications, used by cardiac patients the world over. By next month, they'd be in bloom.

The plantings where Mack had spilled his coffee. He'd been working. Trying, and I'd been—well, I'd been as judgmental as my mother. All he was drinking was coffee. Sweet, milky coffee. Too sweet for me, but not for someone with a sweet tooth. Unless…

"*I knew,*" Sheila had said. Maybe it hadn't been the coffee, or not entirely. All these years, the faithful sheltie had been waiting. Waiting for someone to avenge her mistress. Waiting for someone who would be a friend. Who would understand.

"*I knew,*" Sheila had said. Now I did, too.

Not that I could explain any of this to Creighton.

Chapter Sixty-seven

I was supposed to stay in bed. To avoid an argument, I may even have promised to do that—at least, to take it easy while Jim went into work. He was going to talk to the fire inspector. Figure out how the fire had been started and, from that, by whom. Hoping to talk to Jill, too, once the doctors let him. I couldn't tell what he was thinking, but I knew he'd figure it out. Who had wanted to stop us from speaking. What we would speak about.

In the meantime, I had an older mystery to solve. As soon as he drove off, I got dressed and started walking. I ached like I'd been beaten, and every rasping breath hurt. But the fresh air cleared the last of the cobwebs from my head, and by the time I reached my car I knew what I had to do.

> > >

Judith was packing when I got to the Mont. She told the front desk to let me up, though, and her door was unlocked when I got there. There was no more fight left in the woman. From the look on her face, she was more than ready to leave.

"What happened when you worked for the Wilkinses?" I didn't bother with any niceties. We'd been through too much for that. "I want to know the truth."

"It wasn't my fault, okay?" Judith didn't look up as she folded a blouse. One bag was already packed, the other sat open on the luggage rack, the picture of neatness and order. "It was an accident."

My breath caught, and for a moment I couldn't speak. I'd been meaning to start with the husband. She'd cut right to the wife. "An accident?" I choked out the words.

"I was a kid," Another blouse, patted and smoothed to lie as flat as her voice. With the big shades open on the bright spring day, it was easy to see the care she was taking. The little signs of wear and repair in the once-nice clothes. "A kid," she repeated. "I was working crazy hours. She was on a ton of meds."

"There was a mix-up in her medications?"

Judith shook her head. "No, I was careful. *We* were careful. It was the dosage—or maybe she was just getting weaker faster than anyone knew." She reached for another hanger. Gave up and sat on the bed, facing me. "Melissa Wilkins was sick for as long as I could remember," Judith said. "She'd had congestive heart disease for years. She was on all kinds of drugs that were supposed to kickstart her heart—get it going and keep it steady. And one day, it was all too much."

She brought her hand up to her mouth, as if to stop the words. In the harsh morning light, she looked her age.

"Wilkins blamed you." I kept my voice even and soft.

"No, no, he didn't." I was surprised to see her eyes fill with tears. "He defended me. He told everyone how hard I was working, how diligent I was. But then it came out."

I waited, although by now I knew. "You were lovers," I said finally.

"His wife was sick—bedridden." She looked at me, willing me to understand. "And he was still a vibrant, powerful man."

"And you were, how old when it started? Eighteen? Twenty?" My voice was soft, but she winced anyway. "Your father must have raised holy hell."

"Dad did, yeah." Her voice, low and even, became softer. Hushed. "He was so disappointed. He would have done anything to keep me quiet. To get me out of town."

"I don't think so," I said with growing conviction. "I think he wanted to protect you. To save you. Why else would he keep working with Wilkins except to avoid a scandal?"

She shrugged, but I saw something relax in her. Something give way. All these years, and she had never figured it out. Her father must have seemed so scary back then. So stern. But he wasn't the one who took advantage. The one who...

An idea hit me. "It was Laurence Wilkins who started the rumors," I said, to test it out loud. "It was Wilkins who suggested that you were careless or worse—that you wanted your lover's wife dead."

She blinked up at me. "No, he was furious, when it finally came out," she said. "He still is. After the funeral, he actually accused me of telling Dad that he and I..." Her voice trailed off.

"Wilkins isn't angry with you, Judith. He never was. That was his cover. His excuse." I made my own voice as gentle as I could. "But he wasn't going to start up again with you. Not once he found out what Jill was going to inherit."

She slumped down, shoulders bowed, but she didn't argue. When she looked up at me, I could see the toll it had all taken.

"Jill must hate me." Her voice was flat.

I shook my head. The pieces falling into place. "No, she'll understand." The charm. The connections. The sense of entitlement. Jill spent enough time at County to guess at what was going on, even if Doc Sharpe hadn't shared the details. And at Wilkins' she must have seen some papers—either her boyfriend's or her father's. That was why she'd called. She'd started to tell me about it, before the attack. I hadn't understood.

"She uncovered the truth about his finances," I said now. "That he'd been embezzling." She must have seen something at his house, something that tied in with what the forensic accountant had told Doc Sharpe—or maybe she put two and two together. Saw how he was spending and how little was coming in. "She realized that he didn't love her either. That he was using her. She wanted to tell me, came over to tell me all this last night. Only I..."

I stopped, my thoughts flying back to the scene after the funeral, back to the Canaday house. All the fuss over the food, and how Wilkins took charge of Jackie when she was searching for her father's herbal tea. The "attack" Jill had had, and the disappearance of that tea. "You're lucky you got away, Judith," I said. "Jill is, too. I wouldn't have been surprised if he had married her, and if she too had died of some undetected heart ailment."

"Larry?" Judith shook her head, confused. "What do you mean?"

"It wasn't an accident, Judith." I looked into her eyes. She had to understand. "Larry Wilkins poisoned his own wife with fox-glove. It looked like an accidental overdose because it mimicked the medications she was on. He did the same with your father. I believe it was all planned, keeping him close with their weekly lunches. Getting him accustomed to herbal tea. And finally, when your father grew too suspicious, began asking questions about the books—about County's endowment—spiking that tea. Probably just a little, just enough for someone who already had a bad heart.

"Maybe he got lucky. Your father had a call in to Doc Sharpe at County about the books. Maybe Wilkins managed to add more foxglove during his last visit. We may never know, but he sure knew it worked when Jackie called, frantic, looking for a reason—any reason—to get out of the house. He had the keys, so it would have been easy enough to slip in, to remove the tea, just as a precaution. Do you remember him yelling at her, after the funeral? She was looking for the tea. Looking to serve it, but of course it was already gone."

I thought about Ernesto, about Sheila. I could never explain. Instead, I settled on what I could talk about. "If it weren't for the state lab taking over, your father's death would have been considered natural. As it was, we're going to have to talk to Creighton. Tell him everything, and get them to reopen the investigation."

"An investigation." She hung her head in her hands. "I can't go through all that again."

"He played you, Judith, just like he played both your sisters." I sympathized, truly I did. That didn't matter now. "Once Wilkins realized that there were going to be tests, he did everything he could to foment rumors. Jackie already felt guilty for her…" I paused, unsure how much Judith knew. "For the lapses in her care. And you were already under a cloud here. All he had to do was drag Jill in somehow. Drop a confidential word in the right ears, and she was a suspect as well."

"I can't…" She wasn't listening, and so I left her. She didn't have to do anything more.

Chapter Sixty-eight

Creighton would get on this. I knew he would. But he thought I was still in bed, and, besides, I couldn't wait to tell Doc. I wasn't sure how much Wilkins had stolen or how much the hospital could recover. Still, I was more optimistic than I'd been in days. The old Yankee had taken care of me when I needed help, and now I was going to be able to return the favor. I left the Mont and headed toward County, windows open to the new day.

Not only was Wilkins behind the hospital's money troubles, I realized, he was indirectly behind Ernesto's illness. That poor kitten had been splashed with the tainted tea and only his lack of skill at bathing himself had kept him from ingesting more. I'd seen how the leaves had nearly killed Sheila.

Sheila. With Jill in the hospital, the little dog was on her own. Laurence Wilkins might not actively hurt the sheltie, but he wouldn't take any special care of her either. And if she got out again…if he simply let her out, there was nothing to keep her from that patch of spiky leaves.

She'd be fine, I told myself. I'd been on the road for twenty minutes. I was almost at County. The sheltie had lived with Wilkins for years, keeping her secret close. She must have realized that I had put it together, had interpreted her sacrifice. The old girl would know. She'd be fine.

It was no use. With a squeal of the brakes, I swung a U turn. Creighton might be there already. He might have already taken a statement from Jill. In which case, I could pick up the little sheltie. Find a place for her to stay while Jill recovered. And if he wasn't, well, then, Wilkins would be none the wiser. I never had picked up Albert's ladder anyway.

Creighton's car was nowhere in sight when I got to the lawyer's east side home. I caught a glimpse of a car in the driveway—a late model, big and dark—so I backed out to the street. Just as well, I figured. The lawyer wouldn't raise a fuss with a client there to see me.

I approached the house wondering about his visitor. Maybe Wilkins had been warned. Maybe he had called an attorney of his own. Before I rang the bell, I paused. Evidence—if Creighton weren't here yet, it might still be removed. Stepping back from the door, I made my way around the house once more.

"What are you talking about?" I was right. Wilkins knew something was up. I could hear his voice through the open window as I made my way through the planting. "Have you gone crazy?"

Pointed leaves and a green shoot, the pink-purple buds already forming along its length. Foxglove—*Digitalis purpurea*—my mother's favorites. I picked a few leaves but left the flowers in her memory. The animals out here would know better than to eat it.

"Judith, no!" Wilkins' yell broke through my reverie, and I raced to the window. The shade was down, but slightly ajar. Inside I could see Wilkins, hands raised before him. He was backing up—backing to the other window. Then Judith came into view. She must have driven straight here, gotten into her car the moment I'd left.

She was holding a gun.

"Judith!" I yelled and banged on the window. "Don't do it!"

She kept advancing until both were behind the shade, out of my sight. I heard barking. Sheila yelling, *"No! No! No!"* A high-pitched scream—a ghastly sound—and a thud as something large—a chair, a table—hit the ground.

Then a shot, and the barking ceased.

I looked around for a branch. For anything. Saw Albert's ladder, damp under its tarp, and hauled at it, raising it, staggering, into the air. Falling forward with the weight, with my own exhaustion, I rammed it into the window, shattering the glass. Pushed the shade aside, and then I was through.

"Judith!" I raced up to the woman who now sat, collapsed on the floor, weeping. She had no blood on her. No obvious injury from the gun, which I could now see lay several feet away.

A growl alerted me. Turning, I saw Laurence Wilkins, also on the floor, a dazed look on his face. One arm was outstretched, reaching toward the gun he'd dropped, the gun he had wrestled from his former lover. He wasn't moving. He hadn't been shot, either, but he was pinned in place. Held there by pain, by the small, sharp teeth that an aging dog had sunk into his arm.

Chapter Sixty-nine

"You're lucky that lawyer paid you." I was buying a round. Yes, at Happy's. "Lucky he paid us, too." Dave Altschul had accepted a beer. Mack was sticking to soda water.

"Jill would have made it right," I said with assurance. "Out of the estate." Once she'd regained consciousness, the youngest Canaday girl had been only too happy to tell Creighton what she knew. Wilkins' crooked books might have confused her at first, but his blatant attack on us both—and his ham-fisted attempt to conceal it with a fire—had negated any feelings she might still have for the double-dealing lawyer. She had turned into the star witness, which meant that I could keep myself—and Sheila—out of it.

Judith wasn't so lucky. She had to testify, and that nearly broke her. Not only because of what had happened so many years ago. She had to admit to the gun, to her attempt to use it. I liked to think that her relationship with her sisters would sustain her though. They were there to support her in the courtroom, and she'd moved back into the family home for the duration of the trial.

"She's sticking around?" Dave seemed quite interested.

I nodded. "At least until the wedding."

Randy was marrying her sister—her older sister—at the end of the summer. Jackie must have forgiven his betrayal. Maybe she'd even welcomed it—his attempt at mitigating her worst impulse, at keeping her family safe. By then, he'd confirmed that the note was his, the poor slob's way of dealing with the guilt of their attempted collusion, the rumors he had helped to spread to distract attention from Jackie's panicked flight. Jill wasn't guilty, he'd been trying to communicate. She was helping. It wasn't the way I'd want to start a marriage, but Jill had forgiven her oldest sister, and Judith had agreed to take part in the ceremony. It seemed like the family squabbles were over.

"*Speaking of families…*" An hour later, I was at home, with my tarps and paint. A beer with friends was nice, but I had a cat to feed. Besides, Creighton had said he'd come by later.

"I miss Ernesto, too, Wallis." I watched as she devoured the chopped turkey I'd set before her, and then as she carefully cleaned each paw. "But he's got his own house to look after now."

"*Some mama that one is.*" Wallis didn't think much of Jackie, who'd be keeping Ernesto while Jill finished school. Didn't like that she'd walked out on the kitten, who had bonded with her so quickly, as well as on the dying man. "*Then again, she does need looking after.*"

"Don't we all, Wallis?" I looked toward the window. Saw headlights approaching. Looked back down to see those green eyes appraising me. "No, I haven't figured it out yet, Wallis. But it's spring, you know?"

And I went to open the door.

To receive a free catalog of Poisoned Pen Press titles, please provide your name and address through one of the following ways:

Phone: 1-800-421-3976
Facsimile: 1-480-949-1707
Email: info@poisonedpenpress.com
Website: www.poisonedpenpress.com

Poisoned Pen Press
6962 E. First Ave. Ste 103
Scottsdale, AZ 85251